SURGEONS OF TERROR

RON WOOTTERS

This book is dedicated to Edna and Rosemary

"Surgeons of Terror." ISBN 1-58939-217-5 (softcover version).

Published 2002 by Virtualbookworm.com Publishing Inc., P.O. Box 9949, College Station, TX , 77842, US. ©2002 Ronald Wootters. All rights reserved. No part of this publication may be reproduced, stored in a retrieval system, or transmitted in any form or by any means, electronic, mechanical, recording or otherwise, without the prior written permission of Ronald Wootters.

Manufactured in the United States of America.

CONTENTS

PROLOGUE

I t is summertime in Barcelona, Spain, and the new century is less than six months away. The city and its automobiles are in their usual high gear, except for the people taking advantage of the oasis at the edge of the city.

The Paro De La Ciutadella is a five-by-five block square about a quarter of a mile from the Mediterranean Sea. Trees, benches and vendors line the way for the convenience of the tourists, visitors or people just out for an evening stroll to enjoy the refreshing sea breeze on a hot summer night. Some are there for none of these reasons-for example, the two medium-sized, Arabic men are terrorists, conducting business in plain sight as they walk and talk.

"Have you had a chance to review the documents I gave you?" the distinguished-looking Egyptian man asks.

"Yes," answers the other.

"Can you do it?" he asks.

"Yes, I can," answers the man, "but what about the project I am currently working on?"

"You will have time to do both," answers the Egyptian. "Continue what you are doing, and start planning this one. We are not rushing things."

The two men walk a bit farther together, and then bid each other farewell. The distinguished-looking man turns to walk away when the other man puts his hand out and touches the Egyptian's arm.

"Abdullah," he says, "the plan reads like it will be our last mission."

"Yes, I know," his companion answers. "It is supposed to look like that, but you and several others are too valuable to go to Allah at this time. Maybe another time…but not this one, Atta. We will speak again," says Abdullah Ahmed Abdullah, then turns and walks away.

CHAPTER ONE

I t is springtime of 2000 in the suburbs of New Jersey, and all feel fortunate that the new century did not bring the chaos that was predicted. The weeping willows are now a pretty shade of green, and the red and green buds from other trees are showing a small glimpse of what is to follow in the coming weeks. These are some of Mother Nature's first signals that spring has arrived. The birds are also getting into the festive spirit, with their singing and chirping. They too are happy to see the mild days of spring.

It is a nice day indeed to walk for the morning paper.

The happy, festive mood of spring collides with the genocide of today's world at the newsstand. Once again, terrorists have struck down innocent people in the name of their cause. Fourteen hostages were taken, five women and three young children among them. When the demands of the terrorists were not met, all of the hostages were killed.

People will read or hear about this latest incident; they will feel bad, express their beliefs that something should be done, and then go about their daily lives.

This will not be true for the man who walks to the news stand this morning to pick up the New York Times. He is going to enter the fight against this wave of evil. J.J. Stone will bring all of the resources and power at his disposal to help wipe out this new cancer that is trying to destroy the world.

It will not be official, or sanctioned by the government in any way, but that's okay. The government is still learning how to fight this new enemy of mankind, but they are playing by the old set of rules. With this new evil, the old ways do not always work. For this type of warfare you need a whole new set of rules.

Stone's fight against terror will not be for personal revenge or glory. His ultimate objective will be to help stop the needless slaughter of innocent people caught between fanatics and bullshit politics.

During his walk back from the newsstand, he decides whom he will ask to join him in his fight, and how he will put this group together. John Stone may have lost a few steps through the years, but he is still one of the quickest-minded men in the business community. First, he will form an executive board for planning and support.

He will call Gil Dunn, president of VanCorcoven Firearms Company in Belgium and former Deputy Director of Operations (DDO) at the CIA; John Howard, president of Zerk Pharmaceutical Company; Jeff Dawson, president of International Oil; and Charles

Wilson, president of Wilson Explosives Company.

As soon as JJ returns home, he enters his den. By mid-afternoon he has contacted each of the men and set up a meeting for Wednesday afternoon at his office in Manhattan. JJ does not go into any details over the phone. He simply tells each man he has something very important he would like to discuss with him.

The next item on the agenda is to form a team, and find someone to act as a coordinator between the team and the board. This will be a tough one. He must be a retired man of senior rank, and not a military politician. He must be experienced in combat, not just a desk jockey from Washington. In other words, he must be from the old school, when promotions were due to performance and not butt-kissing. Stone searches his mind trying to come up with the right man, and then a smile appears on his face as he reaches for the phone. After a call to information, JJ dials a number. Three rings later, a man's voice answers the phone.

"Hello, Mac. This is JJ Stone."

"JJ!" the voice answers with surprise. "What the hell do you want?"

A chuckle comes from Stone as he replies, "You haven't changed a bit, Mac. I would like to meet with you, to discuss something very important."

The tone of the conversation changes from light to serious in a split second. These two men haven't stayed in touch over the years, but their friendship has remained strong.

"Anything wrong?" inquires Mac.

"No. But I would like to meet with you at my office in Manhattan, on Wednesday at 4 p.m. Are you available?"

"Yes, I can be there," Mac answers.

JJ will speak with each man separately before he meets with the group. That way, anyone who does not want to be involved can decline without knowing the identity of the others. After JJ gave Mac the address of his office he adds, "I'll wait until Wednesday before I get into any details."

"See you then," Mac says as he hangs up the receiver.

JJ sits back in his chair for a few seconds and reflects on the friendship he and Mac shared years ago. They didn't see much of each other after JJ got out of the Marine Corps, but the friendship stayed intact. Both men are of the opinion that you don't have to see someone every ten minutes just to prove you are good friends. JJ's thoughts are interrupted by his wife Jenny's voice.

"You're in deep thought. What has you so preoccupied?"

"Oh, nothing, Jen. Just thinking about the old days," JJ says.

It's 1:00 p.m. when JJ steps out of his Jaguar in the parking garage below his office and heads for the elevator. Once there, he speaks with each man privately as they arrive. The men that are in agreement will go into the big meeting room. The ones that aren't can leave, with no hard feelings. JJ knows the cut of the men he selected, but even he is surprised at how quickly each man agrees with the proposal that something has to be done.

Mac is the last man JJ speaks with, and now all five are assembled in the room overlooking the harbor. JJ reads down his list of topics. He has the easy ones first: *How will the project be financed?* That's no problem. Each man is a multimillionaire. They will all put in equal shares to support the project. *Intelligence sources?* That's obvious: Wild-man Dunn. He still has contacts in the intelligence community. *Weapons?* Dunn again. He has a whole factory. *How will we handle security? How do we conduct business? How do we select the men for the team?*

After introducing Mac to the other men, JJ calls the meeting to order and the first three issues pass with total agreement. After the third issue is agreed upon, JJ looks up from his agenda and asks with a smirk, "What do I have here, a bunch of yes-men?"

Everyone laughs and responds at the same time with various comments. JJ already knows the answer to that question. Each member at the meeting is a self-made man that will speak his mind and fight for his ideas, but at the same time they are logical and reasonable. If proven wrong, they will accept it gracefully.

"The next issue is," JJ announces, "how do we maintain security for this undertaking?"

"I nominate Dawson," says Mr. Howard, "I figure if he can keep the reason gasoline prices are so fucking high a secret, he's the man for our security."

The room once again erupts in laughter.

"Now, Howard," Dawson responds, "there's a lot of expense connected with the manufacturing of gasoline - especially when you consider all of the gas we have to make for all of those pharmaceutical limos."

"That's right," Howard agrees. "That's why I am recommending we go to Hondas. We will call it Our Generic Limo!"

JJ sits back in his chair and observes the group. He is glad all of the members seem to be hitting it off well. He has had dealings with each man on professional and social levels, and found them all to be quick-minded with a good sense of humor. He also knows that all hell will break loose when this group does not agree on a topic. *That's all right*, he thinks. *It will be like making steel. When all the sparks stop flying we'll have a solid product.*

JJ once again calls the meeting to order. "May I have your attention, gentleman? We have another issue: the selection of a team. I have asked General Mac here to select the men and act as liaison between the executive board and the team. General Mac will choose candidates he feels will do the job, and submit each individual for our approval. Are there any questions?"

"I have some questions," Dunn says. "How will you conduct the selection process?"

"I have an individual in mind," Mac replies, "and would like to submit him for team leader," "He would be the primary source for building the team."

"Will you submit the team leader at the next meeting?" asks JJ.

"I can tell you a little right now. I know his background very well."

All members of the group shake their heads in agreement.

"Who is this man?" inquires JJ?

"We'll call him JC for now. JC is a retired Marine Corps colonel with service in Nam during the sixties, and in intelligence roles during the Cold War. He is qualified in UDT, wears Parachute Jump Wings, and is an expert in weapons and martial arts. Before the Vietnam War broke out, he was trying to convince the general staff to train each Marine in guerilla warfare tactics. I know him personally and can vouch for his character.

"Do you have any questions, gentlemen?"

"I have one question," replies Wilson. "Will the team be made up entirely of Marines?"

"No," Mac replies. "Some may not even have a military background. Each man will be selected for his skills and integrity. Who knows? We may even have Doggies and Swabbies on the team...oh, excuse me. I mean Army and Navy personnel."

Everyone is having a good chuckle as JJ calls the meeting to order again.

"We have four things to cover before we adjourn. First, are their questions about anything we have covered today?"

"No" is the general consensus.

"Second: anyone having second thoughts about our upcoming campaign?"

Once again, the answer is no.

"The third is scheduling the next meeting. Will everyone be available two months from today?"

After checking their schedules, everyone confirms the date.

"Will that give General Mac enough time to recruit a team?" inquires Dunn.

"It should," replies Mac, "if JC agrees to come aboard. We will be selecting names within a few days. I feel the time factor may come into play when we start training as a team. Granted, each member will already be accomplished as a one-man operation, but getting them to work as an expert team may be another matter."

"In that case, wouldn't it be better to get all team players?" asks Mr. Howard.

"I don't think so. As I see it, our missions will be a mixed bag of two-man assignments, one-man ops with a trailer for backup, and team efforts. Another thing we must keep in mind is that this group will function as a traditional team, but it will also function non-traditionally. Therefore, I think it will be easier to convert a loner into a part-time team player than the other way around."

JJ notices Howard seemed satisfied with the General's answer, so he moves onto the last and most important issue. He puts on his most serious face as he continues the agenda.

"Gentleman," he begins, "the last issue is probably the most important one of all. We must maintain absolute security in this matter. If we are discovered, the Federal government and any politician we have pissed off along the way will have a field day with us. We will only discuss this undertaking at our meetings. For an emergency situation, a secure means of communications will be set up. The only contact between the team and us will be through General Mac or myself. I will serve as backup to Mac. This will help to ensure the security of one group if the other group is compromised.

"I know I don't have to dwell on this security issue with this group, but please remember how very important it is. With that in mind, I will adjourn the meeting until June 22, when General Mac will present the team members he has selected. This will include backgrounds, code names and no pictures.

"Meeting adjourned!"

General Mac stays behind to have a word with JJ after the meeting breaks up.

"This isn't going to be a picnic, you know," he says.

"I know," answers JJ. "That's why you must be very careful when selecting the team."

"The team isn't what I'm worried about," replies Mac.

"Then you are concerned about this group?"

"Well..." says Mac. "I know you, but I don't know them, and I think we should set some guidelines."

"Like what?"

"Like, the team will not be used as assassins for business purposes. And what action will be taken if someone purposely compromises this undertaking..."

"Oh, don't worry about these men," JJ interrupts. "They're all top-notch people, and would not even think about compromising the operation."

"What about their families?" asks Mac.

"What about them?"

"What if a family member finds out, and is bent on destroying our efforts. What course of action will be taken then?"

JJ pauses for a moment before responding. "Well, I guess we'll deal with that one when and if it occurs."

"No!' General Mac leans forward. "Procedures must be in place now, so quick action can be taken to either eliminate the problem or strike our tents and fade into the night."

"That's a valid issue," JJ replies. "I wasn't thinking past the board members themselves. We will discuss these issues and set the rules at our next meeting. Do you have any other little gems you would like to drop on me, Mac?"

"Why, yes," Mac quips. "Where in the hell are we going to operate from?"

"I have the answer to that one," JJ answers. "I have a little retreat in Jersey we can use. It's rural enough to carry out training without being discovered. I figure if we go too rural, the local community will be inquisitive about the new people in the area."

"You thought right. How big is this little retreat?"

"Fifteen bedrooms, pool, and a small lake on 3000 acres."

"Oh! A small retreat indeed," declares Mac. "Well, we'll try to make do."

JJ is glad to find out he and Mac will probably work well together, even after all these years.

"I'll take you there tomorrow morning at 0700," JJ tells him. "It will be better during the day. If I took you at night, you would probably have to drop bread crumbs and piss on trees to find your way back."

"Very funny," says Mac. "Is it really three thousand acres?"

"No. It's really just a three-room apartment."

"I'm glad to see you haven't lost your sense of humor. I wonder, though, if you've lost your drinking ability…you being a civilian all these years and everything."

"Lets go find out," smiles JJ.

Mac sets the tone for the night as they walk to the door when he announces, "I don't want you to hurt yourself on my account. You always did blame me when you screwed up."

"Oh! Is that the way it was?" JJ inquires. "All I can remember is wanting to get out of the corps because I could see, even then, you were destined for the general staff, and I didn't want to be around if you became the Commandant. You probably would have replaced the eagle on the Marine Corps Emblem with two pigs fornicating, and changed the motto to Semper Pig Fuckers." Laughter fills the hall as the two men make their way to JJ's favorite watering hole.

The next morning, a silver Jaguar drives down the ramp and into the underground parking garage at Mac's hotel. The Jag no sooner comes to a stop in a parking space than Mac appears beside it.

The passenger side window rolls down slowly and JJ inquires, "Have a bad head this morning?"

"You could say that," Mac replies as he opens the car door. "Even my hair hurts."

"There's a thermos of coffee in the basket. Pour me a cup too."

"Sounds good," Mac replies as he opens the picnic basket.

The Jag pulls out of the parking space and without any hesitation heads up the ramp to the street. A brief stop, a look to the left, a right turn, and they are on their way. JJ never was one to waste time in traffic: he weaves in and out of lanes through the tunnel, and they arrive in New Jersey.

"Will home base be in Jersey, or were you bullshitting me last night?" Mac inquires.

"Yes, it's here. I have a farm in central Jersey that I think is ideal, for many reasons. It's in the country, with no houses for miles, and I own all of the land within a 2-mile radius. It's 50 miles from there to Philadelphia International Airport, 60 miles to Newark and New York airports and 20 miles to several smaller airports. Many train stations are within 20 to 25 miles. I don't have any animals, so I'm going to convert the barn into team quarters."

"We'll probably have eight people," says Mac.

"I'll plan for 12," JJ informs him. "It's a huge barn. It used to be a dairy farm, but the owner wanted to retire to Florida and his kids didn't want to be farmers, so he put it up for sale. It has served as a nice retreat for the wife, family and me, but it will make an even better base of operations."

"Well, you sure are on the way to organizing this venture," Mac says.

"There is one thing that has me stuck," JJ ponders aloud. "You'll select the team, but who will support home base-cooking, food shopping, cleaning, security and things like that?"

"Well, when in-house, the team will handle security. I also have an old salt in mind that can handle the rest, and even chip in if we see any action at the farm. The farm!" Mac says again. "I like the sound of that. Yesterday I was a Marine Corps general, and today I'm on the farm.

"It could only happen in America…especially if you have a peckerhead of a pal who gets you into shit that will probably get you killed, disgraced or both. What a pal!"

"Is this going to continue?" JJ inquires.

"Probably," Mac says as he starts another round of what he calls "humor time."

"Humor time, is it?" quips JJ. "I knew I should have gone to the Navy with this project!"

Mac is just finishing his third round of "humor time" as JJ turns off a secondary country road and onto a packed dirt one.

"Well, at this rate," Mac observes, "I guess we'll be transferring to horseback at the next turn."

"It's only a few more miles up this road and then a long lane, and we'll be there."

"This is nice country," Mac remarks as he scopes out the territory.

"Yes, it is." JJ turns into the driveway. "The missus and I discovered this area about 10 years ago. It's a nice retreat all year long. The house and barn can't be seen from the dirt road, but as you go around a curve and up a slight grade you can see everything."

"Nice. We can use the curve in an ambush, and the buildings are on high ground."

"I hope it doesn't come to that," JJ says, and both men laugh.

JJ had turned what was a big dairy farm into a very nice estate. The main house is huge, with six bedrooms, several baths, an enormous kitchen, big dining room, a den and an entertainment room. Behind the house is an Olympic-size swimming pool. To the left of the house and down a small hill is an indoor pistol range. The barn is empty, but in first-rate condition. JJ presents his plan for the barn to Mac.

"I figure we'll use the ground floor for training, and the second floor for living quarters."

"How are you going to explain the renovations to the workmen?" asks Mac.

"How does a very exclusive bed and breakfast sound?" JJ says.

"A little lame," replies Mac as he checks out the view from the side windows.

"Hey!" exclaims JJ. "If an old paper mill in this area can be converted into condos with each unit going for more than $500,000, I guess we can build what appears to be a bed and breakfast for the very rich, with a three-year waiting list."

"Three years!" laughs Mac. "We'll probably be in prison long before that!"

"What's this 'we' shit, three-star man?" JJ inquires with a big smile on his face.

CHAPTER TWO

A sunbeam is shining through the window as Mac stirs from a deep sleep. The first thing he smells is fresh coffee from the kitchen. JJ is already up and about, in the process of making breakfast.

"Wow," Mac announces as he wanders into the kitchen. "That coffee smells like kick-ass Kona to me."

"It is," replies JJ, "and plenty of it."

Mac starts filling one of many mugs he'll be consuming in the days ahead as he inquires about the agenda.

"The way I see it," JJ begins, "we have the executive board in place. For mutual protection, we do not want any contact between the board and the team. You will be the liaison, with me as backup. Together we will define and fine-tune our objectives. I think constant reviews, now and after we get started, are important to keep us on track with our objectives."

"Good point," Mac approves.

"After we review our plans," JJ continues, "you will start selecting candidates for the team, and I'll begin renovations for home base. If you don't mind, I'd like to be in on the final team selection process."

"Not at all", Mac agrees. "Another pair of eyes may see something I missed."

After a big breakfast the two men, coffee mugs in hand, head for the den. JJ's den is a bit larger than what you would expect. It contains a large desk, a conference-size table, a file cabinet, plenty of windows and a coffee maker.

"I see you still like to spread out when you work," Mac comments.

"Old habit. I like to see what I'm doing."

The two take seats at the conference table and start to plan. First on the agenda is the type of missions they will undertake. Terrorism is a cancer affecting innocent people all over the world-and cancer should be destroyed. Not arrested, *destroyed*.

Completing this objective gets complicated: Two-man teams or the entire team, civilian- or military-type operations? Whom do they target? If one individual with power and/or influence is responsible for a lot of terrorism, he will be the primary target. If possible, they'll cut off the source of finance, whatever it may be. If the money dries up, the terrorists usually do the same. Then they must consider individuals training the terrorists-this applies to people outside the gang being paid for training. And, of course, the terrorist group itself.

"Well that's sort of straightforward," comments Mac.

"I believe in using the KISS method," JJ chuckles.

"I know: keep it simple, stupid. But how stupid do we get with the first item? I mean, how high do we go to get at the source?"

"To the top."

"How did I know you were going to say that?" Mac groans. "I had a nice retirement going; a little quiet, but it beats the hell out of prison or a doze in the dirt!"

"Are you finished?"

"Yeah that's about it," Mac sighs.

"When I was a young lad," JJ offers, "my father told me that people in high places deserve respect as long as they are respectable. When these 'respectable' people start supporting things like terrorism, they deserve nothing. They're worse than someone that's right up front about what they're doing.

"My father also told me people in high places have one asshole, just like everyone else."

"Nice one-liner," Mac chuckles. "And also quite true."

With the first round of planning completed, the two old friends decide to take a walk around the grounds, or "check the perimeter," as Mac deems it. Between JJ's pipe and Mac's cigar, it appears they're trying to lay down a smoke screen along the split-rail fence surrounding the immediate property. They walk for some time before Mac breaks the silence.

"I realize what we're planning is long overdue, but may I ask what incident stirred you into action?"

"No incident," JJ answers earnestly. "I just got tired of seeing innocent men, women, and especially children getting killed or seriously injured by terrorists...or any other group who thinks they have a legitimate bitch. They constantly target defenseless people, and then say 'It was for shock value, or publicity for their cause.' I think it's done because they're either nuts, or cowards. I'll bet they would get just as much-or more-media coverage if they went up against their real enemies.

"But that wouldn't do, would it? Those people would have guns too, and they'd probably shoot back or retaliate with a bomb or two. I'm sure each group has considered these facts, and feel it's much safer to kill the innocent and claim it's better for the cause!"

The two men continue walking, with no comment from Mac.

"Having second thoughts, Mac?"

"No!" he answers quickly. "I was just thinking about what you said. You know, I never really thought about it that way." Mac pauses, then continues: "The innocent are being targeted, and we should try to do as much as we can to stop it. I just have to change my mindset from military fighting to scum extermination."

The two men finish their walk and decide to go out for dinner. The drive is quiet; both men are absorbed in their thoughts.

Mac breaks the silence when he asks, "Where are we going?"

"A restaurant up here on the left," JJ answers.

"Is this downtown?" inquires Mac as they get out of the car.

"Yep," JJ grins, knowing another 'humor time' is on the way.

"Well, let me see," Mac drawls. "We have one blinking traffic light, one general store, what looks to be a town hall, and about a dozen houses. Yeah, a half-dozen new faces will blend right in around here."

"Ya know, I think you took too many blasts to the head at rocket-launcher training," JJ counters.

"Did we finally wake up?" Mac asks with a smile. "I am developing a theory that you may have been exposed to the world of the elite liberal for such a prolonged period of time, that in all probability it has fucked up your melon!"

"Screw you!" JJ fires back. "I'm the same as I always was. I just haven't had a dickhead like you around to bring out the worst in me."

"Well, let's drink to that!" Mac says as he reaches for the doorknob at the restaurant's main entrance.

As they enter, a young waitress approaches them and inquires, "Would like to be seated for dinner, or are you going to the bar first?"

"I think we'll have dinner," smiles JJ.

"Please follow me," the waitress says.

The restaurant is small but cozy, with dark wood the main theme echoed on tables, chairs and trim around the room. Hanging plants and soft lighting make it a relaxing retreat from the fast-paced world of normal living.

"Will this be all right?" asks the waitress as they approach a corner table.

"This will be fine," JJ agrees. The two men take their seats.

"Something from the bar, gentleman?"

"Two large Dewers and water," both men declare at once.

"Will that be two each?" inquires the waitress, grinning as she writes down the order.

"But of course!" Mac replies. "And probably a few more after that."

The waitress laughs as she departs to retrieve the drinks.

"This place reminds me of Tun Tavern," Mac comments as he looks around the room.

"Would that be now, or during your first hitch in 1775?" JJ grins.

"Oh, that's good!" Mac retorts. "You know what I mean."

"Yes. I do know." JJ nods. "I thought the same thing the first time I passed through here, some years ago."

The two continue looking around the room until their drinks arrive.

"Here's to a successful project," Mac says, raising his glass in a toast.

"To a successful project," echoes JJ. Both men consume a hardy amount of their drinks.

As they place their glasses back on the table, JJ says, "This man you have in mind to lead the team-do you think he'll come on board with us?"

"I hope so," Mac answers. "He came to mind as soon as I knew our objectives. He was a Marine Corps enlisted man in the Korean War, and when it was over he possessed quite a few decorations and a battlefield commission. After Korea, he was always into something. Went through airborne jump school, worked with intelligence for a while, doing frogman stuff. He served at our naval base in Cuba in the early 60's. My guess would be he went snoopin' and poopin' in Castro's Cuba more than once.

"After his tour there, he was stationed at Camp Lejeune, North Carolina. That's where I ran across him. In 1962, he was trying to convince any general that would listen to him that we should start training our men in guerilla warfare. I can still remember one of his reasons: 'In the future, there will be more guerilla-type warfare than classic WWII-type combat.' He had the one- and two-star generals thinking, but further up the line I think the idea ran into a 'he's just a captain' attitude. Yeah…'just a captain' who had this idea two years before 'Nam. After that he was a colonel; a mustang."

"A mustang?"

"You remember," Mac urges, "someone who starts out as an enlisted private and goes into the officers' ranks. Under those circumstances, it's not easy to attain the rank of Colonel-but I'm not surprised JC did it. JC is the nickname his men gave him in Cuba," Mac explains, "They're his initials, but I think his men had something more religious in mind. Not to his face, mind you!" Mac laughs.

"He sounds like an excellent choice," JJ approves.

"He is," Mac assures him. "I'll start tracking him down in the morning."

"I never had a chance to ask your opinion on what happened in 'Nam," JJ says.

"I think Uncle Ho read our history books", Mac quips.

"What do you mean?"

"Well, in a nutshell, I think our American Revolution went like this: England was mighty; America was small. They fought a conventional war; we fought an unconventional war. General Washington, for the most part, picked his major battles. To keep this effort going, France, who was an adversary of England, started supporting America with arms and finance. The war went on until the cost got too great and people in England started bitching."

"It looks like Uncle Ho changed the names of the players without changing the ending. America became England; North Vietnam became America; Russia became France. That, plus at least one Benedict Arnold in our government for additional support."

"Oh, that's 'in a nutshell,' alright," JJ exclaims.

"But I think the shell is a little cracked!"

"Oh, yeah?" snaps Mac. "Well I sent a history book over to Afghanistan, and look what happened there, ya dick head banker!"

JJ gives a hearty laugh. This was the way he and Mac went back and forth in the old days. He also knows that if they don't slow down on the booze, they'll have a hair-hurting day in the morning.

It's a beautiful spring day at the farm. The sun is shining, birds are singing...and a gray-haired military man is slowly making his way to the kitchen for some much-needed coffee. When he finally arrives, he finds JJ staring at the coffee maker, watching the brown liquid brew.

"Headache this morning, JJ?" inquires Mac.

"As someone I know once said so aptly, even my hair hurts," JJ mumbles.

"I know what you mean," Mac concurs as he takes up the coffee vigil with JJ.

"Want something to eat?" asks JJ.

"No, thanks. I think I'll just have a few gallons of water after I get my eyes open," Mac grunts.

They're a couple of hurting puppies this morning, but they'd had a good time for it. They know it will probably be a long time before either gets the chance to do it again. Both men are guilty of overindulging on happy occasions, but if they're involved in an important project or under pressure of any type, they tread very lightly or abstain until the project comes to a successful conclusion.

In the middle of the second pot of coffee, JJ announces, "Let's get this show on the road!"

"Spoken like a true upper-class civilian schmecklehead," Mac responds as he stands up and starts walking towards the den.

"What's wrong with 'let's get this show on the road'?" JJ inquires.

"It sounds like something from a circus movie."

"I see. So we're going to use military jargon like 'twenty hundred hours' instead of eight o'clock, and shoot three times, and holler 'halt'."

"Something like that," Mac agrees as he walks into the den. "Where do I sit?"

"You can use the small table by the window," JJ instructs him. "It's not a camouflage phone, but I guess you can make do."

"I'll make do, schmeckle," Mac retorts with a grin.

JJ sits down at his desk and starts planning the renovation of the barn. After a few hours of serious thought, JJ breaks the total silence.

"Mac can I bounce a few ideas off you?"

"Sure," Mac replies as he pushes himself away from his desk. "I was about to ask you the same thing."

"I have a rough plan on how to renovate the barn and still make it look like a bed-and-breakfast," JJ starts. "The first floor will be used for the training facility, and the second floor-the current hay loft-will be converted into living quarters. The center of the second floor will be cut away to expose the first floor, so the doors from each of the living quarters will over look the training area. A walkway in front of the living quarters will encircle the training area below. We'll install two inside staircases, one at each end of the barn, connecting the living quarters to the training area.

"During the renovation, we will say the first floor is going to be used as a dining and lobby area. After the workers leave, we can set up training areas for martial arts, weapons practice, a briefing area and the like. For our own security, a monitoring area will be set up for cameras and listing devices we'll install around the property. Each team member will have a car, registered to a false ID.

"For the barn renovations, I have a local man in mind, a carpenter named Di Nice," JJ continues. "He normally works alone, but he's capable of planning, organizing and recruiting other good men for a big job. For the plumbing he will probably subcontract to Huffer; for electrical, to Nanning.

"Sounds good," Mac approves as he picks up the tablet he's been using. "I've been on the phone trying to track down that old salt I was telling you about, the one that could run the house and take a hand if trouble pops up. Anyway, it turns out he's one of your local residents."

"No kidding!" JJ exclaims. "Who is he?"

"Retired First Sergeant Kiner, Mac replies. "I call him Top Sergeant, or just Top. He's a great cook, and an even better shot with a rifle and pistol. Top Kiner, being a local, can also help promote our cover as a bed-and-breakfast."

"Good," JJ confirms. "Did you get in touch with the Colonel?"

"Yes, I did. I'm flying to South Carolina tomorrow morning to meet with JC. I figure one-on-one is the best way to go with this."

"Well, I guess we're on our way." JJ looks up and says, "I'll take you to the airport and see you off to South Carolina, then I'll look up Di Nice to start the renovations."

"Sounds like a plan to me," Mac grins. "Let's go check the perimeter."

"Let me reload my pipe first," smiles JJ.

The sun is sinking low in the western sky. Both men take a thought break, walking and enjoying the rays from the sun that illuminate the rural setting.

"This is my favorite time of the day," Mac announces.

"Mine too. Maybe we can give other people the time to enjoy it as well, instead of worrying about being killed for no reason."

After that statement the pace of the stroll picks up, and so does the smoking. Break time had just ended.

There isn't much activity at the Philadelphia International Airport in the morning. After the early flights, the pace slows for a while. JJ gets the boarding pass and rejoins Mac by a payphone as he hangs up the receiver.

"All set?" JJ asks.

"Everything is squared away," Mac replies. "JC will meet me at the airport, and we'll drive to a place not far from Hilton Head Island. We'll do most of our talking there. If he comes on board with us, we'll start reviewing possible candidates for the team. If he doesn't, I'll catch a morning flight back."

"About the team," interrupts JJ. "I know that's your turf, but one of our board members recommended someone to me. All he gave me was the name, 'Blue Jay'. Have you ever heard that name before?"

"Oh yeah, I've heard about Blue Jay," Mac responds with a muffled laugh. "He plays by the rules until somebody pisses him off, and then...watch out."

"Do you think the Colonel would consider him?" JJ inquires.

"JC knows him; I'm sure he'll be on his list," Mac says as he moves toward the line boarding his flight.

"Have a safe trip, Mac," JJ shouts.

Mac waves his boarding pass in response as he walks down the hall to board the plane.

As Mac's plane lifts off the runway, JJ is leaving the airport and merging into traffic on Route 95 north. One hour later, he begins tracking down Di Nice. *Let me see*, he thinks. *I'll drive around town first; maybe I'll catch sight of him.* Just as he finishes the thought he sees Di Nice's red pickup truck heading down the street in his direction. JJ stops his Jag and flags down the pickup, and then rolls down the window.

"What's your schedule like?" JJ shouts.

"Finishing up a job right now," Di Nice answers. "Do you have some work you want done?"

"More like a project, with you as the main contractor."

"No problem," He responds enthusiastically.

"When can you stop up at my place?"

"How about tomorrow morning, around 9 AM?" Di Nice suggests.

"See you then." JJ waves as he pulls away from the truck.

JJ feels confident he has made a good choice. He knows from experience, you just tell Di Nice what you want and it gets done.

Well, I guess the next thing on my agenda is to finalize the planning for the barn. With that thought JJ resumes his normal mode of driving: not too fast, but never under the speed limit.

CHAPTER THREE

I t is 11:15 AM when Mac's plane touches down at Hilton Head South Carolina Airport. JC is waiting at the arrival gate, and greets Mac with a warm handshake.

"Good to see you again, sir," JC says enthusiastically.

"Same here," replies Mac.

After collecting Mac's luggage, they head for the short-term parking.

"What are you driving these days?" inquires Mac.

"Well, sir, now that I'm retired, I am acting more like a conservative Southern gentleman," answers JC.

"I see. I guess that means we'll be riding in that big-ass olive drab Hummer over there?"

"That be it, sir," grins JC.

Marines always joke around until the shit hits the fan, and then the joking lamp is put out...or at least dimmed. As the Hummer heads for the airport exit, Mac says, "We have some heavy shit to discuss. Is this vehicle clean?"

"Yes, sir," responds JC. "When you called I knew something was on, so I checked it out good, then drove around for a few hours to see if I had company."

"Good," approves Mac. "You'll see after we talk how important absolute security is in this matter. I will give you a very brief overview of the plan. If you want out after that, no problem. But the more involved we all get in this, the harder it will be to break free."

"I understand," JC says, his voice firm.

With that, Mac launches into the overview. When he finishes, JC inquires about his part.

"Not so fast," Mac interrupts. "Why don't you take some time to think about the consequences: possible hardship, jail...or death."

"Well, sir, it's an idea that's past due, making the powerful assholes in this world pay for their bad deeds. And you know me. I like to contribute if something is going to help our country-or the world, for that matter."

"I figured you would say something like that," Mac says. "You will be team leader. You'll select, train and make the members work as a team. There will be no tryouts. The men you pick, if they agree, are automatically in, so you'll have to be very selective. Still want the job?"

"It's a tall order," JC answers. Then he becomes very quiet.

"Having second thoughts?" Mac suggests.

"No, sir. Just starting the selection process."

It is mid-afternoon when the Hummer turns off the main road onto a winding lane through pine trees. About half a mile later they come to a halt on a white sand beach. Mac surveys the area and almost misses the cabin amongst the large trees. It is constructed of the same type of wood, and blends right into the forest.

"Nice place," Mac approves.

"Thank you, sir. It's a good place to get away, think, relax or plan things."

JC goes into the back of the Hummer and retrieves two briefcases.

"Security check?" asks Mac.

JC shakes his head yes as he moves to the cabin. He first checks the door for his little 'has someone been in my cabin' marker. Satisfied it hasn't been changed, he proceeds to unlock and open the door, move to a wall cabinet and deactivate the alarm system.

"For the amateur contingent," JC announces. Putting both cases on the table, he opens the larger one and removes a device used to search for eavesdropping bugs. He turns it on and starts sweeping the cabin. When he completes the inspection, he opens the smaller case and removes what looks like a miniature radar station.

"Now that's a neat gizmo," Mac laughs.

JC takes a small notebook and pen out of his pocket. After he is finished writing, he hands the book to Mac, who reads: "This scans the room for other listening methods, like shooting a laser through a window and bouncing it off a lamp shade to pick up conversations."

Mac nods.

JC clicks the gizmo on and waits for a while.

"I guess we can do some serious talking now; everything looks clean," JC declares. "The cabin is stocked with food, if you would like to have some chow."

"That sounds good," Mac agrees, and then adds, "I trust you have a beverage as well?"

"I think I may have brought along something," JC grins. "I believe it has a picture of a ship on the label."

"That'll have to do, "Mac says. "Any port in a storm."

Mac and JC have just finished their meal, using the dining time to catch up on each other's lives: what they have been doing, how their families are, and the like. Each had served on and off again for many years in the Corps. Mac spotted JC's potential when he was a general and JC was only a captain. He was way ahead of the rest of the pack on where the world was going, and what they should be doing to prepare for it.

JC also had a great respect for General Mac. Mac was one of the real generals in the US military; not one of those pompous political asses that stay in power during peace time, and then when the shit hits the fan are immediately transferred. Everyone knows being a good butt-kisser does not win wars, unless you are fighting the gay liberation army.

Mac takes a sip of his coffee and says, "Well, JC, you have had an additional four hours to kick this idea around. Do you still want in?"

"Yes, sir," JC replies.

"Then maybe we should get started," Mac suggests, and goes to retrieve his briefcase while JC clears away the dinner dishes. "I guess the best place to start will be the chain of command," he states. "It will be quite a bit different than the usual chain, due to the extreme security that we're using.

"First of all, there is a board already in place to finance, select objectives and give collateral support to the team. Our link to the board will be through the board chairman and myself, but you will not be privy to the identity of any of the other board members. You will know the identity of the chairman, and he will know yours.

"As far as the chain on the other side, if something happens to JJ, I think we will fold our tents and fade into the sunset," Mac continues. "JJ and I go back a long way and I would trust him with my life. The others I don't know that well, so I would not want to continue this mission without him. I do know that JJ is extremely loyal...but don't get me wrong: he's no pushover. If you piss him off you'll know it, and if you piss him off for no reason, he'll probably try to kick your lemon off."

"Sounds like a good man," JC chuckles.

"He is," confirms Mac. "We served together during that unpleasantness with Japan. Both of us were young and inexperienced, but we were quick learners. JJ eventually left the Corps; said there was too much political bullshit during peacetime. Me, being the ever politically correct man that I am, stayed in. Is that a chuckle I detect?" inquires Mac.

"No, sir," JC immediately answers. "I was just wondering if all those political types in Washington, D.C., saw you as politically correct."

"Ah, fuck them," Mac quips. "Some of those assholes made me want to puke. Those liberal ass-suckers want it all their way until something threatens their well-being or takes away some of their wealth. Then they pull their dresses up over their heads and run around in circles shouting, 'Make the nasty man go away, make the nasty man go away'...and that's just the male liberals I'm talking about."

"Are you laughing, Captain?" inquires Mac.

JC, trying to catch his breath from laughing so hard, manages a low "A little," then adds, "And it's Colonel, sir."

"Colonel?" Mac raises an eyebrow. "Oh, that's right. Well, I liked you better when you were a captain."

"Yes, sir," says JC, recovering.

"Okay, JC," Mac grins. "Now that you have that off your chest, I guess we should get back to the briefing."

Mac opens his brief case and pulls out some papers.

"This is a very high-level overview of what we hope to accomplish. Our idea is to make it very expensive for anyone in power, anyone trying to get into power, or any dickhead with a group that uses terror to reach their goals. We are tired of ordinary people suffering at the hands of these monsters. Governments either can't or don't want to help, so we are going to try to do something. This is JJ's idea, and I think it's a good one. Once we get this thing rolling, we must be very careful it doesn't get out of control, or used for the wrong reasons. I have seen and heard things that were done in the name of 'national security' or similar reasons, which were actually done for the benefit of big business. As I said, there is a board already in place. Each member was hand-picked by JJ."

"Can they all be counted on in a crunch?" asks JC.

"That was JJ's primary consideration," Mac replies. "Because if something goes wrong, or a leak occurs, we'll all be in deep shit. The second consideration was the feeling each man has about what is going on in the world, and his willingness to do something about it. Third was the back ground each man brought to this operation. I don't know their identities, but the board reflects a wide array of industry and government contacts that will be needed to support the team. Fourth was the ability of each member to contribute financially to the project. It's going to be a small operation, but it will require considerable financing and resources. I realize this arrangement is different, and its success relies on trusting people in key positions, but JJ and I feel it's the best way to keep security intact for this clandestine operation. Do you see any problems with this?" Mac inquires.

"For myself, I'd say no problem." JC replies. "I know and trust you. But I have to wonder about the members of the team. Some will probably be okay with it, having been involved in the need-to-know business at one time or another. Others will realize this, but are inquisitive by nature and will probably sniff around for answers. What do we do in that case?"

"Well, we can't send them to the unemployment office, and if they're just being inquisitive we'll consider what to do when it happens. We lay down the rules and see if anyone gets nosy. Why?" Mac asks. "Do you have someone in mind for the team that may get inquisitive?"

"Yes, sir," answers JC.

"Then maybe we shouldn't consider them for the team."

"Well that's a thought," JC says, "but we are dealing with a wish list of qualities each man should possess: Loyalty to the team and each other, the ability to keep things to himself, intelligence and resourcefulness, and a background of expertise that will fill one of the team's needs. It's not an easy task."

"That's true," Mac agrees.

"Since we are on the topic," JC continues, "when we start running live missions, the team will require detailed briefings on who and why the action is being taken, and they must be included in the decision process."

"Do you think they'll require that inclusion?"

"The men I have in mind will, and I definitely will."

"Okay," Mac agrees. "I can understand your concerns. But if someone gets captured and the target finds out we're after them..."

JC cuts Mac off in mid sentence. "In that case, the team priority becomes getting the captured man back, doing damage assessment and deciding whether to continue the project or back off for a while."

"I see you have strong feelings about this particular area," Mac says.

"Yes, sir."

"I see your point, and I concur," the General nods. "If the board doesn't like it, they can find another team. Now, let's take a break."

"I'll put on a pot of coffee. I have a feeling it's going to be a long night," JC adds.

Mac is finishing his second cup of coffee and his briefing on JJ when JC makes a motion for another cup.

"Please," Mac responds. "The reason I am going into such great lengths about JJ is because I want you to have an idea of who this man is, and why I jumped on board without any hesitation. Yes, JJ and I go way back, but it is more than that. It's joining a man who wants to protect innocent people, without any reward in money, power or any other type of gain. In addition to the will to do something, he also has the means to finance it and the connections to bring it all together. Did I give you some insight on the man?"

"Indeed you did, sir," JC assures him. "I'm satisfied he is the right man to head up this type of mission."

"Good," Mac says with a smile. "I guess the next item on the agenda is making selections for the team. How many do you think we should have?"

"My initial estimate is eight," JC answers without hesitation. "Seven team members and a pilot that can handle a wide array of aircraft. Of course, he will be used mainly to get the team to and from the target area, but he'll also handle other things if needed, and must be able to keep cool in a firefight."

"Now *that's* a tall order," Mac says. "Do you have someone in mind for the job?"

"Yes," answers JC. "He'll probably bitch and moan about being put into this type of situation, and bug the shit out of us for a bonus if we survive, but he handles himself quite well in a fight.

"The way I see it," JC continues, "projects will be dictated by the circumstances, but never one man alone. He may seem to be alone, but his backup will be there for support if needed. We may run any number and type of teams, or decide to always keep the entire team together and act as one force. We'll make those decisions when we get into the projects."

"When they execute as a team, who will be the leader in the field?" Mac asks.

"Sir, with this kind of group I don't even want to think about it." JC shakes his head. "We'll just have to watch and see what happens when they all come together."

"Shall we call it a night, General?" inquires JC. "I have some people in mind for the team, but I'd like to sleep on it and go at it again when I'm fresh. I usually walk on the beach early in the morning; I'll kick it around again and we can have another session after morning chow."

Mac agrees with a nod of his head. The two men finish their coffee and head for their racks-Marine Corps talk for beds.

"You can bunk in there, General. It's the guest suite at the chateau JC."

"Once again, any port in a storm."

Both men are exhausted: Mac with the flight and bringing JC up to date on the project, and JC with absorbing all the information, making decisions that could cost him dearly, and thinking about the team.

"Good night, General," JC calls.

"Good night, Captain," replies Mac. "Oh, I mean…"

"Yeah, I know," JC cuts in. "You liked me better when I was a Captain."

Mac laughs as he enters his 'suite.'

The morning is still and quiet on the beach as JC finishes his walk and heads for the cabin. Mac has breakfast almost ready, and is pouring two cups of coffee when JC appears in the doorway.

"Smells good," JC approves.

"Looks like I timed it just right," Mac says as he hands JC a mug.

The two men take a sip of coffee, then head for the chow, load up their plates, sit down and start eating. After a few minutes, JC starts the morning session.

"Sir I think our first rule should be that the team members be known by code names only. It will be better for security, and harder for someone to betray the team."

"You won't even tell me their real names?" asks Mac.

"It'll be better that way," JC replies, offering no explanation.

"I can be trusted, ya know," Mac replies.

"Sir, it's not a matter of trust. These men are all very, very good at what they do. Stealth tactics, weapons, explosives…you name it. If you only know them by their code names, and we're somehow betrayed, you won't be suspected. On the other hand, if you do know their names and we are betrayed, someone may make you a gift of some C4, complete with mercury switch, and when you take your morning dump you'll wind up wearing the shit-pot seat as an Easter bonnet."

"Code names are good," Mac agrees. "Besides, I just got that shit-pot seat broken in."

The two men finish breakfast with small talk, knowing that when they start putting the team together their meetings will run into marathon sessions. With breakfast done, Mac and JC once again sit at the 'planning table,' which by default turns out to be the kitchen table. With the radar gizmo running to detect eavesdroppers, the two once again discuss the project. Mac starts the session with a bang:

"Just one pilot?"

"Yes, sir," JC confirms. "Also, I've made some changes. Each man will have the same contract, and it will be very lucrative. Sir, I hope none of that corporate cost-cutting shit comes into play with this project?"

"I don't think we have to worry about that," Mac assures him.

"I hope not, because the first time I see it I'm going to raise hell, and if they don't change it they can kiss my ass good-bye. These men will be risking everything, and I won't have them doing it for peanuts."

"I agree," Mac confirms.

"Well, to start with," JC continues, "the air jockey will be someone I've worked with before. During his tour in the corps, he always seemed to be in the hot spots, or around when us or the Navy were running something in clandestine mode. He was also involved in some black OPS stuff with the intelligence community."

"I selected the remaining members with two criteria in mind: first, their abilities, and second, their language skills. I get the feeling we will be involved in operations all over the world, and if we have members on the team that can converse in those countries' lingo, all the better. As you know sir, this is just basic shit. The real challenge comes in forming a team that can work together without pissing each other off every five minutes. The men I have in mind are mostly independent types, and they enjoy it that way. Bringing them together will not be easy."

"Are you sure you're selecting the right type of men?" inquires Mac.

"I think so, sir," JC answers. "There may be an initial period of adjustment, but when things cool down, hopefully we will have a solid team with mutual respect and camaraderie. If I said that to a civilian they would laugh, but you known what I mean…it's like being in the Corps. When we're in barracks, we raise hell. When we're in the field against the enemy, we give them hell."

"That's about it," the General agrees.

"Some of these men are active, and some have other business interests but take contracts for any number of reasons. Once again, sir, only code names will be used. I'll give a brief background and reasoning for each, but they are all excellent men. Some excel in certain areas, and I'll point that out as we go."

"I guess we'll start with 'Benz': Japanese, heavy in martial arts, been in the contract business many years. 'Panda': Philippine, also into martial arts, takes on contracts from time to time. Regular occupation: engineering consultant. 'Plum' speaks several languages from the old Soviet block countries; heavy military background in special OPS, Green Berets, and Airborne Ranger. He's also a part-timer, owns a small plumbing supply business.

"'Check': Arab, explosives, owns a Middle East restaurant. 'Tick' is Cuban; he does explosives; stock broker by day. 'Bris': primarily a contractor, but also an artist, and a good one. You remember sir, I said seven men plus a pilot would be enough, but I have added two more to the list: 'Pru,' English, contractor, long-range shooter; and 'Met,' German, also a contractor and long-range shooter. I have selected all of these men for their experience, skills and integrity. It also happens we will have the language area covered. As you can see by their nationalities, we have six different languages, and Plum can cover a lot of the old Soviet block countries. All of these individuals can also fit into a situation where that language is spoken. I also doubled up in specialties where possible, like martial arts and long-range shooters, and I can back up the pilot."

"I was wondering when you were going to put yourself in an action role," the General interrupts. "I don't think we can afford that type of risk."

"I wasn't thinking of an active role, sir," JC responds, "just as support and in special situations. Say the entire team is being chased through the countryside of a foreign land, and our pilot is down or can't make the flight. Do you think I'll just sit here on my ass?"

"In a case like that," Mac replies, "we'll probably both be in something, flying somewhere, to get the team out of the shit."

Both men sit back and laugh. Neither has missed too many steps in past years. They may be slower physically, but are quick-minded and have the same dedication to duty.

"Ten?" the General asks suddenly. "You mentioned a ten-man team, but you've only covered nine."

"Yes, I know," replies JC. "The tenth will take some decision-making."

"I'll bet you're going to say 'Blue Jay'," Mac quips.

"Yes, he's the one," JC confirms.

"Well let's hear the pros and cons."

"First," JC begins, "he doesn't seem to respect anything. When we served together he respected me-I think-but he never seemed to take to authority, or the politics that went with it. After he left the military, he worked for the intelligence community, and then became a contractor. I tried to keep abreast of his activities as much as I could for someone in that line of work. He always gets the job done, but has been known to change the game plan if he doesn't like it."

"He has the same type of skills as the others, but has decided not to become a super expert in any one area. He'd rather be very good in many areas. However, there is one skill that seems to come to him naturally, and that's the ability to get in and out of places without anyone knowing he's been there. He's never revealed how he's become so successful at it. People in the intelligence community have tried to find out in order to teach new agents the skills, but he will not budge. All they get is 'It's what I do' and a smile as he leaves the area."

"Do you think he can work with a team?"

"With this team, he would have no problem." JC assures Mac. "The combinations of skills and personalities we have are compatible with his, and he already knows a few of them. I will say this, however: he does like to work alone. My personal opinion is that he doesn't like to rely on other people, and with a team he doesn't take the chances he usually does when he works solo.

"This brings up my main concern," JC continues. "If he gets fired up about something and wants to go and right a wrong, it'll be hard to convince him that maybe it's not a good idea. He does not look for or want any kind of leadership role, but he has a way of getting people riled up just talking about a subject he feels strongly about. Now can you imagine what would happen if he got this team riled up about something, and they decided to take action on their own?"

"Well," the general asserts, "that, I've learned, is a double-edged sword. It can be good or bad. Sometimes you really need a man to get the troops up for something big or nearly impossible. We'll have to weigh his strong points against his shortcomings and make a decision."

"You're right, sir," JC concedes. "I'll ask you to be the objective one in this decision. I served with him in the past, and knowing his tendencies may cloud my judgment."

"There is something you may be overlooking about Blue Jay," Mac adds. "He may have changed in those areas you're worrying about."

"Good point," agrees JC. "From what I've told you so far, what do think of the team...and about Blue Jay?"

Mac sits back and starts to speak,

"To put a preliminary plan like this together with such short notice requires a 'well done' from your former commanding general. You have, of course, required each man to have good primary skills, and experience using those skills. In addition, you have brought additional things to the team, such as language skills we'll need. Each man also has a special skill that can be used if needed. I get the feeling every one will be able to work, either as a team or alone, and above all can be trusted. Very, very well done," Mac announces in a proud voice.

"As for the Blue Jay matter, I once had a situation similar to this. I had an officer in my command with the same type of characteristics. I think the only thing that kept him in line was the fact that he was in the military, and had to play by the rules if he wanted to stay in the Corps."

"How did you handle that situation, sir?" JC inquires with intensity.

The General takes a deep breath and replies, "I waited until I retired, and then asked him to put a team together for me."

"Good one, Mac. I didn't even see that one coming. Do you really think I was like that?" JC asks.

"Does a bear shit in the woods?" replies the General. "I think Blue Jay is a good choice."

"Then that completes the team," JC announces. "Now all we have to do is get them to come on board."

"How will we proceed on that issue?" Mac inquires.

"I have worked with some of these people, and since you have made the decision on Blue Jay…"

JC pauses, giving the general time to respond. Not wanting to disappoint him, Mac finishes, "somebody had to make the decision. We do want to get this project started in this lifetime."

"Well, sir," JC says, "all I know is: Yes, your Honor, it was General Mac's decision to add Blue Jay to the team."

"I knew I liked you better when you were a Captain," Mac says.

Both men start to laugh and head to the kitchen for a break and more coffee. On the way back, JC stops by and checks out the gizmo.

"Is that thing working okay?" Mac asks.

"Seems to be," replies JC. "If it picks up anything, it starts playing a recording to alert us. It plays a tune instead of an alert sound so uninvited listeners won't know they've been detected."

"Then what?" Mac asks.

"Then I get out another gizmo to see if the snoopers are in the immediate area."

"I liked it better when we used two cans and a string," Mac declares. JC smiles as he joins Mac at the table.

"Well, sir, to continue." JC reconvenes the meeting. "If Blue Jay joins us, he can help recruit some of these men. He knows and has worked with a few of them. The problem is going to be the initial story we use to get the men to come on board. We can't tell them the truth until they join us. It's not that I don't trust them; it's more that if they turn us down and then go out on another project, get captured and shot full of drugs, and then spill our project along with what the bad guys really wanted, we could get compromised."

"That could also happen if they're on one of our missions," Mac points out.

"Yes, sir, it could," JC replies. "But we will have more control over the situation. One, the team leaves together, or not at all. Two, if a man goes out alone he will have a second man in the background if needed, and the team will be positioned to react quickly."

"That's going to restrict our activity to one project at a time. What will I tell the board if they want more for their buck?" Mac asks.

"Tell them we are surgeons, and a surgeon does one operation at a time," JC answers. "If he is performing brain surgery, he doesn't also take a boil off your ass just because he has you on the table.

I realize that in the case of politicians it would be tempting to do both at once, since both surgeries would be performed at the same location. But it's going to be one team, one op at a time. If we spread ourselves too thin and get into trouble, who is going to help us?"

"That's probably the smartest and safest approach," Mac agrees, "but I think I'll hold off telling the board until we have the team in place. If they do have a problem with that decision, it will be harder to make any changes at that point."

"Whatever you think is best, sir," JC concedes. "Now for the recruiting story."

After an hour or so, both men agree the original story will contain basically the same facts, but can be ad-libbed during delivery.

"When do you think we should tell them the real story?" JC asks.

"We should tell them before they meet the other members of the team. Someone who has good credentials and is involved in the project should give them the facts. You'll be recruiting and telling them the original story, so maybe I should tell them about the real project."

"Very well, sir, sounds like a plan," approves JC. "I'll start tracking down Blue Jay in the morning."

"I think it will be best if I stay on here at the cabin until you approach Blue Jay," adds the General. "We will use this cabin for our meetings with the men. If Blue Jay accepts your proposal, I'll be here to relay the real story to him. After he's recruited, I'll go back up north and continue planning with JJ. As you contact and get agreements from the other men, I'll fly back for the meetings."

"I guess Phase Two will start tomorrow," JC states with obvious pleasure. "I brought some good cigars with me. Shall we take a walk down the beach before chow?"

"Sounds good," Mac agrees.

JC opens his briefcases and removes two cigars, a 9-millimeter automatic and an ammo magazine. He hands Mac one of the cigars and puts the other in his mouth. He then pulls the receiver back on the pistol, checks the chamber, and then lets it go. After the receiver slides back home he inserts the magazine. As it clicks into place, JC explains, "May as well get into the habit again, sir." Mac nods as he fires up his cigar. The two men leave the cabin and head for the beach. The sun is low in the sky, casting an orange glow over the area.

"This is my favorite time of day," exclaims JC, "the sun…the clouds…the orange glow and casting shadows."

"My favorite time is morning," Mac says.

"Oh, you prefer sunrise and singing birds?" JC inquires.

"No. More like, Oh, I'm still here!" Mac responds. "You start to notice things like that at my age."

JC burst into laughter as he says, "Sir, I think you are going to have a great number of mornings ahead of you."

"You think?" questions Mac. "You're not sure?"

The two men laugh, engaging in a word-fencing match as they continue their walk.

The next morning, the sun has just begun to peek over the ocean when Mac appears in the kitchen.

"Well, I see you're still here," JC says.

"Yeah, I managed to make another one," Mac answers. "What's on the agenda for today?"

"I was going to look for Blue Jay," JC answers. "I know of a few isolated places he goes to train. I'll check them out before I start making inquires. Once I make contact with him, finding the others will be easier."

"Do you mind if I come along?" asks Mac.

"Not at all. Just remember what I told you about him."

JC and Mac have checked out two locations without success and are on the way to a third when JC pulls off onto what used to be a road. A mile or so later, they are parked on the edge of a cliff overlooking a valley. A stream runs through it, bubbling cheerfully along. JC reaches into one of the packs and produces a pair of binoculars and a sniper scope. Mac follows as JC walks over to a small tree, leans against it and starts scanning the valley with the binoculars. In the middle of his third sweep, JC stops, puts the scope on top of the binoculars and re-finds the contact. Once focused, he looks into the scope.

"We got lucky," JC smiles. "He's down there working out."

"Good," Mac approves. "Lets go see if he's interested. I guess you know how to get down there?"

"Yes," JC assures him as they pile into to the Hummer.

The road winds around and finally reaches the bottom of the valley. JC stops the Hummer and says, "I'll walk in and make contact with Blue Jay, sir."

"How far is he?"

"Approximately one mile."

"I'd like to see how good this Blue Jay really is. Why don't we try to creep up on him?" Mac suggests.

"I don't think that would be a good idea," JC advises.

"What do you mean? We're both Marines; we know how to snoop

and poop," Mac says.

"I still don't..." Mac interrupts JC with a "Come on" as he gets out of the vehicle.

JC reluctantly follows. Mac and JC move quietly through the woods, their steps slow and deliberate. When they are within 100 yards of their prey, JC once again looks through the binoculars.

"What is he doing?" whispers Mac.

"He's still working out, with a sword," JC returns.

"A sword!" exclaims Mac in hushed whisper.

"Yeah," replies JC. "If we surprise him too much our heads may have an 'off-the-body' experience."

"Very funny," Mac snaps. "If he's so good, how come he hasn't discovered us by now? I think his reputation is mostly folklore."

"Maybe," JC says, "but we're taking it low and very slow from here on."

The two men start a series of crawls until they come up behind a huge oak tree.

"Time for another peek," JC whispers as he slowly rises up for a look. As he scans the area a voice inquires,

"Did you two old fucks escape from the home again?" It was Blue Jay, on the other side of the giant oak. "I wonder if they pay a deposit on returns-like when you bring back beer bottles."

"Do you know who I am?" Mac asks, his voice somewhere between embarrassed and indignant.

"Why doesn't *he* know who you are?" Blue Jay asks, gesturing towards JC.

"I tried to tell you this wasn't a good idea," JC laughs.

"I know you did, CAPTAIN!" Mac fires back.

Blue Jay gives a big smile and holds out his hand as he says,

"Good to see you, Colonel."

"Good to see you too," says JC as he shakes his hand. "This is General Mac."

"I know who he is," Blue Jay interrupts. "It's a pleasure, sir. I know you by reputation." Blue Jay extends his hand. Mac smiles as he shakes his hand and says,

"Now let me get this straight. It's your pleasure to meet an old fuck from the home with a good reputation?"

"Yeah, something like that," Blue Jay quips.

"I like this kid," Mac approves. "Let's tell him why we're here."

All three start laughing as they move to the clearing where Blue Jay had been working out. After the initial feeler to see how he would react to the idea, it took another hour to bring him up to date-but Blue Jay was in from the start. JC thought he probably would be. He recalls Blue Jay mentioning more than once "all these good people dying because of evil bastards at the top."

"Where do we go from here?" Blue Jay asks.

"You and JC will find the other members on the team list, interview them, and when we have a full team I'll come back to meet with each one of the members.

"Does that mean the Colonel and I won't be telling them the whole story?"

"You will tell them the story to a point, then I'll fill the rest in," Mac explains. "I want to interview each man myself."

"And if you don't like my selection?" inquires JC.

"Then we'll talk about it," answers Mac.

Blue Jay looks at Mac, then JC, and laughs as he says, "Oh I can see this is going to be a fun process." Mac and JC both smile and nod.

"You know," Blue Jay continues, "maybe I won't haul you guys back to the home. But if they raise the amount on return deposits, I'm not making any promises."

"Oh, that's funny," JC answers.

Mac laughs. "Let's get some chow."

"Good idea," JC agrees. "I have three big-ass steaks in the freezer, ready for the charcoal."

"But what are we going to do while they thaw out?" Mac asks, already knowing the answer.

"Well," JC replies, "somebody gave me these green bottles with a ship on the label..."

"Really," Mac says as he and JC start to leave the area.

Blue Jay, still sitting in the clearing, says, "I knew this was going to be a fun process."

The next morning all three men are wearing sunglasses; partly to protect their eyes from the strong South Carolina sun, and partly from the aftereffects of consuming the liquid in those green bottles. JC speaks first.

"Well, sir, I guess..."

Mac waves his hands in the air. "You don't have to yell, Captain. You're not counting cadence for a platoon, ya know."

"Yes, sir," JC smiles. "I guess your head is worse than mine."

"You have no idea," Mac groans. "I should have known better. That stuff probably had a swabbie curse on it for all Marines who drink it."

JC and Blue Jay start laughing and holding their heads at the same time; experiencing something like an ice cream headache. After a brief break to regroup, JC starts again.

"General Mac, what is the schedule?"

"I will fly back to Jersey tomorrow and continue planning with JJ. You men will keep putting the team together. I know I don't have to say this," he says, turning to Blue Jay, "but JC and I have confided in you more than we are telling the others because JC knows and trusts you, and I get the same feeling. We also know that with your skills you will probably find out anyway, but we just wanted you to know."

"I appreciate and respect both of your trusts," Blue Jay acknowledges.

"I never thought I would hear that from you," JC says.

"Well, sir, I always thought it about you. I just never said it," Blue Jay confirms.

The remainder of the day is spent going over the material that was covered the previous day, and the procedures for recruiting the team members.

It is 7a.m. the next morning at Hilton Head. JC and Blue Jay have taken Mac to the airport to see him off.

"I haven't enjoyed myself like this in a long while," Mac announces. "They say it's not the amount of time you spend, but the quality. Where is that more true than in our line of work, where we may all be dead tomorrow?"

JC and Blue Jay smile and shake their heads in agreement as they say goodbye to the General.

As he walks to board his plane, Blue Jay comments, "General Mac is made of what generals should be made of."

"Yes, he is," confirms JC.

They watch General Mac's flight take off, and then turn to their assignment. Blue Jay knows where most of the team members on the list are, and can find the remainder without much trouble. JC is developing a training plan that will coordinate all of their special skills into an extraordinary team…but first they have to find them.

When Mac's flight touches down at Newark Airport, JJ is waiting. Mac collects his luggage and heads for the exit. As he walks into the terminal exit area, the first thing he sees is JJ, wearing a big smile.

"How was your trip?" JJ asks

"Very good," replies Mac.

During the drive home, both men talk about the usual things: the weather, family, and the stock market. The Jag had been left unattended in short-term parking and they feel it's never too soon to implement security procedures. When the two men get to JJ's place in New Jersey, they relax and talk more freely.

"I assume everything went well?" JJ says.

"Extremely well," Mac confirms, and continues briefing JJ on the South Carolina trip. At the end of his report, Mac sits back and says, "So what have you been doing while I've been busting my butt in South Carolina?"

"Well," JJ answers, "while you were on *vacation* in South Carolina, I started putting our home base together. The barn conversion is moving rapidly. I'm working with the architect and including, without his knowledge, areas for devices to detect human presence, and quick evacuation passages should we need them. Shall we go for a smoke and check out the new bed-and-breakfast?"

"Sounds good," Mac agrees.

"Oh, by the way," JJ says with a smile, "you are my new partner in the bed-and-breakfast biz."

"I never was in business before," Mac quips. "I could sell it, move to a small island and have beautiful native girls around all the time. How's that sound to you?"

JJ strikes a match to light his cigar and smiles as he says, "Sounds good…if you live."

Mac lets out a hearty laugh as both men head for the door. It is a warm, sunny day, and a small army of contractors are working on the "Bed-and-Breakfast."

"It looks like they're making good progress on that barn," Mac observes.

"Yes, they are a good group," JJ agrees. "They tore out the inside in no time and are starting from the bottom up. We're using wood for the renovations, and we can make special modifications after the workers have finished. We'll have to go through all the motions of starting a real bed-and-breakfast. Of course, we are already booked up for months and can't see any openings for about a year.

By then, we will probably be dead or in prison anyway."

"Or on an island with a bunch of native girls," Mac pipes in.

"If you live," JJ reiterates. "I figure at the rate the renovations are going, it should only be another month before it's completed. Do you have any time estimates on putting the team together?"

"JC and Blue Jay are going to contact the people who are already involved in some kind of business first. They will be easier to find, and they'll need more time to make business arrangements during their absence. That should cover most of the team, if they're not presently on a contract. Two of the members and the pilot may be harder to find, but I have a feeling Blue Jay will find them."

Six weeks later, after seven-day workweeks, the "Bed and Breakfast" is completed. JJ and Mac have also been busy selecting targets for the team, and have settled on five possibilities. These five will be presented to the Board for selection and approval. If one of the Board Members has an additional target, it will also be considered. If a situation occurs where the board and the team do not agree, the target will be put aside for later consideration. This is one of many procedures and protocols JJ and Mac have put together.

"Well I guess it's time for me to head south again," Mac announces, "and you to get ready for the Board meeting."

"It looks that way."

"I'll put a call in to JC and have him set up the meetings with the team members," Mac continues. "I figure three interviews a day, plus another 4 days to discover any personality clashes. Tentatively, we could start heading up here in about a week."

"Good," JJ says. "I think we'll use a small airline that lands at Mercer Airport, just outside of Trenton," he continues. "We could charter a jet, but that brings attention, and a paper trail. It will be better if the team travels separately on the same flight. After we get settled at home base, you, JC, Air Jockey and myself will look around and set up our own transportation at a nearby airport. I'll lease different types of vehicles for the team members, and have them at the airport when you land. They will also serve as the autos of the guests at the bed-and-breakfast. It would seem suspicious to have neither vacancies nor vehicles in our parking area."

"Okay," Mac says. "When JC gets back to me about the interview schedule I'll be off to South Carolina, and a week later we will move into our next phase."

"That's the way I see it," JJ agrees.

CHAPTER FOUR

I t is a mild late fall evening in New Jersey when the Tri-star touches down at Mercer airport. JJ is sitting in his Jag, enjoying a cigar and taking advantage of the free time to relax a little. It has been a busy few months-selecting a board willing to put their asses on the line and finance the project, finding a man to command the operational side of the project, overseeing the renovation of the barn and the manufacturing of cover stories, setting up dummy companies to finance things like cars or anything else that is needed, and laying a paper trail that leads nowhere.

JJ's thoughts are interrupted when he sees Mac emerge from the small terminal building. Mac spots the Jag and heads for it. To all appearances, JJ is just a friend or family member giving someone a ride from the airport. Mac opens the door puts his bag on the rear seat, then sits on the passenger side.

"How did things go?" JJ asks.

"Very well," Mac answers with enthusiasm. "You would never guess these men are in this line of work. There isn't a hardass among them; they're polite, easygoing and have great senses of humor. But I'll bet they're a little different on a mission. I gave each man a description of the car you have here for them, and they should be coming out of the terminal shortly."

"Good," JJ approves. "The keys and a map to the farm are in each car. I put them in before you landed, and I've been watching the cars. We'll wait to make sure everyone gets started okay."

"Do you have another stogie?" Mac inquires.

"I'm sorry," JJ apologizes. "I should have offered you one."

As JJ and Mac smoke and chat they watch the men come out of the terminal. Each man acts like a stranger to the others and takes his time getting to the parking area. They all seems as though they're just returning from business or a vacation. Everyone locates his assigned vehicle and gets underway.

"These guys are pretty smooth," JJ says with a touch of surprise.

After the last man has left the lot, JJ waits a few minutes, and then starts the Jag and heads for the exit. As they approach the exit JJ says, "I forgot to ask you after your last trip how the Blue Jay situation went."

"Well," Mac begins, "after I helped JC realize he was pretty much the same way Blue Jay is when he was that age, it was easy. But the kid's a pisser,"

Mac tells JJ the story of how they tried sneaking up on Blue Jay. His storytelling ability has JJ laughing in no time. When Mac gets to the big tree and the 'old fucks' part, JJ is laughing so hard he's barely able to drive.

Each man has a different route mapped out to the farm through New Jersey and Pennsylvania, to avoid the appearance of a caravan. JJ and Mac take a route that allows them to arrive at the farm first. As they get out of the Jag, JJ informs Mac he has recruited a 'safe house staff' consisting of Top Kiner, whom Mac had suggested, plus two women the Top recommended. They are good at their primary duties, and are more than qualified to secure home base. "They're retired from contract work, if you know what I mean," JJ tells him.

Mac acknowledges the statement with a nod.

"I had the house staff prepare something light," JJ continues. "Wait until you see the big-ass dining room table I bought. The entire team, including the two of us, can be seated at the same time."

"No shit," replies Mac. "Sort of like the Knucks of the Round Table."

"You mean Knights, like King Arthur," corrects JJ.

"No, I mean Knucks, like knuckle-heads."

"Hee's ba-ack," JJ sings. "And I walked right into that one."

"You usually do," quips Mac.

"Mr. Edsel was right about you," JJ declares.

"Mr. Edsel? How do you know about that?"

"Did I hit a sensitive nerve?" inquires JJ. "Sensitive nerve-you could say that," Mac states briskly. "We were in the middle of a war, and that jerk was trying to scare the enemy into surrendering. I kept telling them someone had tried that with the American Colonies in 1776 and we made it too expensive for them, and that uncle Ho had probably read one of our history books and thought it was a good idea. You have to wonder why the dickheads around the President run the wars instead of the military." Just as Mac is taking a breath, a car pulls up and JC gets out. JJ approaches and offers his hand as he says,

"You must be JC."

"Yes, sir. And you are JJ."

"Yes I am. Mac would have made the introductions," JJ explains, "but I just mentioned Mr. Edsel to him and he went off."

"Oh, spare me," declares JC. "I've been down that road more than once."

"More than once," Mac grumbles. "I still liked you better when you were a Captain."

Shortly after the verbal firefight between JC and Mac ends, the other team members begin to arrive. JJ, Mac and JC stay outside until all have arrived, and then they all head inside the house for more introductions and some refreshments. JJ calls the house staff to the front of the table next to him and starts the introductions.

"Since we are using only code names for the team, we thought it would be a good idea to do the same for the house staff. Let me first introduce Top, or Top Sergeant if you prefer. Next we have the two ladies. We had a problem deciding on code names for them-please don't ask why-but we finally decided on Ladya and Lady1. In addition to duties of a regular house staff, they will help promote the Bed and Breakfast cover in nearby towns, and handle security when the team is on a project."

With that done, JJ introduces each member of the team. After everyone has finished the meal prepared by the house staff and are talking over coffee, JJ gets the team's attention.

"Gentlemen. If everyone has finished, we can go check out your quarters. When in-house, we will be taking our meals here at this table. Now, let's go to the barn and your quarters."

The team members look at each other and shrug their shoulders: *A barn, no big deal.* JJ picks up a large flashlight as they pass through the kitchen, walks out the back door, steps onto a stone walkway and heads for the barn. In the dark of the night as they approach what appears to be a very large building, JJ moves ahead of the group. A few seconds later, he turns a power switch on and the whole place lights up.

"Welcome to our new Bed and Breakfast. We're already booked for at the next 3 years or so, so don't invite anyone else."

The carpenters had done a wonderful job of transforming the barn into a structure that could be seen as a real bed and breakfast-and inside was even better. "As you can see, gentlemen, the ground floor has areas created for meeting rooms, recreation rooms, and a large dining area just like a real country inn," JJ explains. "These areas will actually be the arsenal, the gym, meeting rooms equipped with overheads and VCRs, and a training area for martial arts and the like. If I may use your expert help, we want to set up security, and we thought it better to ask the team first."

All hands agree.

"Good," JJ replies. "JC, Mac tells me you like security gizmos. Could you set up a system for this building and the house? Use one of the rooms as our central security point."

"No problem," JC confirms.

"Mac and I have broken the rest of you into groups according to your skill level in a particular area. They may sound like they overlap, but our plan is to give each group a task, and then we'll review the results from the groups and refine them."

"First, we'll need a defense plan for this building and the house. In the event we are found out and assaulted by unfriendlies, we'll want a plan in place. We'll need sniper and observation positions: I'm an old fart, but placing some people in that silo with night scopes could kick ass at night. As far as training, maintaining muscle tone and reflexes will be a priority, along with personal skills. Martial arts seem to be the team's common denominator, so perhaps this large area we're currently occupying could serve as a workout area. Feel free to order mats from Japan to create the Katami. They're expensive, but I don't want any of you getting hurt using second-rate equipment, because if you do Mac will have to go into the team line-up."

Thinking quickly, Mac gives JJ a smirk and a wave of acknowledgment, middle finger extended full mast.

"To continue with the security topic," JJ resumes, "you all now have code names. We realize some of you men already know each other, but we would like you all to use the code names. You also have forged driver's licenses with false names for outside use, but at the farm, in training and on assignments, the code names will be used. Some of you already had names; JC created new ones for the rest of you. The house team will handle the supply chain. They are former military and contract people. They were good then, and they are better now."

JJ turns to Mac and asks, "Is that a biased statement?"

"Sounds good to me," Mac replies.

JJ shrugs with a grin and resumes his talk. "Concerning weapons, this will be a total team effort for obvious reasons. We will evaluate all the requests against what we think we will need. If all bases are covered, okay. If not, we'll talk about it."

This elicits a chuckle from the team. They are sizing up JJ, Mac, JC, and are becoming more relaxed.

"Let me be totally honest with you men," JJ says. These comments would sound completely glib coming from some turd with a lot of money who never served in anything worthwhile. So, I am going to tell you who I am and why I'm here."

Mac stands up and starts walking towards JJ to stop him from giving away his identity.

"No," JJ tells him. "In for a penny, in for a pound…and I'm in for 2,000 pounds."

Mac sits down and smiles as he mutters, "Same old JJ".

"It may sound simple," JJ continues, "but I'll put it in a nutshell. My name is John Stone, and one day I just got sick of innocent people being murdered by terrorists, so I decided to try to do something about it. I have addressed many groups throughout my career and have developed a sense of sizing up their character and the character of this group is outstanding. I really mean that!" JJ says.

This is not a political rally, so no one in the team applauds; they just flash smiles of gratitude. As JJ covers his military and business background, a bond begins to form between JJ and the team. They are thinking: here is a man who could be sitting back like the other fat cats, living a comfortable life, but he is in the process of trying to protect the innocent people of the world, at a tremendous risk to himself. He trusts us, and we can trust him-after we check him out, of course.

"Always feel free to ask questions," JJ wraps up. "Are there any questions now?" No one responds. "Maybe tomorrow. Well, Mac and I will leave you now, but let me give you all some additional info."

"As you can see, there is a stairway leading to a second floor. Your in-house living quarters are located there. Each room has a temp note with one of your names on it. One of the rooms on this floor has already been set up as a team meeting room. JC has requested you all convene there in one hour for a meeting. He knew you would want time to check out the area; to make sure everything was okay. And with that, I will bid you goodnight."

"Good night," the team replies in near unison.

When JJ and Mac get outside, JJ offers Mac a cigar.

"What do you think?" Mac asks.

"Well we could really wind up in the shit with this effort, but if first impressions are worth anything, these men will not be the cause. You've done a great job, Mac."

"I was just a small part," Mac explains. "JC and Blue Jay did all the selecting."

"What about Blue Jay?" JJ inquires.

"You keep asking that," Mac says. "I told you about my first encounter. After that, I had another sit-down with JC about Blue Jay. He told me not to be deceived by Blue Jay's personality. He has two sides: a humorous, likeable one, and another, darker one. Business is business, but betray him and look out. He thinks 'vendetta' is a good word. JC also told me it's hard to gain Blue Jay's respect, but if you do he will go to the wall with you."

"He sounds like someone who could be manipulated by the right person," suggests JJ.

"I said it was hard to gain his respect. I didn't say he was stupid," Mac snaps.

"Okay, okay. I give in. You are a good judge of character. If you say he's in, I say he's in. So, when did he make you a believer?" JJ asks. "Was it the 'old fucks from the home' incident?"

"JJ, you were a pain in the ass when you were in the Corps and you are a pain in the ass now," Mac pronounces, and both men laugh as they light up their cigars.

In the shadows, another finds humor in their conversation, smiles, and is content with his decision to join these two old salts on this project. He is also happy to know that Mac doesn't think he's stupid.

One hour after the initial meeting, JC convenes the first team meeting.

"I realize we are just getting off the ground, but are there any questions?" He pauses and gets no response. "No one?" asks JC again.

He didn't think there would be. These men are all professionals.

"It's obvious this project is a clandestine operation," he continues, "but with two sides: one military, one civilian. I am sure you all agree that without a military-type operation at the team level, our effectiveness would be weak and disorganized. On the one- and two-man assignments, the civilian side comes into play. Snoopin' and poopin' down Main Street doesn't work too well in civilian life.

"This does not mean you will specialize in any one area or another. The different assignments will determine each man's duties. It may be a team effort with everyone attending, or a one-man infiltration with the team in support. Besides selecting the best, we also tried to cover the languages and nationalities of the hot spots around the world.

"I want to make one thing clear from the start," JC declares. "If anyone has a question or thoughts about anything, please bring it to our attention. No one is perfect, and if anyone thinks there is a flaw in our planning, we want to know. Remember, all of our asses are on the line for this one."

"Okay," JC says finally. "I know you men have had a long day, so I'll see you at 0700 for morning chow."

"I have a question," interrupts Air Jockey, "how did you get the handle JC".

"Well," JC explains, "when I was a captain and the security officer at Gitmo Bay, I would snoop and poop out on the fence line to check our security posts. But, Marines being Marines, they starting keeping track of me, and the man on duty at the radio shake would alert the fence line security if they thought I was on the prowl. Many times I would tap into the EE8 lines to pick up the sentries' chatter and would hear: 'Jesus Christ, is he out again?'"

The team finds that amusing, and laughter permeates the air as they leave the room.

What JC doesn't tell them is the initials are also the first and middle of his own name and that made it doubly funny for the Marines in Cuba.

The next morning at 0700 sharp, all hands are seated at the oversized dining table as Mac and JJ enter the room.

"Ah, good. You are all here," JJ exclaims. "Are there any questions we can discuss over breakfast?"

"'Their is one thing," interjects Bris with his thick French accent.

"What is that?" asks JJ.

"Are you really telling us that Uncle Fudd and his two sisters are going to be responsible for house security?"

Top Sergeant and the two women look at each other and smile.

"Just a puppy," the Top observes. "Just a puppy." Both women agree.

With that, the team bursts into laughter.

"The team wanted to get a reaction," explains Bris, "and I got the short straw."

"Did you all get the reaction you wanted?" inquires Mac.

"Yeah, they'll do," announces the team.

"We have plenty of room at the table," Bris points out. "Why don't you all join us?"

The house team looks at JJ for approval.

"Good idea," JJ agrees. "Why not for all meals?"

The team members all agree.

"Maybe Bris can give the Top some pointers on French cooking," adds Panda.

"Now wait a minute," Bris pleads. "I have already been in and out of the doghouse once, and it's only the first day. Now I'm going to need a food taster before I eat anything. But I probably would have gotten one anyway."

"Let me sit next to that puppy," The Top announces as the room fills with laughter.

"This is good," JJ says to Mac when the room settles down.

"Yeah," laughs Mac. "For a while there I thought we were going to see our first action."

Breakfast continues in a friendly atmosphere. The team knows by the looks and reactions of the house team that they have been around, and are probably good at what they do. By the time everyone had finished his or her second cup of coffee, you would think it was a family reunion.

"I hate to break this up," announces JC, "but we have some work to do."

All agree and get up from the table.

"We'll have to do this again some time," Bris declares.

"How about over lunch?" asks Top.

"Good idea," replies Bris. "See you in a few."

JJ is pleased at the bond forming between the members. *Win or lose*, he thinks, *we could not find a better group.* A few hours later, Mac and JJ take a walk to the barn. The team members are everywhere, working on their assignments. Some are sketching, and others are staring in deep concentration. A few are checking out the perimeter while some set up fields of fire. Mac and JJ enter the barn and survey the area. When they arrive at what once was a silo, they enter the small door. Looking up, they see two of the team members planning for sniper positions, constructing a platform and plotting firing positions that will cover 360 degrees.

"I see they took my advice," JJ smiles.

"Yeah," Mac says. "I'm glad you mentioned it."

Both men chuckle as they leave the silo. Their next stop is the central security point.

"How are things going?" JJ asks as they enter the room.

JC turns and presents JJ with his wish list of gizmos and standard security equipment.

"Can you get these items?" he asks.

"I'm sure there will be no problem with it," JJ assures him.

"What's your game plan?" Mac asks as he looks over the chart JC has created.

"To start with," JC explains, "the two men in the silo, besides working on their sniper assignment, are checking out positions for day and night camera surveillance systems. The men checking the perimeter are also selecting spots for audio surveillance. The video and audio will come into play after the gizmos give the initial alert. It might be a good idea to set up a safe room in the house and hook them up to the surveillance system. This will give the house more protection, especially when the team is away. We should also install a steel gate with a remote control operation at the entrance to the lane. It won't be much of a deterrent, but if somebody blows through it, we'll know they aren't selling magazines."

"Sounds good," Mac approves.

"For a start," JC clarifies.

"You and the other men seem to be making good progress on your tasks," JJ observes.

"Yes," JC admits, "they are good men. We will probably be ready by tomorrow for another meeting to kick around all of our ideas."

"Good show," JJ comments. "Mac and I will be looking forward to it."

JJ and Mac continue their tour, entering the big training area where martial arts will be practiced. Benz, Blue Jay and Plum are discussing the training floor.

"Blue Jay, how are things going?" inquires JJ.

"Good, sir," Blue Jay replies. "Benz, Bean and I are just deciding how far away from the wall the edge of the mat should be."

"Bean? Who is Bean,?" inquires Mac. "Do you mean Plum?"

"Bean, Plum, whatever," Blue Jay answers.

"You know we didn't think up and assign these code names for the hell of it," Mac reproaches.

"Anyway," Blue Jay continues, ignoring Mac, "we have two rooms set up for fitness. One with machines to build endurance, and one for muscle tone and reflex building. This area will be for martial arts practice."

"That sounds good," JJ confirms. "Now, tell me: why do you call him Bean?"

"We go back a long way," Blue Jay explains. "When I was a Marine, he was an Army Green Beret/Airborne Ranger, and he had a spiffy green beanie. Need I say more?"

"No, I get the picture," JJ says. "See you both at lunch."

When Mac and JJ get outside, JJ says, "Mac, I have a feeling we should probably change Plum's name to Bean, right now."

"The names are assigned, and the name we assigned will stay," Mac declares.

"Okay," JJ replies. After a pause he asks, "Are you a betting man?"

Meanwhile in the barn, Bean turns to Blue Jay.

"Mac is a retired General isn't he?"

"Yeah," Blue Jay says. "I should have sung him the hymn."

"The Hall of Montezuma?"

"No the other hymn. Himmm, Himmm, Fuck Himmmm." sings Blue Jay.

"Aw, what's the matter? Did the General ruffle the birdie's feathers? By the way," Bean adds, "your code name is Blue Jay. Does that mean you shit through feathers or something?"

"I changed my mind," Blue Jay snaps. " I think Plum is a good code name for you. You're already shaped like a plum, so why not have the name? Plum! Plum! I like the sound of it already."

"Is that what you like, Feather Shitter?" Bean counters.

It was a sure bet that Benz was going to hear about Plum and Feather Shitter until at least lunchtime.

The next morning after breakfast, JJ, Mac and the team assemble in the team meeting room.

"Okay," JJ announces, "I guess we can get started. JC, why don't you fill us in on security?"

JC stands and walks over to the chart he has created. As he goes through his presentation, all eyes are focused on him and the chart. The occasional question is asked and quickly answered.

The last thing JC addresses is the purchasing of all the equipment he will require. "Most of these items we can purchase on the open market," JC explains. "The surveillance cameras, backup generators and other items are easy, as long as the purchases are small and spread over a large area. When we get into purchasing what Mac calls 'gizmos,' we must be careful not to leave a trail that leads back here. I know one dealer I can get maybe one or two items from without raising any suspicion. Could any of you do the same?"

Everyone in the team raises a hand.

JC gives a big smile and says, "Just wanted to see if everyone was paying attention."

After asking if there are any further questions, JC returns to his seat while the remainder of the team present their assignments. The last item on the agenda is the overall plan for the barn and the house if an assault should occur. This includes all of the previous presentations: security, sniper and defense positions, different attack situation scenarios and how to respond to each. All of the assignments interlock with each other and contribute to the fine-tuning of the plan. When the plan discussion is through, JJ and Mac walked to the front of the room.

"I want to thank all of you for your contributions; they are very impressive," JJ says. "Since you all probably have different weapons preferences, Mac and I will conduct this part. I will ask each team member their preferences, and Mac will create a chart with your requests. Feel free to ask for anything you may require. We want you all to feel comfortable with your weapons." JJ knew they would not have a problem purchasing any type of weapon, because Dunn is the president of an arms manufacturing company.

"The first turn around the table," JJ explains, "we'll cover hand guns. The second will be defense weapons to repel an assault on the barn or house, and the last will cover weapons for your assignments, both military and civilian activities."

The first trip around the table produced a surprisingly small list. The second list consisted mainly of sniper rifles with day and night scopes and automatic weapons for close fighting. *All equipped with silencers, of course*, JJ thinks. If the attackers do not have silenced weapons, part of their cover-up plan is to set off a fireworks display-if anyone survives-to explain any gunfire heard by people in ear range. If it is the middle of the night, we just say it is early evening in Japan or some other place in the world, and we want to be in sync with the celebration. JJ is brought out of his thoughts when Mac says, "I guess we are ready for round three?"

With that, JJ continues the process with Tick, a part time stockbroker whose parents came to the U.S. when he was six years old. Tick starts off round three with a question.

"How serious are we talking? Knocking off a group of terrorist turds, or going after bigger things like a drug lords or wealthy Arabs who are sponsoring terrorism?"

"Yes" is JJ's simple reply.

"Okay then," Tick responds without hesitation, "put me down for a B-52."

"Are we talking about an automatic weapon?," JJ asks.

"No, Boss," Tick replies in a mock Spanish accent. "We are talking about *De Plane! De Plane!*"

Everyone bursts into laughter.

"Fair enough," JJ announces as the laughter subsides. "We haven't gotten that deeply into what our objectives will be, but in two weeks we will brief all of you on the big picture. For now, select weapons for large and small operations. Additional weapons can be supplied at any time." With that, the selection process continues, minus the B52 request. When the last man completes his selection, an impressive list of weapons has been requested. Some are new models, and some not so new, but all very high quality.

"Well that should do it," declares JJ.

"What about the House Team?" JC asks.

"We've already addressed their requirements," answers Mac. "They will not be going into the field, so they require only defense weapons."

"Shall we break for lunch?" JJ says.

All are in agreement, and they begin to leave the room.

"What's your schedule going to be?" Mac asks JC.

"Around the barn, we can work on the sniper's platform and set up camera positions. We'll install the hardware as we get it. Shall we send out team members to get certain items? asks JC.

"No," JJ intervenes, "just give me the item name and where we can get it, and I'll take care of it."

"I'll have the list by tonight," JC agrees. "How do you want to arrange getting the other items we'll need?"

"I leased an empty warehouse in Pennsylvania to a phony company." JJ answers. "I'll have merchandise delivered there, and we can pick it up the same day. The owner is a little shifty, so in order to keep his hands off the stuff, I told him I was fencing goods for a member of the Family in New York. I'll tell the truck driver who makes the first delivery that we were setting up a sting operation. I think he'll believe me, since the cargo will consist mainly of surveillance cameras. Anyway, by the time they all figure it out, we'll have everything we need and wont be using the warehouse anymore."

Mac looks at JC and says, "He was a captain of industry, you know. Aren't you glad we stayed in the Corps? All we had to do was fight our country's battles."

"On the land and on the sea," JC adds.

"And we were always first..." continues Mac.

"To fight..."

"LUNCH TIME!" JJ shouts. "If you two lifers are going to sing the Marine Corps Hymn, I want something in my stomach first."

"Well, we were thinking more along the lines of a narrative presentation," Mac insists.

"Now I am *really* starting to remember why I left the Corps; it's all coming back to me," JJ mutters.

The three men leave the barn, one in front shaking his head and smiling and the other two following behind, laughing like hell.

As the team finishes lunch, JC gets everyone's attention.

"This afternoon we will start acquiring some of the material required for our projects around the barn. Half the team, including the men who laid out the sniper positions, will go with Mac to the lumberyard to get the material to build the platform. The rest of you will go with me to retrieve the closed-circuit TV cameras and monitors. How will we transport the material, you ask?" JJ volunteers before anyone can speak. "Well, follow me."

JJ gets up, walks outside and heads for a smaller building opposite the barn. When he gets to the door he takes out a key, unlocks a massive padlock and rolls the door open. Inside are a large panel truck and a pickup truck.

"Surprised you, didn't I?" JJ states confidently.

"They look almost new," says Blue Jay as he inspects them. "And already you have 23,527 miles on the panel truck."

"I'm afraid the pickup has a slight oil leak," adds Bean.

"And that only has 8,422 miles on it," Benz contributes.

"They just don't make them the way they used to," Panda comments.

"Surprise, surprise," laughs Mac. "I assume we take the pickup with the oil leak."

"Slight oil leak," corrects JC.

"Remember, cash and carry," JJ instructs. "For the lumber purchase just give my name and this address. If they ask who you are, just tell them you're my old gardener."

Mac gives him one of his familial hand waves, with the middle finger extended.

The team appears to be loosening up a little more, laughing during the exchange. This is good. The quicker they get comfortable with each other, the better. They will realize they can trust and rely on each other, and that along with their skills will see them through.

Both trips are uneventful. JC and his group relax and take in the countryside. This part of New Jersey is peaceful, with beautiful scenery. The Delaware River cuts through a long valley separating New Jersey and Pennsylvania. When the convoy crosses the bridge into Pennsylvania, the panel truck and one of the four-by-fours carrying JJ's group continues up a long hill. The pickup and another four-by-four make a right and follow the river. Approximately 5 miles from this point is a rural lumberyard. It would have been faster to go into a small town near by, but small town news bags being what they are, the rural one is better. It will also give JC, who is driving the pickup, and Mac, riding shotgun, a chance to review the project to date.

"I have a feeling these men will make one hell of a team," Mac says.

"It's starting to look that way," JC agrees. "Some of them already know each other, and that should make the adjustment time shorter, not to mention the fact they are all good at what they do and can size up other people very quickly. Getting them used to each other shouldn't be a problem; they just have to get used to each other's styles and adjust to it. This won't require boot camp type training, just some class work and a few casual run-throughs, splitting up the team and running exercises against each other. One-man operational training will be for our benefit. They are all strong, but each man may excel in a particular area and we have to know that when we give out the assignments."

"True," Mac agrees. "The projects will probably cover everything from sniper and team insertions to the civilian clandestine type. It's a very heavy load."

"I think they can do it," JC says confidently.

"So do I," agrees Mac. There is no humor in this conversation.

Humor is thing to be enjoyed by men like these. If one didn't know better, one may not take them seriously-until somebody blows the whistle.

It is late in the afternoon when the panel truck and the four-by-four pull up by the barn and park. JC and his crew are busy building the sniper platform when JJ walks into the silo.

"JC, should we store the cameras and monitors in the security room for now?" JJ bellows.

"That'll work," JC answers, looking over the edge of the platform, "We'll take one of the monitors down to the house when we go for dinner."

"You didn't forget my old gardener at the lumber yard, did you?" inquires JJ.

"No, sir," JC answers. "He's up here with us."

"You're kidding," JJ says in disbelief.

"Shit, I came up that wall ladder two rungs at a time," a voice claims from up on the platform."

"Did you really?" JJ drawls.

"Hell no," Mac answers, now looking down over the edge with JC. "These rascals used me to test one of their contraptions. They told me not to worry, and that they had used this kind of device many times. After the first test run, they all told Check what a good idea it was and wondered why they hadn't thought of it before."

JJ shakes his head and smiles as he asks, "How's the contraption get you up there?"

"You see that rope next to you?" Mac inquires.

"Yes."

"They figure by the time they ran all the way up that wall ladder they would be breathing hard, and it would be difficult to get a decent sight picture, so Check had the idea to install a rope and an electric motor for a fast ride to the platform."

"Ah, hell," exclaims Mac, "a picture is worth a thousand words. JJ, just grab onto the rope with both hands and we'll crank her up."

"Screw you," JJ says without hesitation. "It's Miller time."

"All right!" the team agrees in unison.

JJ and the rest of the men wait in the barn until the silo crew joins them.

"Don't forget the monitor," JC prompts.

"I have it," Bris confirms, and everyone departs for the house.

Bris is the fifth man through the door when they reach the house.

"What's this-a TV for the kitchen?" Top asks.

"Yeah," Bris retorts. "We figured if you started watching Emeril, you might get some ideas. You know, kick it up a notch!"

"I'll kick it up a notch all right," Top grins.

"It wasn't my idea Top, I got the short straw again," Bris insists as he makes a hasty retreat into the next room.

"Stick around!" Top yells, the way Emeril does on TV when he goes to a commercial break.

Everyone, including the Top, has a good laugh as they pass around the beers.

"Are you and the Ladies all settled in?" Mac asks.

"Yes, sir," Top replies. "In fact, we were just saying earlier that with this beautiful house and location, it's more like a vacation than a job."

"Well, if no one discovers our home base, it will probably stay that way," Mac says hopefully.

"I'll drink to that," JJ declares as he raises his beer in a toast.

"What's on the schedule for tomorrow?" asks Mac.

"Well, for me it's into the city with your wish list, but I should be back in time for dinner," JJ replies.

"For us," JC adds, "It's finish the sniper platform and build the camera positions in the silo, around the house and other places. We don't want any blind spots. We will also be digging narrow, deep trenches for the backup electric and camera cables."

"That should keep the 10 of us busy," exclaims Panda.

"Eleven," JC corrects him.

"Make that twelve," Mac says. "I'll help you around here, but don't expect me to come get you if you get into trouble on a mission."

The team looks at Mac and gives him a big smile, knowing he will probably be the first one to show up if anything happens.

"Well, I'd like to make it thirteen," JJ says with a smile, "but I have these lists of gizmos and fire sticks I have to acquire."

"Yeah, yeah," Mac replies.

"It must be nice," Air Jockey muses. "Riding in a big expensive car, right down Madison Avenue."

"Not with him driving," declares Mac. "It's like Rambo in a Jaguar."

Everyone has another chuckle as the Top announces, "Dinner is served."

"Smells good," Bris says. "What are we having?"

"*We* are having Steak Diane with a béarnaise sauce. *You* are having monkey dicks and beans…or franks and beans, if you prefer."

"It's not my fault I got the short straw," Bris grumbles.

"I'll bet you say that to all of the girls," announces Lady1.

"Oh, shit," laughs Ladya.

"They're ganging up on me. How about some help here, teammates?"

"You're on your own for this one, Bris-man," Tic announces.

"If he is in such trouble, how come he has the biggest steak?" Check interjects.

"Oh, do I?" Bris says. "Well, I always did like the house team."

The pleasant banter continues through dinner and for hours after.

When everyone is talked out, they call it a night.

The next few weeks pass quickly. The sniper platform in the silo is completed, along with the positioning of the day and night surveillance cameras. A new gate is installed at the beginning of the lane, also with concealed surveillance cameras. The remaining cameras are installed around the house and the other buildings on the property so that every inch around the area is under surveillance.

JC set up monitors in the designated hutch in the barn and a secure room in the house. With his gizmos installed, he claims he can pick up a frog farting within a quarter mile radius of the barn. The men had done very well. The need for secrecy along with having the team do the work has produced the side benefit of starting them working as a team. It's been fifteen days since JJ mentioned making arrangements to acquire their fire-sticks, and this morning he would tell them they're ready.

"Good morning, men," JJ announces as he enters the dining room."

"Morning, sir," the men reply. The team has come to like and respect JJ and Mac. They know both of them have been there and back, and are going again with this project. They feel the same way about JC, even though he is still young enough to be one of them.

"Well, your fire-sticks are ready," JJ announces. I just have to give a time for delivery."

"Will it be Pennsylvania again?" JC asks.

"Yes," JJ confirms. "But this time we will be there before the truck makes the delivery. Sort of over the hill and down the road, so we can see when the truck departs. I don't want Shifty to get anywhere near this shipment. The delivery will be made between 1 and 2 p.m. We should be there by noon."

"Will we be brown-bagging it?" asks Bris.

The Top sounds off with, "Baloney sandwiches."

The entire team is going for the pickup, and all hands are by the vehicles at 10:15. The truck and two four-by-fours will make the journey. JJ, Mac, JC and the team mount up and head for Pennsylvania and Shifty's warehouse. It is another uneventful trip, with the vehicles spaced out so as not to look like a convoy, yet keeping each other in sight. All three vehicles pull off the road not far from the warehouse.

"It's 11:53," JJ comments, "right on schedule. If a few of you men follow this hill for about 50 yards, you can observe the warehouse area without being seen."

Two of the team members start to peel off from the rest when JJ calls them back.

"I think there is something in the truck for us." JJ grabs the handle and pulls the door up and open. There sit four picnic baskets. "Lunch from Top and the Ladies," announces JJ. "I think this is for the observation team," JJ says as he passes a basket to the men he called back.

"That Top is alright," approves Bris.

"Shall we tell him that?" someone inquires. "No," Bris says quickly, "it will take all the

fun out of everything."

Everyone chuckles and Mac says, "Lets eat."

Top Sergeant has packed them a tremendous lunch. Each basket contains cold chicken, potato salad, coleslaw, dessert and a thermos of strong hot coffee-just the way everyone likes it. Half way through the meal, JC comments, "I think the house team has adopted us!"

"You're probably right," Mac agrees. "I have known the Top for a long time, and I haven't seen him this pepped up in years."

Just then, one of the lookouts rejoins the group to report that the truck has just arrived. An hour or so later, the truck departs and the men resume their journey to the warehouse. As they enter the driveway, they notice old Shifty already on the prowl.

"I knew that asshole would be nosing around,"

JJ says. "Mac, you and I will keep him busy while JC and the team load the truck."

"Why don't we just shoot the asshole instead?" Mac suggests.

"Now, now," JJ scolds, "just pretend you're back at the Pentagon, and act accordingly."

"Now I know I want to shoot him," Mac declares. "pretending he's reaching for his gun."

JJ brings the four-by-four to a stop in front of the warehouse.

"You just missed the delivery truck," announces Shifty.

"That's a shame," answers JJ in a sincere voice. "We could have just transferred the load from one truck to another."

"Aren't you glad we stayed in the Corps, JC?" Mac asks. JC smiles and nods as he gets out of the four-by-four to get the show on the road. JJ and Mac keep Shifty busy with bullshit until the men had completed their work. With the task complete, they bid Shifty farewell and head for the barn and one of Top's great dinners.

The next morning, the team heads for the barn to unpack and inspect the weapons. Around noon they break for a quick lunch, and then go back to work. Around 2 PM, Mac and JJ go out to see how things are going. All of the weapons have been unpacked, inspected and cleaned. Even the house team weapons are inspected and cleaned. Each man has the weapons he requested on display, and is standing behind them. Sniper scopes, silencers; everything is assembled. As JJ and Mac approach, JC announces,

"We thought you might want to see what you're paying for, sir".

"Yes," JJ replies. "I would be interested in speaking with the men about their choices."

With that, JJ walks to the man furthest to his left to start reviewing. As he walks he says,

"This is nothing formal, men, just continue what you are doing." Mac and JC accompany him, and all three are very interested in what the men have to say about their selections. For the most part, it boils down to personal preference. Each man agrees the others' weapons are probably just as good, but it's just a matter of liking the action or the feel of the weapon they've chosen. It takes JJ two hours for the review process. When he is through, JC informs him the ammo will be given out today. The explosives and other goodies are stashed in the silo. There it will be secure and away from the living quarters, for safety reasons.

"The next thing we should do is sight in the weapons," JC says.

"Anytime you want," JJ answers. "I have a cabin in Pennsylvania, back in the hills. Used to go fishing there; haven't used it much lately. It is very isolated, so there won't be a problem with noise and things."

"Sounds good," JC approves. "How about tomorrow?"

"OK," answers JJ. "And the day after that we'll take the house team up. I would take you all the same day, but we should try to have someone here at all times from now on." Everyone agrees.

"Maybe we could cook dinner the day the house team goes to the country," suggests Bris.

"That's a good idea," approves JJ.

"We'll just neglect to tell them until we get them back on the property," Mac adds. "We don't want them to get too excited with anticipation when they are sighting in their weapons."

"I'm a good cook," Bris insists, "and I'll bet the rest of the team are as well."

"Okay," Mac gives in. "Then it's 48 hours before, in the mouth, over the gums, look out asshole, here it comes."

"Very funny, very funny," the team replies. "This guy is a real wise cracker!" announces Met in his heavy German accent.

"Speaking of cooking," JJ says as he looks at his watch, "it's time for dinner."

"Enjoy it, JJ," Mac advises. "It may our next to last meal."

"Yeah, yeah," the team mutters good-naturedly as they all head for the house.

At 0800 all hands, toting their weapons, are assembled by the four-by-fours. As JJ and Mac approach the group, JJ motions towards the building where the truck is garaged.

"We'll be transporting the weapons by truck," he announces. After the truck is pulled out of its parking area, JJ pulls open the back door and climbs in. "I figure if we get stopped by the police for any reason, it will be hard to explain these weapons, so we will use the truck. That way, if we do get stopped, only Mac and I will be compromised-if they find the weapons." He turns and walks towards the front of the truck, pulls two unrelated levers, and a door swings open. He reaches inside, pulls another lever, and a door for the other half of the truck swings open.

"We'll transport them in here. The back wall had padded slots and devices to secure the weapons. Just put them in," JJ says. "The four-by-fours have a similar arrangement for your personal weapons."

"Well done," JC approves. "Lets stack 'em, pack 'em and get on the road."

Each man takes personal care to prepare his weapons for the trip. When they are all ready, the doors are shut and everyone climbs aboard the four-by-fours. The ride through the Pennsylvania countryside is pleasant, and about two hours in the truck turns onto a dirt road that would easily be missed if you didn't know where it was. The truck continues about another mile through the woods before the road breaks into a clearing containing a small cabin with a stream running close by. The truck proceeds to the cabin and stops. The two four-by-fours do the same, and all dismount from their vehicles. Mac is the first to comment on the scenic beauty.

"JC, you see what we missed by staying in the corps?"

"I hear you," JC agrees.

JJ once again opens the back of the truck and climbs aboard.

"Let me familiarize you all with the area," he starts. "Over here to your right, there is a clearing about 300 yards long. Then there are woods again. Behind you there are woods for about a quarter of a mile, then there is a wide path cut through the forest for miles where the power lines run. When I was in the Corps, 500 yards with an M-1 and a peep sight was okay, but these days I know that range isn't long at all."

"I think maybe the reason you are shooting, dictates the range," a serious voice bathed in a French accent comments. "In a one shot-one kill situation, maybe a little closer is better?"

JJ is surprised when he turns and realizes it is Bris doing the serious talking. Like Mac said, when they're back at the barracks, it's fun and games. Out here, it's business.

"Of course, in our business, if a group is in hot pursuit of you, a hit at 1,000 or so yards will slow them down-or at least give them second thoughts," Bris finishes his statement.

"Good point," JJ acknowledges. "Mac and I will set up in the cabin. We'll keep track of the ammo and the empties you bring back. While you folks were still being organized, Mac and I brought out some hay bales and targets and stored them in a shelter behind the cabin. You can use the four-by-fours to transport them into the field to your right. That should do for the initial zeroing in of your weapons. For the long shooting, I'm sure you will think of something."

"Top has fixed us up with lunch again, so whenever you all feel like eating, it will be at the cabin. With that, I'll turn it over to JC."

Without hesitation JC sounds off, "We will set up our 300 yard targets, have lunch, and then start shooting. How's that sound?"

All agree, and without further conversation the two team members that drove head for the four-by-fours and the rest start walking towards the cabin and the hay bales.

"I see why you picked JC," approves JJ. "He is a persuasive manager."

"Persuasive! Oh, that's funny!" replies Mac. "No, that's not the reason. JC has the ability to adapt to a situation. He knows these men are professionals, so he treats them that way. If they were green recruits, it would be another story."

"I have been around a while and seen a lot," JJ responds as he picks up two of the baskets the Top had prepared, "and I have to say these kids are really impressive."

"I know," answers Mac. "I don't really know them yet, but I can tell we will be proud of them in the days to come."

JJ doesn't reply, but he can see Mac is very sincere in what he said. The team sets up the hay bales and targets. Ten team members and JC means eleven targets. With that task complete, everyone collects their weapons and assembles at the cabin. During lunch, the team members start setting the dope, or sight adjustments, on their weapons for 300 yards. These are not the usual 300-yard targets; they are much smaller. JJ had thought they were too small, but Mac just laughed when he questioned it.

"Is everyone ready?" JC asks.

Everyone nods.

"Lets get to the firing line," JC instructs.

Without hesitation the team members move to a position where they can shoot at one of the eleven targets. The ground where the team is shooting from is a bit higher than the ground at the target area.

"This sort on reminds me of the range at Gitmo Bay," JC remarks to Mac. "Once I challenged everyone on the Marine barracks rifle team to get a higher individual score than me. Dammed near cost me two cases of beer," JC smiles at the fond memory.

The team is getting into position when JC walks behind the firing line.

"I am sure you men are familiar with rifle range procedures, but just for an added precaution, I will be the safety officer of the firing line. Everyone will zero in their weapon in their own manner, but I will control firing. With that said, please start when ready."

The team has only been shooting for a short period of time when Mac approaches JC.

"Are you sure these men can shoot?" he asks.

"Why?" counters JC.

"I have been watching through this spotters scope and they aren't any where near the bull."

JC laughs and says, "Look at the red circle on the lower left side of the target. We're using that for weapon familiarity. The bull will be used for zeroing."

"Yeah," Mac exclaims, "and I'm the Sheriff of Nottingham."

Almost as soon as Mac finishes talking, all firing ceases. Mac looks at JC and asks, "Do you think they heard me?"

"Check the targets," JC answers. "I think we're done."

Mac immediately trains the spotter scope on the targets.

"I'll be dammed," Mac exclaims.

"You probably will be, *Sheriff*!" replies JC. "We'll be moving to the long-range shooting now."

"Well don't let them shoot any public service electricians by mistake," Mac bellows. "Damn kids can shoot," he mumbles as he heads for the cabin.

JJ walks out of the cabin and is surprised to see everyone coming back. "Is there a problem?" inquires JJ.

"No," JC replies, "just ready for some long-range shooting."

"Will you be needing additional ammo?" JJ asks.

"Are we supposed to?" says Blue Jay.

The entire team laughs at Blue Jay's answer as they head for the power lines and the long shoot.

"They're real confident in themselves, aren't they?" JJ observes. "Come on, lets watch."

The team makes their way through the woods. Mac and JJ notice Air Jockey moving off to the left as the team gets close to the power lines, but figure nature is calling and continue on. Once in the clearing, everyone is adjusting their slings and scopes.

"There," comments JC, "11 o'clock."

The team looks up and picks out Air Jockey, waving his hat and pointing to a large maple tree. JC points a spotter scope in the direction Air Jockey is pointing, picks up the target and gives a confirmation wave. With that, Air Jockey heads towards the team. The target is a twenty-inch bull on the large maple at 11 o'clock, approximately 600 yards.

"I have it," Blue Jay announces. "Can you see it, Bean?"

"Wait a minute," JJ interrupts. "Who is Bean?"

"Him," answers Blue Jay.

"His code name is Plum," corrects JJ.

"His code name may be Plum, but he's Bean to me," Blue Jay answers in a who-gives-a-shit manner.

"We gave these code names for a reason, and everyone will comply with the rules we set up."

"Whatever," answers Blue Jay.

This sends JJ off. "I'm not used to being talked to that way!" he exclaims. "You will follow the rules or get out!"

Blue Jay, remaining impassive, replies, "The way I understood it, JC is the team leader and Mac is the liaison between you and whoever, so how are you following the rules when you start giving orders to the team?"

Before JJ can reply, Benz says, "Come on, Bean, let's get a sight picture."

"Hey Bean," Panda calls, "I'll bet I hit center before you."

"Maybe!" Bean calls, "and maybe not."

JJ realizes this is a losing battle and decides to keep quiet. Air Jockey rejoins the group and everyone gets ready to fire. On the first round, everyone either hits or comes close to the target. By the second round everyone was on the target and walking towards the bull. In no time all were hitting the bull, and some hitting the center.

"Will this decide the silo shooters?" asks JJ.

"No," JC answers, "the area around the barn is well within 300 yards and anyone can be a silo shooter. This is just familiarization shooting for the weapons."

After everyone had put several rounds in the bull it was time to head back to the cabin. Air Jockey once again leaves the group to retrieve the target. The team cleans up the brass and moves off towards the cabin. When everyone arrives, JJ stands on the cabin porch and gets everyone's attention.

"I have something to say," he starts. "I am used to being a corporate head and calling all the shots myself. To get this project started, I had to get it organized and rolling. Now that it's on its way, I should step back into the role I originally slated for myself. Blue Jay was right in challenging me."

"About what?" Blue Jay inquires.

"I don't know," answers Benz, "something about a roll."

"Hey, maybe we're having hamburgers tonight," exclaims Panda as the team heads towards the hay bales to test their pistols and automatic weapons.

"Are they making fun of me?" JJ asks.

"No," Mac replies, "that's their way of saying it didn't happen, so don't worry about it."

"Just like that?"

"Just like that," Mac confirms.

"I guess I am used to those corporate shits," JJ replies. "Any time you go off on a tangent, you have to smooth out the ruffled feathers afterward."

When the team completes their shooting it is late in the afternoon. They once again clean up their brass, break up most of the hay bales and spread it around the area so the deer can make use of it. After all of the weapons are loaded into the truck they start the journey back to the barn.

The next day JJ and Mac plan to go through the same routine with the Top and the Ladies. The mats had arrived from Japan and the team would spend their day picking up and installing the mats, while Bris,

Check and Tick cooked dinner: in the mouth, over the gums.

Everyone is up and about earlier than usual. Breakfast is at 7 a.m., and everyone going somewhere is on the road by 8. One of the four-by-fours heads to Pennsylvania with the house team. JC and two of the team take the truck to pick up the mats while Benz and the remainder of the team prepares the area. It's almost 1 p.m. when the truck pulls up to the barn with the mats on board. The workout area is ready for the mats to be installed and the team is coming out of the barn to collect them.

The two men with JC go to the back of the truck, open the doors and climb aboard ready to unload the mats. The mats are not heavy; just awkward to carry. As each team member approaches the truck, they are given a mat to carry into the barn, and then they return for another. *They remind me of Marine Corps ants*, JC thinks, *working non-stop*. When the last mat is unloaded, the two men jump down from the truck and closed the doors. The rest of the team is already unpacking while Benz instructs where and how to place them. By the time the four-by-fours return from Pennsylvania, the mats are installed and ready to use.

"Good job," JJ approves. "I guess that's the last item on the home base list. Now we will be training so you all can get used to how everyone functions."

"Lock on training," exclaims JC.

"Lock on this," says a voice in the group.

Mac is surprised when JC starts laughing about the remark. Then he remembers: this isn't the Corps, this is something very different.

"Well I guess we should get started on dinner," Top suggests.

"That has been taken care of," JJ informs him. "A few of the team members decided to give you a break and prepared dinner tonight."

"Ho no!" the Top says. "Please don't tell me Bris is one of them."

"I'm afraid so," Mac confirms. Then both Mac and Top chant, "In the mouth, over the gums, look out asshole, here it comes!"

The team heads for the house for what turns out to be some very tasty dining. Even Top and the Ladies give it three thumbs up. Once again the remainder of the night is filled with laughter. *This group is really coming together*, JC thinks. *We'll take a day off tomorrow, then we start training.*

The team's day off is free time to allow each man to start making the transition from doing what needed to be done around the farm, to getting prepared for what they all do best. To start their preparation, working out with the weights, cardiac-vascular exercises and, of course, martial arts are on their agenda. Each man is proficient in two or more of the martial arts, so the new mats are put to good use. JC is also a black belt and joins in Judo with the team members. Benz, being the top expert in Judo, enjoys randori and keeps an eye on the other players so no one gets hurt(a force of habbit).

Everyone stops and watches during Benz and Panda's randori. It's a grand sight to see martial arts executed with such expert precision. After exercising, each man starts getting focused in his own way: tai chi, meditation, etc. The calm of the afternoon is broken when cursing and swearing is heard from the barn. Out of curiosity, everyone wanders over to see what is going on. The noise turns out to be two men wearing fencing jackets and masks, engaged in a saber match. As everyone approaches the workout area, the taller man delivers a hard blow to the top of the shoulder of the shorter fencer. A second later, a voice yells through the mask of the shorter fencer, "Ya fuckin' green beanie, that hurt!"

Laughter emits from the other mask. The shorter fencer attacks high, then goes low for a cross-stomach attack.

"What the hell," complains the taller fencer. "Do you think we're making sausage or something, ya jar-head fuck?"

This time the laughter rolls out of the shorter man's mask. JC and the team approach Benz, who has been watching the match from the start.

"They were playing so nice until one hit a little too hard, and then everything went to hell," Benz informs the group.

"Who are the fencers?" inquires JC.

"Blue Jay and Bean," answers Benz. "I think they've been through this before."

The match continues until both men are soaked with sweat and probably covered with more welts than you could shake a stick at. When they decide to stop, they face each other and perform the customary salute with their sabers. Then they remove their fencing masks as they walk towards the others. Both fencers have big smiles on their faces.

Around dinnertime all the men are tired, but a good tired.

"If this is your idea of a day off, what will tomorrow bring?" asks JJ.

"I was wondering that myself," JC replies. "These men are so efficient they do just about everything on their own before you ask. The only type of training we'll need will be mostly at the group level for future team efforts. And with the quality of men we're dealing with, that will take no time at all."

The following morning JC and the team are gathered in the team meeting room.

"Well, men," JC says as he initiates the meeting, "we seem to be at the training phase of our project. I realize you are all extremely competent in what you do, but we have never functioned as a team before. Having been around you all and observed how you are already working together, I feel that functioning as a team will not take a long period of time."

"Today," JC continues, "we'll have class work on tactics. Mac and I have set up the first phase of tactics we will be using. I say 'first phase' because with your help we will make changes and fine tune them before we start to train with them. Even when we begin training, we will review and review again, until we are all satisfied. In other words, try to remember when you were in the military and said things like 'this shit is stupid' or 'who's the asshole that thought this up?' Now we'll be the stupid assholes, and we will all talk about it and fix it."

The team members are pleased with what JC is saying. The plan is to use all of their experience and expertise to form the tactics for this team. What a logical thing to do; beats the hell out of some Melba milk-toast egghead back at the Pentagon planning things for them.

"That said," JC continues, "we will start reviewing and correcting our tactics." JC passes out the draft on tactics he and Mac have composed. After the team reads the draft, JC fires up the overhead viewer and started going through it. The week is taken up with chalkboard sessions, overhead reviews and conversations.

Four days later, the plan for basic tactics is finished. The objective is twofold: One, to train with these tactics so each member of the team can get used to his team mates, and two, to have tactic that could be used as is or modified for a particular project. After everyone is seated in the briefing room on the fifth day of the training phase, JC calls the group to order.

"I think we have done a pretty good job developing these tactics," JC announces. "Now we will see how they look in motion. First, we will do walkthroughs to see how they look and feel. After that we will start picking up the speed. We will ask the house team to act as objectives, and they will be armed with camcorders. This will enable us to review our progress. We'll use the morning for practice and the afternoon for review. When we get to night tactics, General Mac and myself will be the objectives." With that, JC asks the team to join him outside for the first walkthrough. JJ and Mac remain seated as the team leaves the room.

"Well," JJ says, "it looks like I'd better call a meeting in New York and start thinking about our first objective."

"JC and I were thinking along those lines," Mac tells him. "We feel the very first objective should be somewhat smaller than what we will be planning in the future. Perhaps some of those drug people south of the border? They seem to be well armed, but not well trained. This will give the team a chance to iron the wrinkles out."

"I agree," JJ confirms. "And I am sure the board will concur. Mac," JJ continues, "making you my backup interface between the board and the team puts you in a position where a lot of people will know you are involved in this, and if something goes wrong it could put you in harm's way."

"So?" Mac shrugs. "You're doing it."

"It was my idea," JJ responds.

"So?"

"Okay then," JJ concedes. "You will come with me to the next board meeting.

Four days later, JJ and Mac are sitting in the conference room in New York when JJ calls the meeting to order.

"I am glad you all were able to attend this meeting today," JJ announces. "I will give you an overview of the team status and keeping in mind they're still in training mode, we will discuss our first objective." Due to the fact that any in-depth knowledge about the team is being kept from the board, the team status takes only 10 minutes of the meeting.

"Now," JJ continues, "we will address the first mission. We have selected a gang in Mexico involved in drugs, kidnapping, murder, and the like. We plan to take out the boss and top members of the gang. This will allow the team to work out any kinks in the execution of their tactics and perform a public service at the same time. Any questions?"

Dunn raises his hand.

"Yes?" JJ acknowledges.

"If we are going to hit this gang, we should put them out of business," Dunn suggests. "If we just take out the top, it will be like upward mobility for the rest of the gang."

"I agree," Dawson says. "I think we should hit them hard."

"How hard?" Mac inquires.

"Hard enough to let them know 'drugs are bad,'" Dunn quips.

"Okay then," JJ intervenes, "we will take a vote. First, on the mission itself." All members agree. "Second, on the modified version of the original plan." Again all members agree. "Mac and I will discuss this with the team, and if they agree, we'll execute the plan in the near future. After that I will schedule our next meeting. More questions?" JJ asks. No response. "Then, meeting adjourned."

One month later JJ is again calling the board meeting to order.

"I'll give you a brief summary on the first mission. The initial plan of taking out the boss and the hierarchy was modified to also include the gang. The boss and over half of the gang were eliminated. All drugs and buildings were destroyed. Being at the right place at the right time, the Team also discovered the boss at the next level. He and his bodyguards were also eliminated. The local authorities believe it was a drug war, but are not sure. The drug people probably think someone is moving in on them, but they don't know whom. This tells me the team is working well together, and can move on to more important targets." With that, JJ walks to the tripod and flips to a page of information about the first of three targets.

"We will again review the targets we are considering. This is Mr. Gonzales," JJ says, "code name Peckerhead Magurk. On the surface he is just another big-time drug dealer, but he is also involved in financing worldwide terrorism. If he and a few of his high-level people are taken out, we think the new management will stop the money that is going to support terrorist."

JJ continues the briefing, with he and Mac answering questions from the board members. After the three possibilities are presented, JJ announces, "If no one has any additional questions we will start the selection process." The board members all look at each other for additional input and agree to vote. JJ gives the board members a chance to make any additional comments, then continues: "Each board member will have a vote. If we do not all agree, we will have more discussion and vote again. If we still don't have an agreement, we put that target aside, add a new target and start again." JJ then asks for a vote from each member. All members select the first target presented, Mr. Peckerhead Magurk.

"Now that we have the who," states Mr. Dawson, "what about where and how?"

"He will be hard to get," JJ explains. "His residence is an old hotel converted into part modern luxury and part fort, overlooking a small village. He helps support the town, so they are all loyal and report any new people that come around. His security force is well armed, and there are security devices around the area of the residence."

"How will the team be able to get to the target?" asks Mr. Howard.

"I'm sure they'll think of something," Mac interrupts.

"I am sure they will," replies Mr. Howard.

The next morning, JJ and Mac are in the team meeting room back at the barn. JJ calls the meeting to order and announces,

"Mr. Peckerhead Magurk will be our next project."

The team reacts as if they have just been told tomorrow's weather forecast.

"Any questions or comments?" JJ asks. After a pause, JC speaks up.

"We have researched each target for the selection process, but have delayed any in-depth study until we knew who the target was going to be. My only comment is that we will not be rushed into any action. Planning is of the utmost importance for success and prevention of casualties." When he finishes there is silence in the room, and he notices everyone is looking at him.

"Oh don't get me wrong," JC smiles, "I don't care about you people. I'm just getting too old to go through all of the bullshit of getting new men on the team."

The team erupts in laughter and someone says,

"And just when we were all thinking about sending him a

valentine!"

When the laughter subsides, JJ shifts the meeting to a serious note.

"I want to assure you we all are in this together. That goes for Mac, the board and myself. It is only for security reasons that you don't know the board and they don't know you. Mac, JC and Blue Jay picked each one of you, and I picked Mac. With that said, I guess we can get to the business at hand."

"What should we do first, JC?" JJ asks.

"Coffee sounds good," JC answers.

"Works for me," Mac adds.

"Coffee?" JJ shakes his head.

"What did you expect?" Mac grins. "A 'One for the Gibber' speech?"

"Screw you," JJ retorts.

The team is taking it all in. They enjoy these men and their verbal battles.

CHAPTER FIVE

I t is a nice sunny day as the tour bus passes a sign that reads El Dorado, 2 MILES. The February sun in Mexico feels good compared to the frigid winter air of New Jersey. Two on the tour will be taking their sightseeing more seriously than the others. Bean, sitting mid-bus, and Blue Jay in the back, are armed with special cameras; they will go their separate ways to perform recon on the town, and especially the hotel on the cliff overlooking the town. This is the headquarters of their next target.

As the bus slows to a stop, Bean and Blue Jay take on the same character as the other tour members, standing, stretching and making small talk. Bean and Blue Jay will be separate, but also together. They will act like strangers, but one will back up the other. On tour with the guide, they will map out the town. When the tour goes to attend Mass at the old Catholic Church, Bean and Blue Jay will slip away to do recon on the hotel. Once again: not together, but not apart.

El Dorado is a quite little town. When the silver mine was in full swing, it was a prosperous place, then it fell on hard times. Then Peckerhead Magurk came to town and things perked up. He purchased the hotel and also started pumping money into the town, mainly for added security for his drug operation. If strangers come to town, the town's people will let him know. If anything out of the ordinary happens, they tell him. This is why Bean and Blue Jay are on a church pilgrimage, just two of the flock taking pictures.

Bean and Blue Jay manage to be on a side street behind the church, heading back toward the main highway just before the bell rings for Mass. They aren't moving too fast, snapping pictures and acting like tourists. Once they get to the main road, Blue Jay has the lead and wanders to the other side and down an alley. He can get good shots of the far side of the hotel and surrounding area from there. Bean hangs back and covers the alley from across the street.

Bean is pretending to take pictures, but is using his viewfinder to select a hiding place for a body, if the need arises.

Pictures taken, Blue Jay wanders out of the alley and Bean takes the lead. He walks down the main road toward the driveway that goes up the hill to the hotel. Blue Jay trails about a block behind taking photos of the town and townsfolk, always keeping his back to the hotel taking pictures.

With his telescopic lens, Bean does not have to get close to the subject matter, and is done quickly.

The two start back through town, heading toward the church, and after walking about two blocks Bean is stopped by what looks like the town tough guy.

"You like to take a lot of pictures, don't you, *senor*?" the tough guy inquires.

"Why yes, I do," replies Bean.

>From the other side of the street Blue Jay almost starts laughing. Under different circumstances, Bean would have just kicked him the balls and called it a day.

"Let me ask you," Bean continues quickly, "I seem to have gotten turned around. The church is that way right?" Bean points in the direction he knows the church is in.

"Yes," confirms the thug.

"Thank you, my son," Bean says as he continues walking.

The thug doesn't want to assault a priest, and Bean is out of range before he can think about it. Lucky thug.

Bean and Blue Jay slip into the back of the church just as Mass ends, and then depart with the tour. They get a third angle of the hotel with the rest of the tour just before getting back onto the bus, and then it's on to Acapulco.

In Acapulco, Bean and Blue Jay stay with the tour in case anyone at El Dorado has gotten curious and followed them. Once they remove all of the film from the cameras and secured it in the moneybelt-type garment they wear around their waists, they hang out around the hotel with the people on the pilgrimage and take daily tours. Two days later, they are on a plane to Mexico City, then on to Newark International in New Jersey.

After bidding farewell to the Polish priest with the Irish accent and the other tour members, Bean and Blue Jay head for long-term parking. It is around 10:00 p.m. when they get onto Route 78 West and start talking about the trip. After discussing all of the funny things that happened and the sightseeing they took in, things get quiet for a while. Then Blue Jay breaks the silence.

"It seemed to me the town tough scared the shit out of you on the street that day we were taking the pictures."

"Is that what the he did?" Bean remarks.

"That pecker-head came close to being the ex-town tough."

"Yeah, yeah," replies Blue Jay as he whips out another one-liner.

The verbal combat continues as they get out of the car back at the barn. JJ, Mac and JC come out of the house to welcome the men home.

"I hope you two didn't argue like this in Mexico," JJ says hopefully.

"No, sir," answers Bean, "except for that fist fight over that broad in El Dorado, we were on good behavior."

Mac and JC chuckle as JJ shakes his head and says, "Top made you up a midnight snack. We'll join you for coffee, if you don't mind."

After the men enter the house Mac says, "The Top will develop your pictures tomorrow and blow up the ones you select. You can give us a brief heads-up in the morning, then we will take the pictures to the team room for a briefing. Let them digest the photos and plan for a few days, then go through it again. Consider suggestions and alternatives. Then lock into a plan of operation."

"As JC stated before the first project, there will be no rushing into any operations," JJ adds. "The better prepared we are, the more effective we are.

"That phrase should be written on something so people can see it," Mac suggests, "How about that big-ass chocolate cake I saw in the fridge?"

"Ya know, it's a good thing you and I didn't go to El Dorado," JJ tells Mac. "One of us would not have made it back. Then I would have that big-ass cake all to myself."

"Maybe," Mac answers as he opens the door to the fridge.

After all had eaten, had coffee and their fill of chocolate cake, they decided to call a night.

Tomorrow was going to be a big day.

"Welcome back," greets the Top as Blue Jay and Bean lead the team into breakfast. "The Ladies have welcome-home gifts for you both." Just as Top is making the announcement the Ladies hand Bean and Blue Jay each a cork.

Lady1 says, "In case you are having any problems."

Ladya adds, "You know, the water in Mexico."

"Oh, that's funny," exclaims Bean as everyone bursts into laughter.

"Now they have the Ladies picking on us," adds Blue Jay, "and us just back from a death-defying mission."

"Yeah, I hear Acapulco is dangerous this time of year," confirms Air Jockey.

"Did I tell you about the fight we had in El Dorado over this stunning female?" Bean inquires as he looks at JJ.

"It's too early in the morning for me," quips JJ as he motions for the cream.

The team continues to laugh and joke around through breakfast. When everyone is finished, JJ calls a brief informal meeting and gives the team the schedule for the next few days. They all seem pleased with how the plan will be developed, and the fact that they would be given time to analyze and offer their input.

"If Blue Jay and Bean will join Mac, JC and me for the initial briefing, we can decide if we want to take on this mission. Top," JJ says, "will you give us the photos as you develop them?" With that, breakfast is adjourned and five men move into JJ's den. They enter the room, and all except Blue Jay find a seat.

"What does it look like?" inquires Mac.

"Well," starts Blue Jay, "at one time I am sure it was a beautiful place to stay. It's a Spanish-style hotel on a mountainside, overlooking a small Mexican village. Something you would expect to see in a movie. Now, it's a strong hold with a hell of a vantage point. The road leading to the hotel is very steep, with several turns. Other approaches are worse. Soft ground, and very steep. Either will hamper any type of quick assault. A night assault isn't a good idea, due to the night vision equipment they probably have."

"This sounds like a tough nut to crack," exclaims JJ. "Do you think we ought to pass on this one?"

"No, I was thinking about a sunset assault," replies Blue Jay.

"Or sunrise," adds Bean.

"That's right," agrees Blue Jay, "that will be determined by the East and West terrain around the Hotel. We will have to use the entire team on this one," he continues, "but since this will be a total destruction mission, we can just turn them loose."

"What do you mean?" inquires JJ.

"That means everyone up there is fair game," answers Blue Jay, "If it was not an isolated site, we would have to watch out for innocents, and that could slow things down a bit. One thing we will have to work on is the quick extraction of the team. Going in isn't a problem. Everyone is watching for people sneaking into the U.S., not the other way round, but after we destroy that site there will be a swarm of folks after us. That's about it for the initial brief," Blue Jay finishes.

"Okay," JJ says. "Any questions or comments?"

"I have a few," JC speaks up. "If you have a choice on the assault time, sunrise may be better. Just as the sun comes over the horizon. People tend not to have their sunglasses on that early in the morning. I realize that when the sun is at a certain angle sunglasses don't help much, but why give them any kind of help?"

"Good point," agrees Blue Jay.

"I was also thinking about the extraction," JC continues. "If we need transportation for the entire team, a plane is in order. Something that can sneak in under radar and land in the desert. I'll talk with Air Jockey about it. I have a plane in mind." JC smiles. "I forget the name, but I'll know it when I see it."

"Well, with that ray of enlightenment," exclaims JJ, "I guess we can get the pictures from the Top and head for the team briefing room to present it to them."

Bean, Blue Jay and JC all nod their heads, stand and walk toward the door. The Top is just finishing up the shots they requested be blown up to a bigger size when he hears JJ inquiring about the status of the pictures.

"Just finished," replies Top as he appears with the photos.

After briefly reviewing them, JJ announces, "I think we are ready for the team briefing?"

All agree and walk to the door and the barn.

After two weeks of briefings and training, the last team meeting is in session.

"I have one last question," JJ says. "I know you are going to assault in the morning from the East at sunrise, but how will you get into assault position at the top of the ridge?"

"Well sir, we'll use kill suits, and a slow all-night crawl," Blue Jay answers. "I'll be observing their security through night-vision goggles and giving the team start and stop commands. We will start around 9:00 p.m., and will be in position before daybreak."

It is a calm morning as one of the security people walks around the hotel checking out the area. He finds nothing out of the ordinary. *Nobody would dare bother with us anyway*, he thinks to himself.

The sun is just starting to peek over the distant mountains as the guard stops to light a cigarette. He just finishes the third pull of his last cigarette, when a round from a silenced .22 Blackhawk hits him between the eyes. Bean usually likes to fire two rounds, but from six feet away even Blue Jay could make the shot. As the guard falls to the ground, a mass of vegetation and foliage comes to life at the top of the ridge. Everyone will use silenced pistols until the alert is sounded at the hotel. Then automatic weapons will come into play.

The team forms a skirmish line as they quickly move toward the hotel. Another guard appears from around the corner and joins his fallen comrade. As the team approaches the hotel, without hesitation, they divide into two groups. Bean leads one group to the left and Blue Jay leads the other group to the right. All are in communication with each other, but no talk is necessary. Each man knows the plan and can improvise if necessary. As Blue Jay's group turns the corner, two more guards hit the ground, and another on Bean's side.

"We are lucky today," Bean whispers into his Com gear.

"Hold that thought," replies Blue Jay.

Bean's group is moving quickly, approaching a terrace at the back of the hotel. *No one in sight,* Bean thinks to himself, when all of a sudden, a man stands up and starts stretching. Everyone in the group goes into freeze mode, but the man has already seen them and starts sounding the alarm. "Ah, fuck!" mutters Bean as he takes his usual two shots to shut off the alarm. Everyone in Bean's group puts their silenced weapons away and readies their automatics. The plan is that whoever gets discovered first will switch to automatic weapons. The other group will stay silenced as long as possible. This will draw the bulk of the force to the ongoing fire and allow the other team to get behind them or attack from another angle.

Bean's group finds cover, and when another group from the hotel arrives at the patio they open fire. At the same time, Blue Jay's men are moving quickly around to the front, taking out the two doormen. Quickly pulling the bodies aside, the group crouches down as more of the drug lord's men rush to the patio. As the group passes through the lobby area, someone yells out something in Spanish.

"We are getting company," whispers Tic, the Cuban member of the team.

Blue Jay quickly instructs, "Tic and Blue Jay will take these two quietly. Everyone else, go to auto."

Two men approach the door cautiously. A split second after one of the men called out for the guards at the front door, Blue Jay and Tic appear in the doorway and dispose of the unwanted company. Without hesitation the group moves toward the gunfire on the patio. As they get close, Bris takes up the position of rear guard. Once in position, Blue Jay alerts Bean's group and they stop firing. At the same time, Blue Jay's group opens up. When Blue Jay's men stop firing, Bean's people rush toward the patio and the opposition is naturalized in short notice. Bean looks at Blue Jay and says, "Now for the main man."

The team forms up and moves back toward Bris. As they approach him the groups again split up. Blue Jay moves back through the lobby and Bean goes down the stairs where additional rooms are located. Blue Jay's group quickly checks the dining room and kitchen. No main man. With that done, they move to rejoin Bean's group. Bean is doing the same, and the groups meet in the lobby.

"Where in the hell is he?" Bean grinds out.

"Let's check outside," answers Blue Jay.

As the team gets outside and starts checking the grounds they see two men running down the steep road leading to the town.

"They are out of range for these weapons," remarks Bean.

"I know!" answers Blue Jay as he looks at the fleeing men through field glasses.

"That's Peckerhead and his Number One, if I'm not mistaken."

"Sneaky little bastard, isn't he?" remarks Bean.

Just then, one shot, then another ring out, and the two fleeing figures fall to the ground.

"We don't call them Met and Pru for nothing,"
remarks Blue Jay. "They are our insurance polices."

"Did anyone run across any money?" inquires Blue Jay.

"Yes," Panda replies, "a whole shit load of it."

"Well a few of you go get a bunch," Blue Jay orders.

The men look puzzled.

"For the town folk," explains Blue Jay. "This may be a toll road."

As the men reappear with the money, Tic is pulling the hotel bus up to where the men are standing. As he opens the door Blue Jay exclaims,

"Nice getup."

"This mask is hot as hell. Do you really think it's going to fool anyone?" inquires Tic.

"Well, I don't think we will be interviewed by CNN at the

bottom, but these days one never knows," quips Blue Jay.

"With the dark sunglasses, hat pulled down low, the bus going like hell and money flying out the windows, it may work."

"Lets get," exclaims Bean.

A quarter of the way down the hill, the bus stops to pick up Peckerhead and Number One.

"With that mask you do look a little like Number One there," Panda assures Tic. "That may come in handy, since you will be the only thing those people with guns down there will be able to see."

"Take a seat, *in the back of the bus!*" Tic orders Panda.

As the bus continues down the hill Blue Jay announces, "We'll try money first. If that doesn't work, be careful who you shoot."

Each man takes up a window seat along each side of the bus and positions himself so he is out of site.

"We are about 100 yards from the bottom of the hill," Tic informs everyone.

"Remember, when you get to the main road turn left and don't stop for anything," orders Blue Jay. "I'll be throwing this money out the window. They will think we're a scared Peckerhead running for his life. Once they see the amount on these bills, a riot will probably ensue as we haul ass down the road."

When the bus is approximately 50 yards from the main road, a man walks out into the middle of the hotel road and starts waving at the bus.

"A man wants me to stop," Tic informs Blue Jay. "What shall I do?"

"Hit the gas and lean on the horn. I'll start throwing the money, Blue Jay answers.

The big man standing in the road is the local law, and on Peckerhead's payroll. He seems to be unsure of what is going on. It is the hotel bus, and at that distance it looks like Number One is driving. As the bus bears down on him, he starts moving to the side of the road and slowly reaching for his gun when he notices someone is throwing something out the bus window, something that looks a lot like money. As the bus speeds past him he is showered with hundred dollar bills, and quickly forgets about his gun and the bus. Tic wheels the bus left onto the main road, with cash still flying out of the window.

Seven miles out of El Dorado, Tic turns onto a dirt road that winds through the hills. After a mile and a half, he brings the bus to a stop and two of the team get off the bus. He shifts the bus into first gear and slowly turns it off the road. Fifty yards from the road is a canyon, and Tic drives the bus toward it as the two men cover the tire tracks and continue their efforts as the bus moves to its destination. When the bus comes to a stop in the canyon, everyone gets off.

Three of the team go to retrieve the three Volkswagens they used to get to the canyon. Tic removes his disguise with great relief and joins the other team members, who are changing from kill suits to civilian clothes. After the two dead bodies are removed from the bus and put into the VWs, Blue Jay walks to the back of the bus and starts spreading gas on the seats and floor. Not too much, he just wants to destroy anything that could be of use to the police. Blue Jay puts a match to the trail of gas he created and leaves the bus. The bus ignites with a low roar and in no time the interior of the vehicle is an inferno.

"We want to knock this down before too much smoke is generated," says Blue Jay as he reaches for a fire extinguisher.

After the men are sure the fire is out, all but two get into the three Volkswagen convertibles. The cars depart the same way the bus came in: slowly, with one man per tire track covering their trail. When the cars get to the road, they purposely form a staggered line for their trip to the main road. This should cover the bus tire trail on the dirt road.

Ten minutes later they are at the main road, where they again turn left and continue at a respectable 55 to 60 miles per hour. With no lights, traffic or towns to deal with, one hour later they are 50 miles away from El Dorado and turning onto another dirt road.

Mexico is mainly desert, but this part is mountain too. The three VWs climb up, then down the dirt road. It was a good idea to use these cars. They are air-cooled with good traction, and they are still made in Mexico, so they will not draw too much attention. After traveling 15 miles on the dirt road, the VW convoy comes to a halt.

"Did you forget to confirm our reservations?" Bean inquires when he notices that no plane is waiting for them.

"What are you complaining about?" Blue Jay responds. "It will give you a chance to work on your tan."

The team sits patiently waiting for the plane. After an hour they hear the faint noise of a prop engine. Blue Jay breaks out his field glasses and starts searching the sky. A few minutes later he confirms it's Air Jockey.

"See if you can raise him on the radio, Panda."

"Roger," replies Panda as he puts on his headset.

"So, did you get lost, asshole?" Panda says.

"Get knotted," is the reply from Air Jockey.

"He said he'll be right down," Panda relays to Blue Jay.

"I'll bet he did," smiles Blue Jay as he scans the area for any movement.

The plane flies parallel to the dirt road, then makes a left bank and comes in for a landing like a big-ass bird.

"Holy shit!" the team exclaims as the plane comes to a halt.

Within a few minutes, the VWs are approaching the plane. The tail ramp is lowered and the Volkswagens pull right inside.

"Are there any tires left on this bucket of bolts?" Panda inquires to Air Jockey.

"Take it up with the pilot." Air Jockey points toward the cockpit as JC pokes his head around the corner.

"Nice landing, sir," Panda announces.

JC waves his thanks as Air Jockey pushes Panda and calls him, "Pilot kiss-ass."

When all of the gear is loaded and lashed down, JC starts to taxi the plane into takeoff position.

"Hold onto your shorts," advises Panda. "Wild Thing is at the controls." Panda's words are still ringing in the air when the plane starts hauling ass across the desert.

After what seems to be a long time someone inquires, "Are we driving to the Mexico City Airport so we can take off from there?" Just as the team starts to laugh, the plane jumps into the air. After climbing to a reasonable, but low, altitude, JC banks the plane to the right and heads for the sea and their escape route. Blue Jay makes his way to the cockpit to speak with JC.

"I see we still have a full team," comments JC.

"Yes," replies Blue Jay, "quite a group. Most of the time things are anticipated and in progress before I can give a command."

"They are good men," agrees JC. "I would hate to lose any of them. I like them all." He notices Blue Jay is taken back by his words. "Yeah, I know. In the past I always kept up that hard-ass attitude for the troops, but inside it was a different story. Besides, you are the one in the front lines calling the shots. I'm too long in the tooth to be out there with the team."

"Oh, I can understand that," Blue Jay says. "For a minute there I thought that was you flying into Mexico, landing and taking off in the desert, then sneaking out again under the radar. But now that you cleared that up, I feel better."

Air Jockey is amused by the conversation and inquires, "Where did you get this piece of flying shit anyway?"

"Sears War Surplus Catalog," quips JC.

"Well if you keep landing and flying it this way you'll be ordering from the catalog again soon," Air Jockey returns.

"Is that what I'll be doing?" snaps JC. "Well, where did you learn to fly? Pussy Airways?"

Blue Jay sees where this conversation is going and says, "Well I can see you men want to chat," as he moves to return to the team. When he reaches the rear he reminds the team to make sure Peckerhead and Number One have their seatbelts on, and is not surprised when he gets the reply "already taken care of."

Air Jockey and JC have completed their chat and are skimming across the Pacific Ocean. Air Jockey is hard at work looking for any sign of traffic.

"See anything?" JC inquires.

"Nothing," reports Air Jockey, "air or sea."

"Lets do it," commands JC.

Air Jockey clicks on the Com unit and announces, "Past 10 mile mark, nothing in sight."

With that announcement, the back ramp of the plane is lowered. Blue Jay orders, "Everyone hook up."

After checking that all team members are, Blue Jay informs Air Jockey they are ready. JC pulls the plane into a steep climb. As the plane approaches a 45-degree angle, the Volkswagens start rolling to the rear of the plane. The steering wheels have been tied down so they will roll straight back. The VWs quickly pick up momentum, and the first, then the second roll off the end of the ramp. Then Peckerhead and Number One take the dive.

"Well, they're off the plane," says Panda. "Now all we have to worry about is sinking an unsuspecting ship Wild Thing didn't see. I can see the headlines now: Cruise Ship Sunk By Beetle."

The ramp is raised as the plane returns to level flight, then banks to the left toward Guatemala. It has been arranged that a group of drug smugglers, with ties to Peckerhead Magurk's terrorist organization, will purchase the plane. They will take delivery in Guatemala at a deserted airstrip they often use. It is sunset when the plane is on final approach at the airstrip.

"Now remember, we are Arab terrorists," Blue Jay instructs the team. "Keep your faces covered, and Check will take the lead and do all of the talking. These clowns think they are bad, so keep your cool."

All of the men nod their understanding. In a few minutes, the plane touches down with a relatively smooth landing. As the plane rolls down the runway Panda states, "Air Jockey must be behind the wheel."

"Pilot's pet," Check replies with a smile.

"Lower the ramp half way down," orders Blue Jay, "so we can see what is going on. I don't want any surprises from these yahoos."

The plane finally rolls to a stop and the ramp is lowered to the ground. The team quickly files out and stands a short distance from the plane. Check, with Blue Jay and Bean standing on each side and a step to the rear, starts the transfer.

"Money for the plane?" Check states.

The leader of the smugglers' group steps forward with a briefcase and hands it over to Check. Holding the briefcase with both hands, Check turns to Bean and motions for him to hold it. He obeys. Check opens it, looks at the money, and then closes it again. He then gestures with his right hand that they can have the plane. Part of the arrangement was the smugglers would supply transportation for their brother terrorists, and they have. Two Suburbans are parked along the side of the strip.

The props were left running so the plane could depart as soon as the transaction was completed. When the plane is loaded with drugs, the smugglers raise the ramp and get into position to take off. The security force that came with the smugglers climb into their vehicles and wait for the plane's departure.

Quietly, Blue Jay gives orders for the team to check the Surburbans for booby traps, and for Pru and Met to scout the area for any additional men.

As soon as the plane starts down the runway, the smugglers' security force departs.

"Is that real money?" inquires JC.

"Looks that way," answers Check as he puts the briefcase on the hood of one of the vehicles and opens it.

"Look at that moolah," exclaims JC.

"Excuse me, sir," inquires a confused Panda, "I have a question."

"What is it?" inquires JC.

"Well," Panda begins, "first we knock off a drug king pin running a terrorist group. Then we turn over a plane so the smugglers can run more drugs and supply the terrorists?"

"What plane?" JC interrupts.

"That plane!" exclaims Panda, pointing.

JC looks in the direction of the plane that's just left the runway, holds up a little black box and presses the red button. An instant later, the plane erupts into a ball of flame.

Panda looks at JC with big-eyed surprise and says, "You mean to tell me you had that much explosives on that plane, and you were landing and flying like it was some kind of hot rod?"

"Yeah!" JC answers. "Scary, ain't it?"

Panda looks directly at JC, then at the team and says, "Scary, ain't it?"

"That security force will be coming back to see what happened, so we'd better get into position," instructs Blue Jay.

The team spreads out into defensive positions. The security vehicles came to an abrupt halt when they heard the plane exploding. Their bright red brake lights can be seen easily as dusk settles over the desert. They sit for a few moments, then the red lights go back to normal as the brake pedals are released. Instead of making a U turn, the force continues in the same direction, but a lot faster.

"I guess they are going for reinforcements at the ranch," states JC. "I'd say it's time for us to skedaddle as well."

"Lets load up," yells Blue Jay, and team members start showing up out of nowhere and pile into the Surburbans. The driver of each suburban is wearing night vision goggles, so no lights are required. If the drivers stay off the brake pedals no one will know they are on the move. When the two groups are about five miles down the road, they start changing into civilian clothes. The kill suits, camouflage utilities and weapons, except for the silenced .22's, are put into the American tourist bag each man is carrying. Blue Jay is in the front seat checking out a map.

"We have about 30 miles to go," he announces to the driver. "You and I better get changed into civvies."

The suburban pulls over the side of the road, followed by the second. The driver and Blue Jay change seats with two of the team members as JC and the driver of the second vehicle do the same. Within 15 seconds, both vehicles are back on the road. Forty minutes later, the first group is driving past a small airport.

"Looks quiet," Blue Jay says into his Com unit. The other group has dropped off the pace and is trailing about a mile behind.

"You pull in and unload," orders JC. "By the time you start heading for the plane we will be in place to cover you."

"Roger that," Blue Jay answers.

The first vehicle unloads and the men start heading for the plane. The second vehicle has parked and, except for the driver, all have gotten out. When the first group gets halfway to the plane, the second group starts. It is a moonless night, and pitch black outside. Air Jockey walks up to the side of the plane and pounds on the door.

"There's nobody home!" Mac yells as he opens the door to the jet.

When the door is completely opened on the Lear business jet, Air Jockey goes aboard and to the cockpit to prepare for takeoff. JC and the second group arrive, and both groups get on the plane. Air Jockey fires up the engines, turns on the plane's lights and starts taxiing as he talks to the tower, requesting takeoff permission. After a brief delay, a sleepy voice from the tower gives the okay and the Learjet streaks down the runway.

"Who's driving?" Panda asks.

"Air Jockey," replies Mac.

"Well, I guess we won't be buzzing the tower, so I think I'll get some sleep."

"Did I miss something?" Mac asks.

"I'll fill you in," Blue Jay laughs. "It's a long story."

By the time Blue Jay gives Mac a short briefing on the mission, the jet is over the Pacific Ocean. Once the plane is off Guatemala radar, the plane drops down, turns south and returns to the airport it flew out of two days ago. The airstrip does not have a tower, so as long as you stay under radar it's possible to sneak in and out. The Jet gets refueled and takes off. After a brief stop in Jamaica, it's back to Jersey. The team takes the opportunity to get some sleep as Air Jockey and JC take turns piloting the plane.

It's 0700 in Jersey when the tired Learjet limps to a stop in front of the hanger at Mercer Airport. Air Jockey is the last man to leave the plane, and he heads for the hanger. Inside the hanger he is greeted by the Learjet's chief mechanic.

"Good flight?" inquires the mechanic.

"Yes," replies Air Jockey, "but I think she's a little tired. Those people know how to party. Here," Air Jockey says as he hands the mechanic what looks like a cardboard suitcase. "A bottle of Jamaica

Rum for you and each member of your crew, and this for the morning after." He hands over a bag of Jamaica Blue mountain coffee. The mechanic is surprised and pleased with the gifts, and thanks Air Jockey several times as he walks to his car. Like the other team members, he is good-hearted when it comes to the average person. On the other hand, none of them could give a rat's ass about the rich and powerful who think they are better than everyone else.

After Air Jockey gets into his car, he lights up a cigar and sits there recalling the past three days. *I'm no stranger to dangerous clandestine operations, but these people really rock and roll. I wonder what the future will bring?* He thinks. Then he takes the cigar from his mouth, looks at it and says aloud, "And who in the hell got me started smoking these things? It was that brash pilot JC. I'll have to mention it to him. They could affect my health-if JC's landings don't beat them to the punch." He smiles as he starts his car, peels out and heads for the exit.

Air Jockey is the last to arrive at home base. As he enters the dining room where everyone is having coffee, someone asks, "Get lost coming from the airport?"

Before he can reply, JC announces, "I'm not surprised," trying to get the troops stirred up.

Air Jockey doesn't disappoint him when he comes back with, "Not surprised, huh? Well, who wants to talk about the almost-kamikaze landing in Mexico?"

"Oh, don't bring that up," pleads Panda, "I won't be able to sleep tonight."

JC is laughing when Mac inquires, "Am I detecting some criticism about your flying skills, JC?"

"Ah, they're all pussies, Mac," JC retorts.

That really gets the ball rolling. It almost gets quiet once, until Met and Pru tell the Top about their importance the day the team assaulted the hotel.

"I say, Top! The long guns carried the day," starts Pru.

"The main people would have gotten clean away if it wasn't for us," adds Met.

Pru and Met both know the team would have gotten the two main men even if they had missed, but this was their entry into the Bullshit Derby that was on going. Realizing that, Top helps them out with, "I'm not surprised; you can only do so much with those automatic weapons."

The other members look at each other and smile as Bean says, "Oh this is good!"

Knowing it will make the other team members really crazy, Met and Pru start demonstrating how they got the big bad guys, and the conversation takes off like popcorn in a microwave. As things start to quiet down again, Bris says,

"So maybe we should have just stayed in town having tea and

crumpets, while you two smoked out the bad guys with your long guns?"

"Thanks for the lead-in Bris," announces JJ. "While you were away, I came across some new toys that may come in handy some day. I have them in the team room. Let's go check them out, then start our debriefing."

The team adjourns to the briefing room and finds two .50-caliber rifles displayed on the table. The members are instantly attracted to the weapons.

"These are the same type of weapons Special OPS use," announces JJ. "I would like all of you to get familiar with them. I guess Pru and Met will be the primaries. They may come in handy in the future."

"If you had these in Mexico," Bris says to Pru and Met, "you probably could have knocked the entire hotel down."

"Or made it too hot for anyone to stay in there," replies Pru.

After all have inspected the new weapons, JJ calls the meeting to order.

"I think we can break this down into three parts. First, Mac can cover from Jersey to Guatemala and back; second, JC from Guatemala to Mexico and back; and third, Blue Jay with the main part of the debriefing, the assault on the hotel." At once, all joking and laughing is exchanged for a serious atmosphere. As Mac presents his part of the debriefing, JJ scans the team. *Is this the same group that was here a few minutes ago?* he thinks to himself. *The look on each face has changed from good natured to someone you probably wouldn't want to mess with if you saw him on the street. I can only imagine what those faces look like in a combat situation.* When JJ comes out of his thoughts, Mac is just finishing and is turning the briefing over to JC. After JC's presentation the team breaks for lunch, then regroups for part three. Blue Jay's part takes the entire afternoon. It was a very smooth operation, but this team is striving for perfection. It is evening when all of the team members are satisfied. JJ stands and announces,

"I would like to say you men have done an excellent job. I can honestly say I am not surprised."

"When you have been around as long as I have, you develop a sense of judging men, and that's why I knew you would do well."

JJ is taken aback by the team's reaction to his words. They are all very quiet, and almost sad, as though no one had ever given them a compliment before. JJ looks at Mac, who is also picking up on the reaction. Without hesitation JJ continues:

"Except for Mac. I am surprised the plane was still there for your return trip." Mac, realizing what JJ is doing, quickly fires a series of one-liners that changes the solemn mood of the team as they file out on their way to dinner

The next day Blue Jay talks Bean into making a booze run with him. After taking everyone's order they depart for one of the local liquor stores. Today, it is Riverview. After loading up the goodies, Blue Jay pulls out of the parking lot and heads north.

"Where are we going?" inquires Bean.

"A little drive to clear my head," answers Blue Jay.

Bean knows that is bullshit. He has known Blue Jay for a lot of years, and going for a ride to clear his head is not his forte.

When the car gets about 4 miles outside of Riverview, Blue Jay makes a left turn into a state park situated along the Delaware river. Blue Jay stops the car and gets out with a paper bag in tow. Bean follows, knowing something is up. When the men are seated at one of the picnic tables, Blue Jay produces a child's writing toy. You write on the tablet-like surface, read it, then lift up the outer sheet and the writing disappears. It takes Bean about two seconds to figure out what is going on as Blue Jay starts his first correspondence:

I am going to find out who is on the board. These business types aren't like the government. I think JJ is OK, but who are the others? And if push comes to shove, will JJ be taking a dirt nap with us to cover the Board?

Good point, Bean writes after reading the message. Blue Jay resumes his writing. *The board isn't just rich; they have access to all kinds of hardware and intelligence. If they know who we are and we do not know them, we can wind up in deep shit.* Bean nods his head yes. *If I disappear, you will know why. Tell the team what is going on.*

After exchanging a few more notes, Blue Jay and Bean stand and start walking toward the river. At the riverbank Blue Jay takes a lighter from his pocket and lights the corner of the tablet. The flames slowly turn the tablet to ash that falls into the river. When the only thing remaining of the tablet is the part they did not write on, Blue Jay throws it into the river. Bean is wondering if this is all overkill, then remembers with today's technology, someone could probably tell you when gnats are having sex.

"Nice area," comments Blue Jay.

"Yes, it is," replies Bean as both men turn and walk back to the car.

CHAPTER SIX

With the second mission completed, the team has some down time. Some leave to check on the businesses they own, and others take a vacation. At least one of the household staff, and at least two of the team members always cover home base. Everyone works together and adjusts their schedules accordingly. JJ and the board use this time to select the next target before presenting it to the team for review.

World terrorism is not a big organization, but has many smaller units, JJ thinks to himself as he drives to a board meeting. *That makes it hard for a government to destroy it with one campaign, but the fact that they're small makes it better for our team. Also, we don't have to follow the same rules the government does. It's not like a real war, where each side tries to follow the rules of engagement. The terrorists have no rules, so we have no rules.*

It is late afternoon as JJ pulls into his spot at the parking garage in downtown Manhattan. He gets out of his Jag and on the elevator, the door closes and he is gone.

Five hours later, JJ reappears in the parking garage, accompanied by another man. They are holding an apparently serious conversation. They are not loud, but judging from the hand movements, something is very wrong. This activity has not gone unnoticed. In New York City, with the UN and other government organizations, you never know who's under surveillance, or why. JJ seems to be reassuring the man, and he calms down. After additional conversation, the man continues to his car, as does JJ. They both leave the parking garage and head in opposite directions.

The person observing from the shadows moves quietly from the garage and continues to a car parked on a side street, then gets in and starts the engine. *Well, this doesn't look good*, thinks Blue Jay. *I'd better get back to the barn before JJ-and the way he drives, that isn't going to be easy.* Blue Jay puts his Z28 Camaro into gear and quickly gives chase. Blue Jay knows JJ will beat him out of the city, but if he drives like hell, he may be in position at the barn to see what the problem is. As Blue Jay comes out of the Jersey side of the Holland tunnel, he knows JJ must be ahead of him. Blue Jay quickly changes lanes when he can to close the gap between him and his prey.

He finally catches sight of the other man going down Route 22. *Well, JJ, how am I going to get past you without you seeing me?* he wonders. JJ is in deep thought, and answers Blue Jay's question as he passes the merge onto I-78, the quickest way back to the barn. As Blue Jay speeds up the ramp, he thinks it would be nice if JJ takes Route 22 toward the barn…but he knows better. The man will be pissed off that he missed the I-78 ramp, and cut over from 22 to 78 farther down the road.

Blue Jay downshifts the Z28 and moves to the left lane. In no time he can see the I-78 Express Lane West sign overhead. *Just what I need*, he thinks, as he once again downshifts and moves to the express lane. In twelve minutes, he's at the I-287 exit and quickly navigates through the merge to I-287 south. He tries to stay around the speed limit on route 202 between Somerville and Flemington. There aren't many cars on the road, but he keeps an eye on those distant headlights behind him that seem to be closing the gap. *Is it a state trooper, or JJ?* he thinks.

The traffic light just before the Flemington circle is turning to amber as Blue Jay passes through the intersection. As he enters the circle, he looks into his rear view mirror to check out the car that has stopped for the red light.

"Shit!" he exclaims as he shifts his car into a lower gear. "It's the Jag."

As quickly as possible without exceeding the speed limit, he maneuvers around the circle and continues down 202 South. He knows it's going to be close, but he's confident he'll make it. At the Mt. Airy exit, Blue Jay turns onto a small two-lane country road. The road has a lot of curves and hills, but the Camaro doesn't seem to mind. With its wide tires, excellent traction and acceleration capabilities, it was made for this type of driving.

As he approaches a stone bridge that spans a small creek, a deer suddenly runs across the road in front of the car. He didn't have to swerve to miss the deer, but it did break his concentration and when he looked back to the road he realized he was not going to make the curve before crossing the stone bridge.

"Ah, SHIT!" he exclaims as his hands and feet start working to prevent a major accident. First the car tries to make the curve and cross the bridge, but the distance and speed won't allow this maneuver. The Z28 continues the turn and is on its way into a 360-degree spin, but it seems more likely the car will hit the bridge.

Blue Jay can't believe how fast his hands and feet are moving; as though some unseen force has taken over his body to show him how it's done. He looks down and sees himself shifting gears and pumping pedals automatically, and the next thing he realizes, he is standing on the brakes as the car slides sideways across the bride. The width of the tires and the low center of gravity keep it from rolling over, and the slide continues the length of the bridge, not making contact with the stone in any way.

As the Z28 slides off the end of the bridge it comes to a halt. Between forcing the brakes and turning the power steering unit hard to the left, the engine has stalled. Blue Jay sits behind the wheel reflecting on what just happened. Not to mention he was not sitting in the middle of a wreck, the Z28 also made it across the bridge without a scratch.

"Thank you," Blue Jay says out loud. Then he turns the key to see if the engine will start.

JJ comes to a stop in front of the house. He usually parks by the barn, but he had called ahead, and Mac would be waiting for him. He enters the house and proceeds to the den. Mac is sitting in one of the deep leather chairs as he enters the room.

"What's the scoop?" Mac asks.

"A problem has come up," JJ tells him. "This whole project could be in trouble before it even gets started."

"How?"

"It goes something like this," JJ explains. "Wilson, as you know, is one the Board members. He has a nephew that is somewhere between an opportunist and a good-for-nothing. Well, this nephew and Wilson's sister are visiting him at his home for a few weeks to do the NYC scene; Broadway and the big sights. Apparently, the boy likes to snoop around, and one day he found a note in Wilson's desk that made him curious."

"How curious?" inquires Mac.

"Curious enough to find a safe that was left unattended for a few minutes-and the situation has progressed to blackmail. Wait until you hear this," JJ shakes head as he continues. "Wilson asks him how much he wants, but the nephew doesn't want money. He wants one of Wilson's storage facilities signed over to him. He figures he can make a fortune selling the explosives on the black market, and probably to the very people we are after."

"What's going to be done?" Mac asks.

"I don't know yet," JJ replies. "Wilson is supposed to meet with his nephew tomorrow evening at one of his facilities up in rural northwest Jersey. I haven't eaten since breakfast. Have you eaten?"

"Yes," answers Mac, "but I'll keep you company if you want to get something."

Outside one of the den's windows, a voice in the dark whispers, "Well, somebody better know what's going to be done."

The next morning Blue Jay is flying through Riverview in his Camaro. He spots a pay phone and pulls to the curb. Figuring Bean will be at his store, he dials the number. A man answers and Blue Jay asks to speak with the owner. When Bean comes on the line he asks, "Do you deliver in the area of Bull Island in New Jersey?"

Bean recognizes Blue Jay's voice immediately, and waits for a punch line. When none comes, he replies, "No, I am afraid we don't," and hangs up the phone. He realizes his friend wants to meet at Bull Island; what bothers him is that he doesn't know why. After fooling around the office for a few minutes, he gets into his car and starts the drive to Bull Island. Blue Jay is sitting in his Z28 when he pulls up.

"We got trouble," Blue Jay announces. "Follow me, and we'll park your car in Riverview. I'll fill you in on the way."

Bean nods and the two cars head for Riverview. Once his car is parked the Z28 heads for Route 202 North. Blue Jay tells him about the activities from the night before. Bean waits until he's finished then says, "I guess we have to find out the location of Wilson's facility in North Jersey."

"Before tonight," Blue Jay adds.

Outside of Somerville, Blue Jay pulls into a mini-mall area and purchases two $20 calling cards, and the two men head for a bank of phones. Fifteen minutes later they have the location and are back in the car.

"Okay, where exactly is Quarryville?" Bean asks.

"You don't know?" exclaims Blue Jay.

"No, I am afraid I don't," snaps Bean. "Do you?"

"Of course I do," claims Blue Jay. "You follow 287 past Route 80 for a while, then bear left."

"I see," comments Bean. "Does the bear have a name?"

"Of course," Blue Jay answers.

After a minute of silence Bean says, "Well, are you going to tell me?"

"Yes," answers Blue Jay as he pulls up to a pay phone, stops the car and grabs a laptop computer from the back seat. "Just as soon as I double-check the maps on Yahoo...ya-hoooo."

"I knew you didn't know where it was," Bean grins.

Blue Jay laughs as he plugs the phone receiver into an adaptor on his laptop and dials a number. He gets onto Yahoo, clicks on Maps, and in a few seconds has the location.

"Pretty fancy, isn't it?" inquires Blue Jay. "You're probably not used to this level of sophistication with the business you run."

"Yes, it is sophisticated," admits Bean. "But if you get food poisoning, can you shit in it?"

Blue Jay laughs out loud, and Bean joins in. After he disconnects the phone and puts the laptop in the back seat, Bean says, "So we go up 287 past Route 80, then what?"

"No," replies Blue Jay.

"What do you mean, 'no'?"

"We follow 206 all the way up."

"But you said we had to go past Route 80," Bean insists.

"No, I didn't!"

"Ah, you asshole," Bean quips. "I don't think you even know where we are right now."

"Yes, I do!" Blue Jay pulls the Z28 back onto the highway and heads north.

It is a give-and-take trip until they reach the northwest corner of Jersey. Several miles outside of Quarryville, Blue Jay and Bean start looking for an entrance or sign that will show the location of the meeting place.

"Boy, this is a good place for an explosives facility. It is rural, and with all these hills, if it ever went up people might not even know about it," Bean comments.

The Camaro slowly makes its way around the winding road. As they approach a plain dirt path, they notice a small sign at the entrance: A Wilson Facility.

"Oh, that's quiet," Bean laughs. "Like it's a think tank or something."

"Now that we have the location, we have to park the car out of sight and go on a little patrol," says Blue Jay.

When Blue Jay finds what he feels is a good place he pulls the Z28 off the road and into a group of trees. He parks so the front end of the car is facing the road. This way, no reflections will be picked up from the taillights, and when they get out they'll put tree branches in front of the car. This, in addition to the dark blue coloring and low silhouette of the Z28, will make sure no one notices it in the woods. The two men get out and Blue Jay opens the hatchback, removes a pair of night vision binoculars and hands them to Bean. He then opens a case and removes a camera and a telephoto lens, which he attaches to the camera.

"It's going to be a recon patrol," Bean observes.

"Yes," Blue Jay confirms. "We have to know who this guy is and who his contacts are. He must have someone holding stuff for him if he's blackmailing his uncle on this."

Bean agrees as Blue Jay closes the hatchback. Both men take a closer look at the area.

"We'll follow that ridgeline back to the entrance road and see what kind of vantage point we have."

Bean nods and both men start moving toward the climb. They stop just below the top of the ridge, find a large tree and use it for cover as they look over to get a bearing, then return to just below the ridgeline and start their patrol. After a few more observations, the two men are at a good vantage point. They lie along the ridge in a direct line with the front of the warehouse.

"Once you get past that low-profile entrance, this place becomes high-tech." Bean observes. "No guards, but that fence and gate are state-of-the-art security. I'll bet they have motion sensors inside, and a quick-response team for this location as well."

The sun is just setting when a silver Corvette wheels up to the gate of the facility. A young, spoiled-rich-kid type gets out of the car and walks to the gate. Blue Jay realizing this must be the nephew, gets him into focus, and starts shooting pictures. In the middle of this process, he comments, "That's strange."

"What?" Bean asks.

"This turd has a security card for the front gate. He's letting himself in."

"Maybe it's a done deal," suggests Bean.

"Maybe," replies Blue Jay.

The nephew wastes no time in getting to the warehouse. Leaving the gate open, he drives the 'Vette to the front of the building and opens the large sliding doors. After finding a light switch, he checks some of the contents of the facility. As he surveys his newfound wealth, a Jeep Cherokee pulls up to and passes through the still-open gate. After the Jeep comes to a stop, a distinguished-looking man opens the door and exits the vehicle.

"Is that Wilson?" inquires Bean.

"I think so," Blue Jay replies. "He was the one talking to JJ in the parking garage."

Darkness sets in as the two men have what appears to be a heated discussion in the warehouse.

"I think I'll check out the area to see if anyone else is around." Bean starts scanning with the night vision binoculars as Blue Jay observes the two men in the warehouse through his camera lens.

"It looks like this meeting may be coming to an end," Blue Jay relays to Bean. "Wilson just handed some papers to the nephew."

"I wonder what this turd is up to?" Bean muses as he passes the binoculars to Blue Jay.

After Bean points out the location, Blue Jay focuses in on the back of some guy's head who is also in a direct line with the facility, but at ground level.

"He looks like he's doing the same thing we are, watching the meeting," Blue Jay guesses.

Bean is now manning the camera, and tells Blue Jay the meeting is breaking up in an unpleasant manner.

"This turd is also starting to move," reports Blue Jay as he tries to get a better focus through the binoculars. He has him in perfect focus when he changes his position. As the man looks back toward Blue Jay and Bean's position, Blue Jay gets a brief look at his face.

Without hesitation, he says, "Let's get the hell out of here."

"Why, what's the matter?" asks Bean

Blue Jay is already on his feet and searching for something to try and cover their tracks as he replies, "Do you think the people will know about it?"

Bean looks puzzled for a second, then asks,

"You mean the people living in this area?"

"Yes," answers Blue Jay. Bean quickly joins Blue Jay in his efforts.

"Who did you see?"

"Dunn."

"You're shitting me," a surprised Bean says. "But what makes you think the place is going up?"

"Lets just say I also just found out where those two new .50-cal weapons came from."

"You're shitting me," Bean reiterates.

"No," continues Blue Jay. "I think this nephew fucked with the wrong uncle."

"But if something happens to the nephew," Bean points out, "whoever is holding the kid's stuff will go public with it."

"I hear South America can be nice," Blue Jay utters. "These old farts are going to screw everything up. If he survives the blast, I'll have to have a chat with Mr. Dunn to find out what he had in mind with this little adventure."

Bean and Blue Jay try to cover the disturbances they've created on the ridge, and then leave the area as quickly as possible. If they are observed by anyone, they could become part of any investigation that may spring up. As the two men on the ridge are departing, Wilson is driving toward the open gate. As he passes through he continues to a point just past Dunn's position and applies the brakes. Dunn has already acquired his target: a box of nitro that has somehow found its way into the middle of a stack of other boxes filled with plastique explosives. As the Jeep comes to a stop, Dunn squeezes off a round. The .50-cal erupts and sends an incendiary projectile toward the warehouse.

Dunn realizes he doesn't need incendiaries for the nitro, he just wants to be sure where the round is going. It's been a while since he has been in the field. The round races toward the target as Dunn watches through the scope.

"Close enough," he mutters as he stops looking through the scope and prepares to get up. At that moment the .50 strikes the nitro. Dunn is prepared for a hasty retreat. After dark, he had moved onto a rocky surface and spread out a large plastic sheet before taking up a position. All he has to do is pick up the .50 by the handle, grab the plastic sheet and hall ass for the Jeep.

Dunn is at the Jeep when the second series of explosions starts. Wilson has the back door of the Jeep open, waiting for Dunn's arrival. Dunn hurls in the rifle, followed by himself, and yells, "Go!"

With that, Wilson takes off while Dunn is still reeling in the plastic blanket. When the Jeep reaches the other side of the ridge, Wilson stops, gets out and closes the back door. Dunn is busy dismantling the .50 so he can put it away in case they're stopped. Wilson gets back into the driver's seat and heads for the main road. When they reach it he turns north. At the same moment, Blue Jay and Bean have just pulled onto the main road and are also heading north. As the two cars speed into the night, Bean checks the road behind them.

"I see headlights," he announces.

"Let me guess," says Blue Jay. "Larry and Curly are also heading north. We'll have to put some distance between them and us." He presses hard on the accelerator.

The Z28 responds, and within seconds is traveling too fast for the secondary road. Once again, the wide tires and low profile pay off. In a matter of minutes, the distant headlights are lost in the curving road and high hills.

"When I checked the maps on Yahoo, I noticed this road goes into New York state," Blue Jay says. "I think we'll follow it, then cut across to Pennsylvania and down to home base." Bean shakes his head.

Both men are quiet as the Z28 races towards the New York border. Finally, Bean breaks the silence.

"How do we proceed now?"

"I see it this way," Blue Jay explains. "We are not supposed to know who the board members are, and vice versa. But on the other hand, we have to know what they had in mind when they disposed of the nephew. Did they leave the project exposed? Do they have the same type of plan in store for us to cover their tracks?"

"That boy is always thinking," announces Bean.

"My main concern is finding out who the nephew got to hold his stuff for insurance."

"Now I'll be wondering about this shit," Bean remarks.

"You won't be wondering for long," Blue Jay assures Bean. "I am sure the board will have a meeting after what happened tonight, and they're going to have a guest visitor. Me."

"Want me to come with you, just in case?" Bean asks.

"No," replies Blue Jay. "I want you to stay out of sight tomorrow. I will call your cell phone with a code word. Black means everything's okay. White, you call the team and tell them to clear out. You don't have to go into details, they will remember the contingency plans we set up when we started this project."

"What about Top and the Ladies?" asks Bean.

"Have a meeting with them and explain the situation," Blue Jay answers. "If the team is in trouble, so are they."

"I'll call you before I go in," Blue Jay continues. "If I don't call you within an hour, assume the message is white. My guess is JJ will be on the road early tomorrow morning, and Mac will probably be with him. I'll follow at a distance, and to make sure I don't lose them, I'll put a tracking device on the Jag tonight." The two men continue their discussion and planning for the 'what ifs.'

Early the next morning, Blue Jay has taken up a position in the barn that gives him a clear view of the Jag and the house. At 6 a.m., JJ and Mac leave the house, get into the Jag and proceed down the lane. As Blue Jay moves toward the Camaro he switches on the tracking device, and the small screen comes to life. *This modern technology is neat*, he thinks. *This thing tells me where I am and where the beeper is, and constantly changes the map background to show me the exact locations at any given time.*

As he closes the car door, he checks the screen again. *JJ is moving extra fast this morning. It will be a quick trip to the city,* he guesses as he turns the key in the ignition. When the two cars move onto Route 78, they are separated by about three miles, but Blue Jay will close the gap when they get closer to the city. When the Jag comes out of the Holland Tunnel, the Z28 is about 1/4 of a mile behind.

"Okay, JJ, where we going?" mutters Blue Jay.

After a series of turns, JJ pulls into the same parking garage he occupied a few nights before. *Well that's good*, Blue Jay thinks. *No one is panicking...yet.* The Camaro circles the area looking for a place to park. It's early, and a parking spot is available behind the office building. Blue Jay turns off the engine and starts calculating. Under normal circumstances he wouldn't do this in broad daylight, but these aren't normal circumstances. He then shifts his attention to the building, gets out of the Z28, walks around to the front and lights up a cigar. Dressed in overalls, a Yankee ball cap and sunglasses, he almost doesn't recognize his own reflection in the big window at the front of the building.

"Running a little late," he mutters as the newspaper truck comes around the corner. Blue Jay walks to the curb to meet the truck. A young man is preparing to jump off the truck and take a stack of morning papers into the newsstand in the lobby.

"I'll take them in for you," Blue Jay offers.

"Who are you?" asks the young man.

"I'm new here," the man in overalls replies. The young man hesitates and Blue Jay adds, "I'm not going to run away with them."

The young man finally agrees, and Blue Jay takes the bundle. Inside the lobby Blue Jay walks to the newsstand and delivers the papers to the visually challenged man behind the counter. Blue Jay exchanges a few pleasantries with the man as he checks out the lobby area, finds what he is looking for and moves on. As he walks through the door of building maintenance he is greeted with, "May I help you?"

"My company told me to come here for a clean-up."

"Clean-up? Our staff is responsible for that kind of stuff."

"Well," says Blue Jay, "maybe they were trying to be nice to the staff here. Somebody must have a touch of food poisoning or something. This clean-up involves vomit and number two, if you know what I mean." Blue Jay sees the subject matter is starting to bother the lady this early in the in the morning, so he adds:

"I hope nobody slipped and fell in that stuff. Of course if you want to do the deed, I won't feel bad."

"No, that's okay," the lady replies as she waves him away.

"Can I borrow this mop and pail?" Blue Jay asks

"Take it," the lady replies, still waving him on.

Before the lady can change her mind, Blue Jay is down the hall and at the freight elevator. As the door opens, he sees a security guard leaning against the back wall. Blue Jay quickly gets on with his pail and mop and pushes number 11. The doors close.

"You always wear sunglasses inside?" inquires the guard.

"Scratched my eyeball yesterday, and the Doctor told me to wear them," replies Blue Jay. "I'm supposed to be home, but who can afford to do that?" he adds.

"I hear ya," the guard says as the elevator doors open on three and he gets off. As the elevator continues its journey to eleven, Blue Jay thinks, *I'll have to compensate Bean for that food poisoning and shit routine. I wonder how much a pail, mop and elevator ride would be worth?* As his thought comes to an end, the doors open on the eleventh floor. The man in overalls gets off, walks down the hall with mop and bucket in tow and finds Suite 1106. After discovering the door is locked, Blue Jay resorts to knocking. Around the third series of knocks a voice from the other side of the door asks, "Yes, what is it?"

Blue Jay looks up and down the hall, then moves close to the door and says, "I'm here about the shit."

"Is this some kind of joke?" the voice asks.

"I wish," Blue Jay replies. Then he hears another voice from behind the door. This one he recognizes. After a brief discussion the door opens and two men are facing him. As Blue Jay removes his sunglasses he says, "Well Mr. Dunn, I'm here to see how much shit you have stirred up."

Dunn smiles and says, "I was wondering when you would show up." Then he looks at the other man and says, "This pecker always has to know everything that is going on, or he isn't happy."

"Well I'll be happy, happy," the man with the mop and bucket announces, "if you tell me you have everything covered."

Dunn motions for him to come in, and all go into the larger room where the board is meeting. As they enter the room, JJ's mouth drops, Mac laughs and the others look stunned.

"Blue Jay," announces Dunn.

"And this is Mr. Wilson," Blue Jay volunteers. "You are one of the reasons I am here." JJ's face turns to one of knowing as he suggests all take a seat.

"Well, Blue Jay," JJ says, "would you like to start explaining?"

Blue Jay acknowledges and begins with, "Lets fast forward past the big boom in North Jersey last night, and go right to the point: what did the nephew do with the information he was using to blackmail his uncle?"

The statement surprises everyone...except Dunn.

"That has been taken care of," Dunn speaks up.

"How?" inquires Blue Jay.

"That's on a need-to-know basis," Dunn tells him.

Blue Jay looks at his watch and says, "Well, if I don't make a call within the next fifteen minutes, the team will disappear."

"Does that mean everyone knows?" JJ erupts.

"No," answers Blue Jay calmly. "But I have made arrangements to protect the team."

Dunn looks at JJ as he starts to speak.

"This problem started about a week ago. Wilson was approached by his nephew, who offered not to go public with certain information if Wilson met his demands. Wilson got in touch with me, and we started planning what to do. The first step was to find out if the nephew was working alone, or if he trusted someone to hold the information for him for insurance. We did find out he was in touch with a friend of his, an attorney with the same moral fiber as the nephew. Further investigation revealed the nephew did give his pal the attorney an envelope to hold for him, and probably gave him instructions on what to do if something happened to him."

"We know about the nephew," Blue Jay says. "So what about the envelope?"

"Wilson has the envelope," answers Dunn.

"And the attorney?"

"The attorney doesn't practice anymore," replies Dunn.

Blue Jay can tell by the look on Dunn's face what that means.

"Any questions?" Dunn says.

"Just one," Blue Jay replies. "Was anyone outside the current group involved in all of this?"

"No," Dunn quickly answers.

Blue Jay scans the room looking at each member of the board. He then takes out his cell phone and dials a number. When Bean answers, Blue Jay says "black." Bean repeats the message, and both hang up.

"Does that mean the team will be gone?" inquires JJ.

"No, the team is still intact," says Blue Jay, "but I think if this type of thing happens again it should be handled differently."

"I agree," affirms JJ. "We'll take it up at our next meeting. If no one has any additional questions, I think we can adjourn." Everyone agrees, and JJ sets the date for the next meeting.

"I guess the maintenance man should leave before we do," Dunn states, "so I'll see him to the door."

With that, Dunn and Blue Jay stand and walk toward the door. As they approach the exit Dunn says, "Now I have a question for you. What did you mean by 'handled differently'?"

"I meant using me or another team member for that type of thing," Blue Jay replies.

"What makes you think we didn't?" inquires Dunn. Blue Jay

looks him in the eye as Dunn says, "You haven't seen JC around for a week or so, have you?"

"Oh, that's funny," quips Blue Jay. "If it's true."

As he opens the door for Blue Jay, Dunn says, "Don't forget to return the mop and bucket before you leave the building, there's a good lad."

Blue Jay smiles as he walks out the open door and continues down the hall. *He could have gotten JC involved in this, or he could be just busting my chops,* he thinks. *Either way he's got me thinking, and he knows it. The fuck-face. Well I guess I'd better return the mop and bucket like a 'good lad.' What is he, English now? The old fuck.*

CHAPTER SEVEN

I t has been several weeks since the nephew episode, and no one has said a word about it. It seems any loose ends have been taken care of. Wilson took a million-dollar loss on the deal, but the nephew had his mother, Wilson's sister, as the only beneficiary.

The entire team has been at home base for about a week, and now that they have trained and been on two projects together, they are in maintenance mode until the next project. This consists of keeping up their endurance, reflexes and other skills by fencing, karate, Judo, long-distance jogging and personal drills the team members have developed over the years. Each man knows what he has to do. Any individual who thinks they can train hard constantly without losing their edge is mistaken. The object is to go into maintenance mode, and keep within striking distance of that edge.

Today seems to be Judo day. It's not planned training, but Benz and Panda are on the mats working out, and the team naturally seems to show up wearing their Judo Gi's, and start to randori with each other. This is just to get them warmed up before each team member asks Benz or Panda to randori. No one has ever thrown Benz. He is a Judo expert of the highest caliber. The entire team likes and respects him, but the challenge is there, and they try every tactic they can think of to throw him. Benz knows this, and enjoys it. He laughs and talks to his opponents as they try their best. Benz lets them practice their attacks, but they can always tell school is out when they find themselves flying through the air on the way to the mat.

"Looks like the troops are warmed up," Panda says to Benz.

"I noticed," replies Benz.

The two men stop their randori and bow to each other, a courtesy done before and after performing all Japanese martial arts.

"Blue Jay," Benz calls.

Blue Jay bows to his opponent and walks over to Benz. The two bow and assume the normal Judo grip: the right hand grasps the lapel, and the left grasps the sleeve at the elbow. As the two men start moving around the floor, Blue Jay attempts a foot sweep with no results. Benz' foot doesn't even move on the mat. Next Blue Jay attempts Hane Goshi, or spring hip. Again, his opponent remains immobile. This continues for a few minutes, and Blue Jay is in the middle of a *what can I try next* thought when his brain alerts him that something is happening. By the time he realizes what is going on he's in the air, and should be in the process of performing a break fall when he hits the mat. Benz always helps the team members with their landings, and they are grateful, knowing he could probably throw them through the mat if he desired. Blue Jay picks himself off the mat and assumes the randori position once again.

This time I'll watch for an attempted hip throw and try to block it, then counter it. He has been studying the way Benz and Panda randori, and noticed the way Panda blocks with his hip. The two men once again move around the floor. When Blue Jay doesn't attempt a throw, Benz starts moving in for a hip throw. Blue Jay sees it coming and immediately throws his right hip. When the two hips collide, Benz' attack is countered. He is both surprised and pleased as he compliments Blue Jay on the move, but Blue Jay realizes he wasn't studying hard enough. As a result of their collision, all of his internal organs feel like they are bouncing off each other. Benz asks him if he's all right.

"Yes, I'm okay," answers a shaken Blue Jay.

Benz bows, and Blue Jay does the same before he goes to the side of the mat. The team observes him as he leaves.

"My insides feel like a pinball machine," Blue Jay announces. Everyone, including Benz, laughs.

When the laughter dies down, Mac's voice rings out. "Don't you children get hurt; we have a mission coming up."

Air Jockey replies with, "It's your turn with Benz, Mac."

"I'd like to," Mac says in mock disappointment, "but I forgot my Judo gi again."

Mac is always stirring up the troops-mostly because he likes them. If he didn't, it would be business only. That's true for all of the team members. If they don't like you, they don't bother. Mac continues his announcements with, "After lunch we will be having a meeting in the team room. JJ is going to present another project for your review."

"Will you-know-who be on pilot duty for this one?" a voice from the team inquires.

"Ah, they're all pussies with no sense of adventure," JC calls.

Everyone bursts into laughter.

"On that note," Mac announces, "I guess we can break for lunch."

It is 1 p.m. and the team is assembled in the conference room talking with each other when JJ and Mac arrive. Mac takes a seat as JJ heads for the front of the room. The team gets quiet when he gets ready to speak. JJ starts his presentation with, "Good afternoon men." The team responds in kind.

"This one is going to be complex. We once again have a situation where drug money is being used to finance the terrorist, but it has a few twists. Cocaine is being shipped from Columbia to Jamaica, then to Cuba. It is then transported by land from Santiago to Matanzas. High-speed boats transport the goods from Matanzas in Cuba to various points on the coast of the US. I'll try to explain why it is done this way. We have some facts and, I am afraid, some guesswork. You'll see what

I mean as I continue."

"We know for a fact this is on going. We also know that explosives are being smuggled along with the drugs, and delivered to a person or persons in the US. And now, this is where the guesswork comes in."

"Why are the drugs shipped from Columbia to Jamaica? Is it to conceal direct connection to Cuba, or is it just a staging point? We think the packs of explosives are earmarked somehow, and mixed with the packs of cocaine after they are shipped to Santiago in Cuba," JJ continues. "It's obvious that the land transportation part is to get it into position for the move to the US."

"And here are the things we don't know. One, do the drug lords in Columbia know about the terrorist connection? We think no. They are in it for the money, and they know if some kind of terrorist activity is traced back to them, Uncle Sam will get serious about wiping out the drug trade. Two, we know high-level people in Castro's government are involved, but not whether Castro knows all or part of the operation."

"The target for this operation will be in Santiago, Cuba. The reasoning is that the people with the connections to the Columbians and the facility where the drugs and explosives are all in Santiago. Someone has come up with a plan that I think is a little hairy, but the team will give it a yea or nay. Any questions at this point?" JJ inquires. A hand is raised.

"Yes?"

"What about the Columbia site?"

"We are trying to focus on the terrorists. These drug connections just keep popping up," answers JJ. "If we find out later they are in the terrorist business, then they will become a target." Another hand goes up.

"Why Santiago?"

"That will be addressed during the hairy plan presentation," JJ replies.

"Anyone else? Okay then," he continues. "I have given you the high-level view of this project. I'll now turn it over to Mac for the more detailed part of the briefing."

As Mac walks to the front of the room he remembers back to his days in the Corps when he always tried to start a class or briefing on a humorous note to relax the group. This group doesn't require that, but Mac does it anyway, just for the hell of it.

"Good afternoon, men," then after a slight pause Mac says, "You too, Air Jockey."

Without hesitation Air Jockey responds with, "Good afternoon Mr. Hairy Plan Man!"

Mac looks at JJ, who is enjoying the exchange, and says,

"These kids are rough."

"I know," JJ agrees.

When things again get quiet, Mac starts his briefing.

"The reasoning for Santiago is twofold. First, of course, is the destruction of the facility and the bad people. Second, we also need a plan to draw some or all of the high-level people involved to the facility, where they can be included in the destruction phase. If we merely destroy the facility and the Columbian connections, the high-levels will just reorganize and be back in business in no time."

We need to execute a plan that will cause a lot of commotion and questions in Cuba. As for the high-level people, most of them are not terrorists themselves. Some are in it for the money, and others have a hard-on for the US. In both cases, if too much attention is drawn to them on the subject, they will stop participating in the endeavor."

"Now for the basic part of the plan," Mac continues. "First we will fly the team to Montego Bay, Jamaica. The team will deplane in normal dress, with suitcases containing equipment needed for the project. After renting transportation, using cash and bogus credit cards as security, the team will proceed to the general area where the boats make their runs to Cuba. You will make whoever is in attendance at the site disappear, then borrow a boat and make the crossing to Cuba. Hopefully, anyone who notices you will assume it is just another run to Cuba. Timing the arrival at Santiago for after dark, the boat will come in the entrance to Santiago Bay and dock a few miles from the objective. After camouflaging the boat, the team will proceed to the facility."

"The following afternoon in Jamaica, after making it known around the airport that one of the passengers wants to be flown to Georgetown in the Cayman Islands, the plane will depart and wait in Georgetown."

"Now, here comes the tricky part," Mac explains. "We know when big shipments will be made from Santiago to Matanzas. We need a plan that will one: eliminate the people in Santigo with the contacts in Columbia and destroy the drugs and explosives stored in the warehouse. Two: create an incident that will bring government attention to their operation. Three: eliminate as many of the high-level people running this operation as possible. As you can see, this is the hardest part, and if you can come up with a plan you all feel comfortable with, we will go; if not, we don't go. We have figured out the basics for getting you there and back. You have the rest to consider."

"What is your plan for the return trip?" inquires Bean.

"Returning to the boat you borrowed in Jamaica," Mac replies, "you will leave Santiago Bay, turn east and hug the coast. You will head for Guantanamo Bay and slip onto the base at Leeward Point. There are a lot of salt flats on that side of the base, but close to the sea there's enough cover to hide the team-especially with the way you folks can camouflage yourselves."

"I know what you're thinking: how do you get off the base and out of Cuba? Well, do you remember the man that wanted to visit Georgetown?" Mac continues, "He is going to make arrangements to visit his old buddy Admiral Fox, the current base commander at Gitmo. That night, the team will move in close to the airstrip at Leeward point and rendezvous with JC, who will give you empty garment bags, false ID cards and dog tags. After the team changes back into civvies, and with the new Marine Corps hair cuts, you will all get before the trip, you will look like a group of officers getting a ride to Jamaica for a liberty call. Then it's just a matter of the Hairy Plan Man giving you children a ride back to the States."

The team members look at each other and wonder if they can pull it off. It will be ambitious and complex, but they are all good at what they do, have already worked together and are familiar with each other's mode of operation. Blue Jay raises his hand.

"I have two questions, and correct me if I'm wrong. This mission has several objectives. We disrupt the traffic of drugs and explosives, and eliminate as many high-level people in the Cuban organization as possible, okay. But bringing the smuggling to the attention of the Cuban government? What is that about?"

"We want to see what kind of response we get from them," JJ answers, "Their reaction will dictate any future action against them."

"My second question is this," Blue Jay continues. "The last time I checked, there were mine fields on both the Cuban and American sides of the fence line surrounding Gitmo Naval Base. How do we 'quietly slip through' two mine fields to get onto the base?"

"I told you it was hairy," Mac says.

"We didn't know you meant anal hair," remarks Air Jockey.

"Anyone else?" Mac inquires.

After a few moments Mac confesses, "I realize this is a lot to digest for the first briefing. Lets take a break and get some coffee. JC and the rest of you can reconvene in about an hour to talk it over."

With that, everyone stands and starts heading for the house, mulling over the presentation silently. The in-and-out part wasn't too bad, except for those minefields. The plan would have to be complex and simple at the same time, KISS methodology. Thirty minutes later, every one of the team members is back in the conference room and JC is again going through Mac's part of the briefing. This time it is taken apart and inspected. What ifs and contingency plans are discussed. This process continues up until the dinner hour, and then the team reconvenes after dinner.

Late that evening, everyone is satisfied. Tomorrow they will start kicking around the hard part. JC will list the objectives on one of the boards at the front of the room. On another he'll list ideas from the team for each objective. A third board will be used for team input, to add to or take apart each idea.

For three days the team works on a plan, and finally agrees on a shell, or working copy. The following morning, the team breaks into pairs and starts putting their plan to the test. Two pairs for shooting-one shooter and one spotter apiece-will work with Blue Jay. Two pairs for explosives will work with JC and Bean. The shooters plan to use the .50-cal rifles. The large rounds of the weapons would deal with the wind better than a smaller cal at 800 yards, and with multiple targets they'll strive for one round, one kill.

The spotter for each shooter will help locate and ID the primary targets. The first shot will be quick, but after that the firing comes fast and furious. The entire team will be in constant communication with each other and while the spotters and shooters are trying to locate targets, they will also be listening to the other pair to make sure they are not on the same target. This could get a little confusing, so they will practice a little with Blue Jay. That means when Blue Jay brings testing to an end, it's either a no-go or the shooters will be able to eliminate targets faster than the project will actually require.

JC and Bean select the type of explosive that will be used. Hopefully, JJ has or can get the type of explosives the bad guys usually ship. This will lessen the possibility of discovery; if it's the same type, it won't be obvious that someone from the outside is involved. JC probably already has the remote detonators covered, but timers will have to be selected.

Two days after the team decides on the working copy of their plan, JJ returns to the farm after a brief holiday with his wife.

"How are things going?" he asks.

"Quiet," answers Mac.

"Quiet!" exclaims JJ in a loud voice. "We are not paying for quiet."

"In one of those moods, JJ?" Mac says. "Remember, you're not in the corporate world. You give these people a project, and then stand back."

"I guess I'll have to look into things myself," JJ snaps. "It seems I can't depend on you."

"Knock yourself out," Mac snaps back as JJ storms out the door.

As JJ approaches the barn, he catches a glimpse of someone at the other end and proceeds in that direction. As he gets closer he sees Bean sitting in a chair, reading a book.

"Is that all you have to do?" inquires JJ in an uppity tone.

"Pardon?" Bean says as he looks up.

"What are you doing just sitting in that director's chair?" JJ demands.

"Directing," answers Bean.

"Directing?" JJ fumes. "Directing what?"

"Tests," replies Bean as he turns the page on the book he is reading.

JJ is beside himself as he asks, "Where is JC?"

"In the barn."

JJ starts for the door behind the barn.

"Wouldn't go that way," Bean advises.

"Why?" snaps JJ.

"Just wouldn't," answers Bean.

Ignoring Bean's advice, JJ storms toward the back door. He is halfway there when Bean's wristwatch alarm goes off, and almost immediately a loud bang sounds and JJ is covered with mud from his shoes to his hat. If he weren't so furious, he probably would have had a heart attack. He looks back at Bean, who is checking his watch and saying, "Getting real close." Then he looks at JJ.

"What happened?" Bean inquires with a smile.

"What happened!" explodes JJ.

"I told you not to go that way," Bean says.

JJ throws his hands in the air and continues to the back door. As he enters the barn, he finds the shooters and their spotters lying on the floor looking through small scopes at little pictures on the fall at the far end of the barn. Blue Jay is sitting on a stool behind the four men, watching and listening. Each man is wearing a Com headset and talking very low.

JJ walks over to Blue Jay and demands, "Where is JC?"

Blue Jay motions for him to be quiet. JJ doesn't take the hint. "Where is JC?" he says again.

Blue Jay looks up at him, covers the mike on his Com unit and yells, "Go the fuck away!"

"Who do you think you're talking to?" JJ demands.

"I think I am talking to a man that just shit himself on the outside."

At that statement, JJ storms off and out of the barn. Bean who had been taking it all in, walks over to Blue Jay.

"So, you're having problems with management again. You never did have any respect for authority, and I am sorry to say things haven't changed."

Blue Jay flips him the bird and continues concentrating on the shooters.

"Yelling at the big boss," Bean continues, shaking his head. "We'll probably all get fired."

"Who cares," Blue Jay finally replies. "We'll all probably get killed on this one anyway."

"Yeah, probably," Bean agrees.

As their conversation continues in the barn, JJ storms into the house and slams the door. Mac looks up and laughs as he says, "I told you to stand back."

JJ looks at Mac and intones sarcastically, "I told you to stand back. I told you not to go that way. I hate my job," exclaims JJ, then breaks into laughter and sits down at the kitchen table with Mac.

"You're right, Mac. These kids are rough, and they don't respect anything."

"I don't think that's altogether true, but it's close," Mac says. "They remind me of this turd in the Corps I knew. He was the same way they are, and he finally got out. Oh, wait a minute…that turd was you."

"Very funny," JJ shoots back as he stands up. "I'm going to change my shitty clothes," he announces, then leaves the room.

A few seconds pass, then Mac hears JJ exclaim, "No, ladies, I did not poop myself on the outside."

Laughter fills the air as Ladya and Lady1 enter the kitchen. Mac looks up at them and says, "I think I'll have to have a talk with the team and house staff about harassing poor JJ."

"You're going to what?" exclaims Ladya.

"Yeah, like you aren't leading that parade," Lady1 chimes in.

"I'm surprised to hear you children talk like this," Mac answers in feigned shock. He has to pick on someone until JJ gets back from changing his shitty clothes.

Eight days after the initial briefing, the team is ready to review the plan with JJ and Mac. Having finished breakfast, they are assembled in the team meeting room. JC is presenting the plan.

"I'll begin with a review. To accomplish all, or as much as we can, of the objectives and get back alive, we have come up with the following. After getting into position in Santiago the night before the big shipment, members of the team will attach explosives and detonators with timers to the undersides of the truck beds. As far as setting the timers, we have to take an educated guess as to what time they will be somewhere between Santiago and Matanzas. This will make the Cuban government aware that something has happened."

"The team will also conceal additional charges to be set off remotely in the area of the warehouse, where the explosives are stored. When the explosions in the trucks occur, it will draw attention to the trucks. If their shipment also goes up, it will really draw attention in the towns and countryside around Santiago. Ideally, the bad guys will think the explosives they're shipping are unstable, and call a meeting at the facility to check things out."

"By the time the big shots in Matanzas hear about it and drive to Santiago, it will be after dark. We have been working with pictures of the primary targets; any additional targets will be a bonus. When all or most of the primary targets arrive, the team will strike by setting off the explosives in the warehouse. I don't think anyone will stop to ask questions before exiting the building."

"As the primary targets emerge from the building, Pru and Met, working with spotters, will try to hit the primaries as soon as they leave. Hopefully, we'll get at least two more of them before the others figure out why they're dropping. Blue Jay will control the detonation of the explosives to keep them off balance, even after they leave the warehouse. The other members of the team will maintain security for the area and the escape route."

"We will be using the .50-cals with silencers at long range, so we should be able to get off a lot of rounds before the hostels either react or haul ass. Blue Jay will call the break-off and detonate the remaining charges. That, in addition to the team being between 500 and 600 yards away from the target and in the dark, should allow for a clean departure. If it's all right, we'd like to start serious preparation tomorrow."

JJ looks at Mac, and they both nod in agreement.

"I think the cabin in Pennsylvania will be a good place for shooting and minor explosives drills," JC continues. "All other preparations can be done here at the barn."

"Have you reviewed the in-and-out portions of the project?" asked Mac.

"We are still going over that part," replies JC.

"Is there anything in particular the team sees as a problem?" Mac.

"Well, I did hear 'Fuck a mine field' several times in our planning sessions," JC admits.

JJ is concerned by this, and asks, "Are you working on an alternative?"

"Now and then," JC replies.

"Where else could they enter the base?"

"Here or there," JC again responds.

JJ shrugs, then looks at Mac and asks,

"If you have to change the timetable of your original plan, when will you be able to extract the team?"

"Sooner or later," Mac answers.

"I hate my job," JJ says again.

"Ah, we'll figure it out," Mac assures JJ.

"You people just keep me around for laughs, don't you?" inquires JJ.

"No, no...well, sort of," Mac replies.

"I'm going to start charging fines for unnecessary humor at the expense of the barn owner."

"Fine this," Mac answers.

"I'll bet Mrs. Mac always has a problem fining it during romance time," quips JJ.

"Oh, that's funny," answers Mac. "I'm happy to see you aren't PMS-ing any more."

"Can we assume the meeting is adjourned?" inquires JC.

JJ and Mac both look at JC, then at each other as JJ asks, "Who is this man?"

"I thought he came with you," answers Mac as they both stand and head for the door.

The next day, everyone is up and at 'em early in the morning. JC had a training schedule in place the night before for this project. There are too many 'what-ifs' to let go to chance. What if they have a problem with the boat during their escape? What if they have boat trouble between Jamaica and Cuba? Should they 'borrow' two boats?

JC wants each man's endurance at its peak, and Blue Jay has to know how hard he can push the group as a whole. The daily schedule consists of an individual run at their leisure before breakfast. After the morning meal it's planning in the team room, followed by circuit weight training before lunch. In the afternoon, the team members work on their part of the project: spotters and shooters, or explosives. They hold a three p.m. team run, then dinner at five.

All of the men keep themselves in good condition; now they're merely working toward their peak. Except for the days the team goes to the cabin in Pennsylvania, this will be the daily schedule. One week before the team leaves for Jamaica, they will switch to a lighter workload. This will give their bodies a chance to regroup; a little rest after hard training helps them work better and faster.

The last two from the morning run have just returned and joined the rest of the team in walking off before they shower and go to breakfast.

"How are we going to deal with those mine fields?" Bean asks Blue Jay.

"Fuck a mine field," Blue Jay replies. "We aren't crawling through that shit, especially if someone is hot on our ass."

"Aw, don't you like mines?"

"No," answers Blue Jay. "Don't like snakes either, and if I ran into a snake in a mine field I wouldn't want to be responsible."

"So, you have something else in mind?"

"Yes, but how quiet it's going be is anybody's guess."

With breakfast finished, the team members are seated in the meeting room. JC announces he would like to present an idea for the team to kick around for a while.

"As you all know," he explains, "everyone is using the weapons they prefer. May I suggest that for this project we all use the same type of weapons? One of the reasons I say this is that if things go bad and your escape route is cut off, Castro's people may be chasing your asses through the hills for a while. If we have to sneak in and drop you care packages until we can figure a way to get you out, using the same type of ammo would make it easier to keep you all supplied. It's also nice for sharing during a firefight. With the Mexico project, and I am sure other projects, using your favorite weapons is not a problem. But this time you will be on an island, possibly being pursed by government troops. Think about it."

"Why don't we discuss it now?" Blue Jay suggests, and the team agrees.

"Did you have any particular weapons in mind?" interjects Bean.

"Funny you should ask," JC quips.

"I am so surprised," Bean drawls. "Who'da thunk it?"

"Well, as luck would have it, I do have a suggestion prepared. First, I would choose 9 millimeters for the ammo. Second, with the exception of the shooters, each man will carry an H&K MP5 with a silencer. It fires 800 rounds a minute, holds a 30-round magazine and an effective range of 88 yards, and when the stock is not extended it's only two feet long. This will come in handy for transportation, before and after the project. As you know, the Seals and other special OPS groups use this weapon, so we know it's is reliable."

"The side arms will be Berettas, also with silencers. With that, I'll open it up to the floor." JC announces, and the team members remain quiet, thinking over the proposal.

"For myself," starts Check, "what you're saying makes sense, and I have no problem with the selection of weapons. I prefer my weapons because they're what I am used to, but I see no problem using the MP5's."

"Do we all agree with that?" asks JC. All seem to, but then a hand goes up in the back of the room.

"Yes, Tic?" JC calls.

"The MP5's will be good while we're at the warehouse," Tic says, "but if we get into a situation where we're being pursued through the mountains, the short gun isn't going to keep the bad guys at bay."

"Good point," JC replies. "Thank you for bringing that up. Number four on my list is the Remington 700 titanium lightweight. It weighs only five and a half pounds. After it's broken down, with the scope and a few rounds, you won't even know you're carrying it in your pack."

"Won't even know you're carrying it in your pack," mutters Panda, then mimics JJ by adding, "I hate my job."

"What's this?" inquires JJ as he and Mac walk through the door carrying two boxes each. "Someone else hates their job as well? Let's start a club." He looks at JC and says, "Here's the stuff you wanted for the .50s. I have the Gen II day-night scopes, and Mac has the AWC Turbodyne silencers. Ah, Mac and silence. Do they go together?" JJ is feeling frisky this morning, and Mac is still half asleep.

"Don't you people use anything with a reasonable price tag on it?" JJ complains.

"Do you want to kill bad people, or pinch pennies?" a voice in the room inquires.

"Well, JJ, now that you have brought up the subject," JC quickly responds, "we do require a few more odds and ends."

"Now what?"

"10 MP5's, 12 Beretta hand guns, all with silencers, 7 Remington 700 lightweight breakdowns, a shitload of 9mm, and some 30.06 rounds."

"Is that all?" JJ groans.

"No. We also need two drag bags for the .50s."

"Two drag bags," echoes JJ.

"I already have it written up," JC announces as he hands a sheet of paper to JJ.

"I can understand his dilemma," offers Blue Jay. "It's not like he has an arms dealer he can just give that list to and presto, he has the stuff."

That smart ass, JJ thinks, *he knows that's exactly what I'm going to be doing when I give this list to Dunn.* Ignoring Blue Jay's comment, JJ takes the list and says aloud, "No problem. Anything for the troops."

Mac, who is now fully awake, sees his chance to retaliate for the silence remark.

"That's the spirit. What do you want to do, kill bad people or pinch pennies?"

"Would you like anything?" JJ asks Mac.

"Yes," Mac confirms with a grin. "One of each."

JJ just looks at him.

"Hey," Mac continues, "I need something while I'm protecting the aircraft on foreign shores."

"So you're telling me you would engage in a shootout if someone tried to take the plane?"

"Well, I would try to sell it first," Mac says. "But if we couldn't come to terms, there would be hell to pay."

"There would be hell to pay," JJ mutters, echoing Mac's statement as he walks toward the door.

"I guess you've forgotten about my no-nonsense, fierce nature when we were in the Corps together?"

"Yeah, yeah," JJ singsongs as they leave the room. "All I remember is that you couldn't find the shithouse without a gunnery sergeant leading the way."

JC, still looking toward the doorway, announces, "I wonder which one will be the first to figure out I already included Mac in the count?"

Three weeks later, preparation for the project is in full swing. Planning and dry runs at the barn have given way to live fire drills at the cabin. JJ and Mac accompany the team today, and in the morning they watch as Bean and the explosives group run through the drill of planting the charges, retreating to their original positions, then timing the explosions.

About two p.m., JJ and Mac decide to go for a walk-or snoop around, as Panda would say. The two discover JC standing by himself in the middle of a field, looking through field glasses as they approach him.

"Can't find the team?" JJ intones, trying to be amusing.

"Can you?" challenges JC, still looking through the field glasses.

"Given time, we probably could," Mac says.

"I doubt it."

After a few moments of silence, a group of silhouettes pop up 600 yards away, and within seconds, ten feet from where the men are standing the underbrush jumps as the two .50s start firing at the silhouettes. The spotters select the target, and as soon as the shooter acquires it the spotter looks for the next one. The teams have the target area divided by clock time: Pru covers 6 to 12, and from 12 to 6 is Met. Of course, if one runs out of targets, they automatically acquire targets in the other's time frame.

JC has attached pictures of the main targets to the silhouettes. Since the team doesn't know which are which, the drill is to take out the bad people as fast as they can. Of course, there are other pictures among the silhouettes, so they have to be sure before they shoot. As the second volley from the .50s gets underway, a minor explosion occurs behind the silhouette area. These explosions will be much larger when they go off in the warehouse. When the shooting stops, only two silhouettes remain standing.

"Ricky Ricardo and Fred Mertz have survived," announces JC as he stops looking through his field glasses. "They're the innocent bystander silhouettes I mixed in with the bad guys."

A few seconds later, a series of small explosions occurs in the silhouette area and the ground comes to life in the immediate area, gets up into a low crouch, turns and starts moving toward the three men. The five team members don't even acknowledge their presence as they move quickly past them. JJ turns to continue watching their movements, and discovers that the remainder of the team has also come to life behind them and is leading the way out of the area. At that point, JC offers some info.

"The first five are the shooting group: shooters, spotters and Blue Jay. When Blue Jay gives the word, the activities begin. Blue Jay also controls the detonations of the explosives that Bean and the other group will have planted in the warehouse the night before. Bean's group will also set up area security for the shooting group. With night vision equipment, they can stay behind the shooters and still maintain security. If things don't go well, the two groups can use a leapfrog-type withdrawal. Air Jockey is training with Bean's group and will fill in if necessary. Otherwise, he'll stay with the aircraft."

"Very impressive," Mac says to JC.

JJ is still watching the team as they disappear into the woods.

"What do you think, JJ?" asks Mac. JJ does not reply. Mac looks closer at him.

"Something wrong?"

"The looks on their faces took me back a lot of years," JJ explains. "I have seen their barracks faces, but these faces are much, much different."

"Are we ready to go?" Mac asks JC.

"Yes, sir."

"JJ, do you have the dates for the shipments in Cuba?" Mac inquires.

JJ comes out of his thoughts and replies, "Ah yes. There will be one next week."

"Are we in agreement for next week then?"

The other two men agree.

"Then at the morning meeting, we'll run it past the team. If there are no major concerns, it's a go."

CHAPTER EIGHT

I t is eight a.m. as the Learjet rolls to a stop in the Montego Bay airport. The team, dressed like businessmen on holiday, stays on the plane while two of their group go make arrangements to rent two Jeep Cherokees. An hour later, the two vehicles pull up next to the plane. The team, acting like they are there for fun in the sun, leisurely get off the plane and make small talk about the nice weather as they put their gear in the back of the Jeeps. Inside, the light-hearted conversation continues.

"Oh, I see we have a driver," announces Bris. "To the nearest whorehouse, James, and don't spare the horses," he commands.

The Jeeps move through the airport to one of the exits. The light-hearted appearance the team had been putting on for anyone who may have been watching switches gears to serious, thoughtful discussion as the Jeeps travel up highway A1, The Queen's Drive. A few miles before arriving at St. Ann's Bay, the two vehicles pull off the highway and onto a small dirt road. After they are out of sight of the highway both Jeeps are stopped and put into four-wheel drive. Then the lead Jeeps turns to the left and starts a slow cross-country trek. They proceed until they're well off the dirt road, then stop.

The team members disembark, unload the Jeeps and start unpacking. Military field packs, web gear and kill suits appear from the soft luggage. MP5's and two drag bags containing the .50-cal rifles are taken from the garment bags.

Once everything is unpacked, the men strip off their casual dress, revealing the camouflage utilities they are wearing underneath. They quickly put the casual dress into the now-empty luggage and return them to the Jeeps.

After donning their packs and kill suits, each man checks his side arm, then his MP5. The .50s will be used later, and will remain in the drag bags until needed. With weapons checked, locked and loaded, Blue Jay calls for a Com check. Each man acknowledges he can hear Blue Jay. Then, one by one, each speaks into his Com to make sure everyone can hear him. Once Blue Jay is satisfied everything is set he calls, "Let's move out."

Two members of the team take the lead, and the remaining men spread out behind them. It is approximately two miles up the coast to the speedboat site, and their first objective.

The team has been moving pretty fast, but as they get closer to the objective they switch to a slower, more cautious pace, checking each noise and movement in the area. These people probably don't have any security posted, but it's better to be sure than be sorry. The lead gives a hand signal for everyone to get down, and each man slowly lowers himself into a kneeling position. Objective in sight, Panda whispers into his Com mike. With that, Blue Jay moves to join Panda. The two men survey the entire area, then watch the activity for a few minutes.

"Remember," Blue Jay whispers into his mike. "If any kind of communication gets out from them, the mission is canceled."

"There are nine that I can see. Half are around the boats, and the others are around the shack that probably has a communications link to Santiago."

"Let's move in," he commands.

The men drop into a crawl and move up to the edge of the foliage, where they are still concealed. When they are in place, Blue Jay announces, "Count off." Using a predetermined code, each man identifies what target he will take out.

That completed, Blue Jay asks, "Anyone not clear?" The Com units remain quiet. A few seconds later he says, "Let's do it."

A hail of rounds flies through the air, each finding its mark. The drug runners fall like dominos. Even as the targets are still falling to the ground, the team members are on their feet and moving toward the objective area. Blue Jay and Panda head for the shack and the communications gear, and any additional people. There is no one in the shack.

"Remember, we are just disabling, not destroying this gear. This place should look the same, in case visitors show up after we're gone."

Panda acknowledges and Blue Jay moves out of the shack to check on their transportation. Check and Tic are already checking out the boats, starting each one and listening to the engine run. Everyone on the team has been taught the basics of driving these boats, but the two of them are into racing speedboats on the ocean for recreation.

"How do they look?" Blue Jay inquires.

"They all seem to be in good shape," Tic replies.

"I guess they figured they couldn't afford a breakdown or a delay in delivering their cargo," adds Check.

"Pick the two you think are best, keep another and disable the rest. Remember, disable neatly," Blue Jay reminds them. As he walks up the small dock toward the beach, the rest of the team are already in the process of carrying the bodies toward the boats.

"Which one?" the first man inquires. Tic motions to the last boat tied up at the dock. The man goes to it and deposits the body.

"How is that ball coming, Bris?" Blue Jay calls as he rushes past.

"Almost there," Bris answers as he displays a new soccer ball, almost totally inflated. As the men complete their assigned tasks, they meet at the shack.

"Let's clean up," orders Blue Jay, and the team moves into the underbrush. Each man knows the approach he took, and after walking into the brush about 10 yards retraces it, covering any telltale tracks and spent cartridge casings. When this part is through, the team is on the beach.

"Time for soccer," announces Blue Jay. The team divides into two groups and goes through the motions of playing a game. Their main objective is to cover any unusual imprints in the sand, and to give the impression that the boat crews are getting hyped about the good soccer team Jamaica has fielded the past several years.

"That should do it," announces Blue Jay, "lets load up." The team puts the soccer ball in the middle of their makeshift field and heads for the dock and the boats. Blue Jay is the last to leave, double-checking to make sure everything looks normal. The team boards their assigned boats: one shooter and spotters in each boat, and the explosives group divided between the two, Bean with Check and Blue Jay with Tic. If one of the boats is lost, they will double up and continue. With everyone on board, Blue Jay takes a last look at the boat containing the bodies.

"Will they stay secured?" he asks.

"Everything is ready," affirms Bean.

"Let's do it," Blue Jay orders, and the two men board their separate boats. Tic pulls slowly away from the dock. When he's clear, Check starts to navigate his boat into position behind him. Bris is driving the third boat, and pulls in behind the other two.

"Let's keep it reasonable," Blue Jay suggests.

"Understood," answers Tic as he increases speed.

About a mile out, Blue Jay says over the Com link, "You see anything, Bean?"

"Looks clear."

"Let's hold up here." The drivers cycle down their engines to a stop, and Bris navigates his boat along side of Check's. After throwing a line to the other boat, he disappears into the bowels of the craft and a minute later he reappears. The boats are still side-by-side, and Bris moves to Check's boat. With Bris aboard, the line is tossed back and both boats slowly move off.

When they are at a safe distance the boats again stop and Bris removes a remote detonator from his pocket, arms it and presses the red button. Giant air bubbles explode on each side of the third boat as the explosion ruptures the bottom. The vessel quickly sinks as seawater rushes into the gaping hole. In seconds, it is gone. The two remaining boats hold their positions for a minute to make sure there are no surprises.

"All right, let's get there," Blue Jay says, "but don't burn up the engines. Remember, we will need these boats again later." He reminds the drivers because he knows they are both very competitive, and often go against each other in races off the coast of Florida.

"No problem," two voices confirm on the Com unit as the boats come to life and haul ass for Cuba. *I'll bet this is going to be the fastest run these boats have ever made to Santiago*, Blue Jay thinks.

The team is an hour into their voyage when a truck comes to a stop by the shack back in Jamaica.

Three men get out and start questioning each other about the vacant beach and missing boats. One of the men tries unsuccessfully to us the communications unit in the shack. When he rejoins the other two, he notifies them about the unit not working.

"I'll try to get through to Santiago," one of the men announces as he takes a cell phone out of his pocket. Before he can get a dial tone, a round passes through his head, and in almost the same second the man next to him drops to the ground. The third man attempts an escape, but is taken down in his tracks as the other two were. All is silent for a minute, and then two figures emerge from the landscape and move toward the bodies.

"I wonder how many more there are?" one inquires.

"I don't know," answers the other. "We'd better hide these three and get back in to position." With that, the bodies are disposed of and the men melt back into the landscape.

Tic and Check know the time schedule well, and the two boats arrive off the mouth of Santiago Bay at dusk. They'll race another day. Maintaining a low rate of speed to avoid attention, the boats stay in the middle of the channel that leads to the entrance to the bay. It is dark now, but with night vision goggles the boats have no problem navigating the channel as it curves to the left, then back to the right. About halfway between Santiago City and the entrance to the inlet that leads to Bay, Blue Jay tells the boats to head for the starboard shore.

"According to my positional gizmo, that little cove we saw in the photos should be right in this area."

"That looks like it there, at 1 o'clock," Bean's voice informs everyone over the Com link.

The two boats make for the cove. With cliffs going straight up on all sides there is little chance of the boats being discovered from land. They maneuver into the cove and position themselves on the same side, one behind the other, with the bow facing the main channel. When the boats are secured to the side of the cove, each man breaks out a small square and starts unfolding it. While this is going on, Bris and Bean meet on the back of the second boat.

"This looks like a hard climb, even in daylight," Bean muses aloud.

"It's only 50 feet straight up, then it goes into a 10-degree angle for another 20," Bris tells him as he finishes tying the laces on his climbing shoes. "With these goggles it won't be bad." He surveys the cliff face as he chalks up his hands. "I will try to find a place along the way to secure a biner for the belay line, in case I slip. If I can't, I'll just play through."

"It's a plan," agrees Bean as he feeds out some of the belay line to allow Bris to proceed. Two of the team members pull the boat close to the cliff to allow Bris to reach the face of the cliff. He gets two good grips and he's off. Bean is manning the belay line and trying to locate good handholds Bris can use. With the squares unfolded, the rest of the team is in the process of hooking them together. Each piece is camouflaged to look like the rocks on the face of the cliff. Once together, there will be enough to cover both boats, and from a distance they will blend into the rock face behind them. By the time Bris gets to the top of the cliff, the camouflage curtain is together and the first boat is half covered.

Bris whispers "Off belay" into the Com unit. Bean attaches an MP5 and a second line to the belay and replies, "Take it." The second line and the MP5 quickly move up the face of the cliff. Within seconds, Bris confirms, "Both lines are secured."

With Bris on top, that means eight more have to make the climb. The first two up join him in security positions. The next two pull up the packs while other members work with the camouflage curtain. When that is completed, two more men make the climb. The last items pulled up are the drag bags and the explosives, followed by the last two men. Once everyone is topside, the ropes used for climbing are well hidden. They will be used to rappel down to the boats on the return trip.

When everyone has their packs and kill suits on and are squared away, Blue Jay whispers, "Move out," and once again two take the lead and the others spread out. The warehouse is only a few miles away, and for good reason: it is isolated from the other warehouses in the area. There are no fences, but armed guards are present 24-7. There is no lack of hills in this end of Cuba, and this will come in handy if the team has to leapfrog out of the area. The shooting group can lay down a field of fire while the security group takes up positions on another hill in the direction of the boats.

When they'd been at the barn looking at photos, some of the team remarked that one of the areas looked like The Devil's Den at Gettysburg, where the union snipers, in positions on high ground around Little Round Top, laid waste to the confederate infantry at the bottom of the hill.

The team is moving quickly but cautiously towards the objective when Blue Jay orders, "Let's hold a minute. My global positioning gizmo says we are getting close."

"I have a feeling it's over this next hill," the point announces.

"Probably so," agrees Blue Jay. "Everyone hold up here."

"Bean, you're on me," commands Blue Jay, and two figures move quickly and quietly up the hill. Near the top they go into a crawl until they can see over the ridge. Both using their night vision gear, they survey the area.

"This looks like the place," Bean says. "And this is the hill we'll be shooting from. Those photos and intel sure came in handy."

Blue Jay puts his hand over his Com unit mike. Seeing this, Bean does the same.

"I guess we should send that fuckface Dunn a Valentine in appreciation."

Bean smiles and shakes his head. "You always did have problems with management."

"It's what I do," quips Blue Jay as he removes his hand from the mike and whispers, "Break out the .50s." Met and Pru unsaddle the .50s from their backs, open the drag bags and start assembling the weapons. First, they remove the receiver group and attach the bi-pod. Next the barrel is attached to the receiver group. The scope and magazine are already in place. Once the barrels are set, each man attaches a silencer to the end. With the safeties on they pull the bolts all the way to the rear, then forward and down, securing a round into the chamber. Pru looks at Met to confirm, then whispers, ".50s ready."

"Move out," a second voice calls over the Com unit, and the team goes into motion. At the top of the ridge, Bean is checking out warehouse security and the route he and the explosives team will be taking. Blue Jay is scanning for fields of fire for the .50s, and also scouting the area for anyone in warehouse security that may be scanning with night vision gear.

One by one, the remainder of the team arrives at the top of the ridge. Blue Jay lets them check out the area for a minute, then announces, "That bush and foliage on our right flank can be used for cover and a base of fire for the .50s." The shooting group turns their focus to the area Blue Jay has designated. Before morning, they will be a big part of the bush and foliage on the right flank.

Bean has the explosives group focusing on the route to and from the warehouse. They will stick close together in case of a firefight. Once at the warehouse, while two are planting their explosives the other two will serve as security, then they'll switch out. They have enough shit to bring down the warehouse and send the trucks to Mars. As the shooters and spotters move to their positions, Blue Jay joins Bean and the explosives group.

"What time you thinking about taking off?" Blue Jay inquires.

"Before we got here, I was thinking three a.m., but with all that hoopla going on we could probably do it now."

"That's what I was thinking," Blue Jay agrees. The men start preparing. The detonators are the last things to be checked, and the men are ready. Blue Jay huddles with them before they depart.

"Now remember, don't push your luck. If you get into trouble, back off. If you get into a firefight, back off, and the .50s will tear those guys some new assholes to cover your escape. We are not after body counts, we are after curtain people that will cripple or hurt this organization badly. Okay?" The group nods their agreement.

"Let's do it," Bean says, and the men move off and disappear into the underbrush. Since the timing has been moved up, the shooters and spotters have put the .50s into a temporary position to support the group in case of trouble. An hour later, Blue Jay, who has been keeping an eye on all of the activity at the warehouse, raises his eyes from his field glasses.

"Have you picked them up yet?" Blue Jay asks Benz who is one of the spotters.

"I think that's them snooping and pooping on the far right corner of the warehouse," Benz replies.

"I got 'em," Blue Jay says. "It's nice that these people are having a wild-ass party tonight."

"Very nice," echoes Benz.

The explosives group is in position, and makes entry into the warehouse. While Bean and Tic stand guard, Check and Bris locate the explosives stored in the warehouse, then using sticky strips attach two charges to the underside of the pallet they're stacked on. They then conceal other charges in the same end of the warehouse, but not too close to the pallets. When their charges are placed and armed, they take up security positions. Bean and Tic immediately move forward, placing two charges in the warehouse, and then go to the door they'd just entered through. All four men stay low as they move up the side of the warehouse to the parking area where four trucks sit waiting.

Bean and Tic remove two charges from their packs, each equipped with timers and two special gizmos JC attached to them. The gizmos on each charge have the same numbers on them. One of them stays with the charge, and the other is detached and stays with the team. Since the team will not know which truck or trucks will be used the next day, all must have charges attached to them, but only the ones being used to transport the stuff will be destroyed. The ones remaining cannot explode, or the plan won't work.

The explosives team will keep track of which trucks are being used and after they are loaded and start on their way, the DIG and then the RED button will be pushed on the part of the gizmo the team has. This starts a digital clock that will detonate the explosives 60 minutes later. If armed when the red button is pushed, the charge detonates immediately.

"Starting from left to right," Bean instructs, "you take the third and fourth truck, I'll take the first and second.

With an explosive charge in each hand the two start crawling towards the trucks. Tic arrives at the third truck and Bean continues to the first. When both are in position they stop and all four men carefully check out the area before they continue. You never can tell when some turd out for a stroll will go unnoticed and screw up your well-laid plans.

"Turd at 2," Bris whispers. Bean's focus shifts to 2 o'clock as the other two continue scanning the area for additional turds.

"Got him," confirms Bean.

"You don't need night vision gear to see this guy," Bris offers. A second later, the red glow from a fine Cuban cigar shines through the dark like a big-ass lightning bug.

"Let's do these trucks, then wait and see what Fidel with the cigar is going to do before we move to the other two." Bean advises. Tic and Bean are slow and cautious as they attach the charges. The sticky strip should hold the charge in place, but the charge also has a strap used to secure it to the truck, in case the strip fails. The first two are in place and Fidel is still puffing. Another five minutes go by, then the smoker stands up and stretches, and returns to the party.

"All clear," Bris alerts the team.

Bean and Tic proceed to the other two trucks and quickly attach the charges. They are ready to join the other two when Check whispers, "Turd at 10." Bean and Tic both look in the direction indicated. A few seconds later, Tic whispers, "Oh, good. This asshole is hollering for the guy who is supposed to be on guard duty, and he's heading this way."

The quick-walking man in khakis is on a beeline for the area where the trucks are parked. Bean and Tic freeze as Check takes out a .22 Blackhawk and makes sure the silencer is on tight. The man is now at the first truck and still yelling. He checks the cab, then looks underneath. Shouting louder now, he proceeds to the second truck and checks the cab. He is in the process on bending down to check under the truck when a voice calls out from across the road, "Sir, are you looking for me?"

The man in khaki stands up straight and yells, "Stupid ass, who do you think I am yelling for?" and quickly moves across to meet the man who had called to him.

"It's our pal Fidel with the cigar," Bris informs the others.

"Let's get while he is getting chewed out," Bean orders. "To thank him, we'll try not to shoot him tomorrow night."

Bean and Tic rejoin the other two and they take a different route back to the group. When they return, the shooters are almost through camouflaging their position and themselves.

"Well, that was fun," Bean relays to Blue Jay.

"We saw," replies Blue Jay.

"Fidel with the cigar held us up and saved us in the same night," Bris offers.

"The guy getting chewed out?"

"Yeah," answers Bean.

"We'll have to cut him some slack if he shows up in our scopes," Blue Jay says.

Bean's group picks security positions, and with help from Benz, Panda and Blue Jay camouflage themselves while Pru and Met keep watch. By the time the sky begins to lighten in the east, nothing looks out of place. Once again, there is just a hill with a big bush on it.

At nine a.m. the loading of two trucks is in full swing. The team keeps close tabs on the selected trucks, 2 and 3, and what is being loaded onto each one. Which truck are the explosives being loaded onto: 2, 3...or both? Having seen it up close, the explosives group's eyes are glued to every movement around the warehouse.

"Bris," Check whispers over the Com unit, "at 1 o'clock, inside the main door. Look at the box that guy is carrying."

"Give that man a cigar," Bris responds. Both men focus on the box's destination.

"Truck 2," Check whispers, as the man hands the box off to another man loading the trucks. Bean removes the device for truck 2 from his pocket and puts it on the ground next to him. A few minutes later, Check is again on the Com unit.

"Bomb-Boy is back with another box." Check and Bris watch his every move.

"Truck 3 this time," whispers Check. This time Tic removes a gizmo from his pocket and puts it on the ground next to him. The loading of the trucks continues. With the explosives boxes in the middle of the trucks, additional boxes of drugs are stacked around them. As a finishing touch, several layers of legitimate cargo are stacked on top and around the drugs and explosives. Thirty minutes later, tarps are pulled over the back of both trucks to cover their loads.

"They're getting ready to roll; let's get these gizmos ready." Bean says as a group of men congregates at the rear of the trucks.

Bean and Tic pick up the devices they had put on the ground, pull out a small antenna, flip the switch to DIG and a green light blinks into life. Each man's attention is now returned to the trucks. Bomb-Boy and a driver board truck 2. A driver and another man climb into truck 3. At the same time, a bunch of hooligans with automatic weapons pile into a van. The van and the two trucks start up, and the van leads the way out of the compound and onto the road leading to Santiago City, followed by truck 3, and then truck 2.

"Ready Tic?" Bean inquires.

"Ready,"

"Do it." Bean hits the red button on his gizmo. The green light goes out and the red light flashes on, indicating the transmission was made.

"Got red?" Bean asks.

"Red," Tic replies.

"Sixty minutes," Bean alerts the team.

That means the trucks will go up at 11:17, Blue Jay thinks as he checks his watch. *By the time the word gets to Matanzas and they react, some of our targets should be showing up by the end of the day to investigate. So far, so good.*

With phase two underway, the team settles into a general recon atmosphere. The sun is hot and getting hotter, but Tic doesn't mind. He recalls, back when he was a little boy, growing up in Mariel down the coast from Havana. They were good times. His family was poor, but if a little kid has enough to eat he thinks more about play than being poor. At 2:43 p.m., Tic's daydreaming about the old days is interrupted by a voice on the Com unit.

"Company just entered the compound," Blue Jay whispers.

All eyes are focused on the warehouse. Benz and Panda are glued to their spotter scopes, trying to ID the visitors. Two men get out of a new Audi sedan, and are immediately joined by men from the warehouse.

"These two look like our primary targets," Benz announces.

Panda confirms it a few seconds later and adds, "They must have already been in the area."

Decision time, Blue Jay thinks. *We are in close for a dusk or night shoot, and leaving the area in the dark. If we take these two now, it's going to be hard to hide in broad daylight while we're on the move...but if they try to leave, that's what we will have to do.'* While the two men are still talking with the warehouse crew, a Mercedes comes speeding up the road, pulls into the compound and stops by the group of men that are talking. A new face gets out and starts yelling at the other two. Seconds later, a truck full of militia pulls up, and an officer climbs out and joins the group of men.

"Tic, can you make out what they're saying?" Blue Jay inquires over the Com unit.

"He's talking really fast, but I think he's one of the big guys our intel missed."

Blue Jay gets on the Com. "The first two that showed up are at the top of our list, and if this guy is over them, we'll take them and that officer out if anyone starts to leave. Then I'll fire off everything in the warehouse to help cover our exit." *In range for a night shoot-and-scoot, and almost too close for a day shot, but who knew.*

The new man continues yelling and starts pointing toward the warehouse.

"Target the unknown first," Blue Jay orders, "and the other three in any order."

It is decided that the new face is in Met's time frame. When Met and Pru are set up on their first two targets, Benz and Panda range and keep track of the other two. After a final burst of yelling, the new face turns towards his Mercedes.

"Ready," Blue Jay's voice whispers over the Com unit, and both shooters prepare to fire.

After taking two steps, he turns back to the men to yell and finger-point some more, then turns again to get to his car.

"Do it," commands Blue Jay, and two .50-cal rounds fly on their way. When Blue Jay hears the two muffled shots, he sets off the first charge in the warehouse. As the shooters expel the spent cartridges and chamber new rounds the spotters are still keeping track of the next two. Benz whispers:

"Pru, mark is still reacting, 2 o'clock."

Then Panda: "Met, Militiaman on the move, heading for the Mercedes. 9 o'clock."

Pru drops his second target before he can react. The militia officer reaches the Mercedes and takes cover behind it, looking through the car windows. Met takes aim and fires at the officer. The heavy round passes through both side windows without being deflected and kills the officer instantly. With all four targets dispatched, and while Blue Jay is setting off the remaining explosives, the team does a quick crawl off the hill. They probably would have gone unnoticed with all of the excitement at the warehouse, if it weren't for the sergeant that showed up with the militia. He sees which direction the four men were thrown when they were hit, and figures the rounds had to come from south of the compound.

After taking cover the sergeant removes his pack, takes out a scope and attaches it to his rifle. As he lies on the ground, he scans the area with his naked eye, looking for any type of movement to the south. On the hill he picks up on a little movement. He quickly shoulders his weapon and scans the hill thorough his scope.

This guy should be in Special Ops. He probably wouldn't play ball with the Commies, so they shit-canned him to the Militia.

Everyone is off the hill except Blue Jay, who is timing the explosions with the movement of the team leaving the hill. Knowing they haven't been discovered yet, Blue Jay moves slowly and is almost off the top when a round kicks up the dirt a foot from his face. Blue Jay stops and listens, and when no other rounds hit he knows it's not just bullshit fire. Someone has him in their sights.

"Ah, shit," exclaims Blue Jay, then announces "leapfrog" into the Com unit as he crawls and rolls, never in a straight line.

"Bean, we'll take the first stop and cover. Have your group proceed to the second and break out your lightweights."

As he rolls to the down side of the hill, another round hits the crest and kicks dirt over Blue Jay.

"Who *is* that guy?" Blue Jay inquires.

As soon as Blue Jay is off the hill, his group takes off for the first stop, quickly followed by Bean's group. The two groups are executing a contingency plan they'd hoped they wouldn't have to use. Blue Jay keeps looking back for signs of the pursuit he knows will be coming. Blue Jay catches sight of a green hat coming over the hill they just left as his group reaches their first stop. They halt and get into firing positions while Bean's group continues to stop number two.

Blue Jay is already in the process of breaking out his lightweight as he kneels on the ground. He quickly assembles the model 700, and as he chambers the first round he says, "That JC must be a fucking Gypsy."

No time for a scope. Just iron sights, calculate the distance and watch the wind. The .50s are already popping as Blue Jay looks up to survey the scene. As he scans from left to right, he sees someone scanning him. The man shoulders his weapon to take aim, and Blue Jay quickly does the same. Blue Jay acquires his target, squeezes the trigger and hears a click as the firing pin strikes the round in the chamber.

"Shit," he exclaims as he pulls the bolt to the rear to expel the bad round. As he chambers a new one, a round from his adversary whistles past his head. Blue Jay has kept the rifle in a firing position, and without flinching takes aim and fires. The man flies backwards. After that first round whistled through, the spotters were already looking for the enemy who was shooting straighter than the rest.

"He's still alive, but you took him out of the chase." the spotters announce.

"Lets focus on the warehouse people," orders Blue Jay. "If we ding them first, it may make the militia men slower; more cautious."

The command is no sooner said than done, and two more warehouse people go down for a dirt nap.

"Let's move," orders Blue Jay. His group passes through Bean's group and proceeds to the third position.

Once there, Blue Jay sees they are getting out of the open terrain and into a foliage area.

"Bean," Blue Jay calls into the mike.

"Yeah?" a voice answers.

"On your next move, stop and set up with us."

"Roger."

Bean's group is in position with the shooting group. Talking on the Com unit, Blue Jay explains the plan.

"On the next exchange, hit them hard then take off for the foliage area and make for the boats. Drop off your 30.06 ammo by me as you leave. Pick me up on the beach a few miles east of here."

Blue Jay has the scope attached to his lightweight and is making adjustments as the men file by, dropping off the ammo. The last man in the team stops and falls into the prone position next to Blue Jay. With his scope already attached he asks, "What did the rangefinder say?"

"300 Yards."

"We using the clock for targeting?"

"Yeah," replies Blue Jay, then adds, "until you start missing. Then I'll have to turn the clock ahead."

"Fuck you," replies Bean as he takes aim at his first target. After a few of the pursuers have been dispatched, Blue Jay notices activity on his left front.

"Looks like they are going to try to flank us," he relays to Bean.

"Range me." He tosses the range finder to him. "When I used to do this for a living, I had a Marine Corps Scout on the finder, but I guess now I'll have to settle for a doggie that used to wear a green tam."

"The leader is at 250 and on the move," replies Bean.

"Got him," answers Blue Jay. He takes up the slack in his trigger squeeze and mumbles, "Come on, stop for a second." Two seconds later, the round is on the way.

After Bean hears the shot he announces, "They are trying a double flanking movement; you range me," and tosses the range finder back to Blue Jay.

As Blue Jay is locating a target, Bean says, "Fucking Jar Head, I'm surprised you don't want to charge down the hill shooting and screaming John Wayne is all."

"3 O'clock, 225, stopped," replies Blue Jay.

"Got him," Bean confirms.

After Bean fires, Blue Jay suggests, "It's time to mogate."

Both men crawl down from the ridge and into a crouched position, moving towards the foliage. They will leave a false trail in a different direction than the team took, then double back and head northeast toward the pickup point. After setting the trail, Bean and Blue Jay are heading for the rendezvous point when they hear gunfire nearby.

"Well, that's not good," Blue Jay comments as he looks at Bean.

The team has reached the site where the boats were stashed, five had already rappeled down to the boats and are removing the camouflage as Tic and Check start the engines. Benz and Panda are preparing to rappel down when a Cuban Patrol discovers them and a firefight breaks out. Unknown to the team, militia patrols had been started around the warehouse area. Someone in the Cuban government wanted to protect the source of income the drug running brings in.

The militiamen on the truck at the warehouse had been on their way to relieve this unit, who has been out on patrol for three days. Benz and Panda are in a good defensive position, but cannot get to the edge of the cliff to rappel without being shot.

When the shooting starts, the men already in the boats man the ropes and quickly climb up the sheer wall, but when they try to get over the top they come under serious fire.

"No, No," yells Benz, "You'll never make it. You'll be sitting ducks if you try to get over the edge. Just throw over some 9mm ammo."

After a quick look over the edge of the cliff to get their locations, Bris tosses two mags up. A few seconds later, additional mags are underway.

"Looks like we have ourselves a little Mexican stand-off," Panda comments.

"But we can't stick around," Benz replies.

The Cuban patrol isn't thinking stand-off as they quickly maneuver into position to charge.

Bris and Check have already went down to retrieve more ammo when the militia charges. Benz and Panda are a little surprised they made this move, but click the MP5's to automatic and came up firing. One, two, and then three militiamen drop, but the rest keep coming. Benz is down low, putting a new mag in his MP5, and Panda is dropping down to do the same, when the entire militia unit charges their position. As Benz rises up to fire, a militiaman is right on top of him…but he doesn't fire his weapon. The militia has been told to take them alive so they can chat later-mistake number one. The man lunges at Benz with his rifle, knocking the MP5 to the ground. Without hesitation Benz grabs the man by his jacket and pulls him forward at the same time spinning and driving the back of his right leg up between the other man's, and both go airborne. As they return to Earth the militiaman is on the bottom, shaken up considerably.

At the same time, Panda is being overrun. He grabs the first man's rifle barrel with his left hand and swings his right arm around the man's neck as he drives his hip into his opponent's lower abdomen. A quick turn, and they are also in the air. Panda spins, and his man also lands on the bottom. A quick kick with the back of his boot to his groin and he is out of action.

Benz is up and making for his weapon when a huge man jumps in front of the MP5. He's a mean- looking turd, about 6-foot-5 and 250 pounds. The man smiles as he draws a large knife and moves toward Benz. The man in charge of the patrol is yelling something in Spanish, but the big man waves him off. Benz backs up toward the cliff and ends up without much space to maneuver. The big man makes a few small moves, nothing serious, as they move closer to the edge.

Benz doesn't know much Spanish, but he takes a shot. When the other man figures out he is trying to say something bad about his mother, he gets enraged and charges Benz.

In picture-perfect action, Benz blocks the knife attack and grabs the sleeve of the knife hand, pulling the man toward him and breaking his balance. At the same moment, he grabs the man's shirt with the other and pulls hard with both hands. When it looks like the big man is going to fall on him, he rolls onto his back and plants his right foot into the man's lower abdominal area. The big man loses his forward balance completely as Benz pulls him down, then he gives an extra-hard push with his right foot, so the man will not fall on the boats below.

As the man goes flying over Benz's head and the cliff beyond, he grabs for Benz and catches his sleeve. The weight of the bigger man starts Benz sliding over the cliff, but he can't keep his grip and continues his fall. Benz is slowly sliding over, trying to grab onto something. Bris, on the first boat quickly grabs one of the rappelling ropes and runs to the back of the second boat. Holding onto the rope and giving it a lot of slack, he looks to be in the process of cracking a whip. As Bris drives his right arm forward, the rope makes a wide arc as it heads in Benz' direction.

"The rope," Bris yells to Benz.

The rope sails over Benz and lands at his right side. He grabs it with his right hand just as he slides over the edge. Panda is trying to come to Benz' aid, but he is surrounded by militiamen yelling at him in Spanish.

"Down, Panda," drifts over the Com units. Panda raises his hands and gets down on one knee, then the other, then lies down on the ground.

A second later, two of the militiamen go flying into the others as if someone had just given them a swift kick. Almost immediately, the cracks of two rifle shots are heard. As the militiamen turn in the direction the shots came from, another two fall.

Benz has regrouped and is peeking over the edge of the cliff. As the militiamen scamper for cover, one turns and points his AK-47 in Panda's direction. Before he can squeeze the trigger, two rounds hit him almost simultaneously: one 9mm to the side of the head, and one 30.06 in the back. The man falls to his right front, dead before he hits the ground.

Panda wastes no time in getting to the edge of the cliff. Benz still has his 9mm pointed toward the militia.

"I'm all right; get on the other rope," Benz tells Panda.

"Take off." The familiar voice comes again on the Com unit.

Benz puts his 9mm away and he and Panda rappel down to the boats. As they land the mooring lines are cut, and the boats pull away. Bris takes the first to where the inlet meets the channel and looks both ways for traffic. He doesn't want any collisions on the way to the open sea. Both craft then move to the right side of the channel and put on some speed.

While the rest of the team escapes, Bean and Blue Jay have been shooting and moving. The militia men aren't sure how many they're up against, and the way whoever it is shoots, they're happy just to stay low. The unseen shooters remain until "in the channel" comes over the Com link. Then they fade away and continue moving toward the pickup point.

CHAPTER NINE

Back in Jamaica, more people are approaching the boat landing.

"What the hell is this?" Air Jockey inquires over the Com unit. "Are these assholes selling boat rides when they aren't running drugs?"

"It looks like a local police unit," responds JC from the other side of the road. "I wonder what they want, driving leisurely down the lane in the middle of the day to a drug-running operation."

The police unit drives past the spot where JC and Air Jockey are concealed and come to a stop by the shack. The two men get out of the car and look around the area.

"Hey, mon! Is anyone in the bushes?" one of the officers yells. Of course, there is no reply.

"Ya know, mon, it is strange no one is here," one says to the other.

"But three of the boats are gone," the other replies. "Maybe they had a special run to make."

"Maybe," the first says, "but I have a feeling."

"Your feelings are usually pretty good," the other cop says, "so let's have a look around."

The two men move onto the beach.

"Are they getting into sports now?" one officer asks as he picks up the soccer ball. The two walk down to the dock, where the remaining three boats are moored.

"If someone steals these boats, there will be hell to pay," the man holding the soccer ball exclaims.

"Yeah, mon!" the other replies. The two men move slowly back to the beach and toward the shack. They again look into it.

"Do you think we should use the radio to make sure everything is in order?" inquires the officer holding the ball.

"Okay," agrees the other. "Maybe it will get us a little extra in our envelopes." Both men enter the shack.

"This damn radio won't work," exclaims the ball carrier, "I'm going to call that number they gave us for emergencies." He walks outside.

As the officer removes a cell phone from his pocket, Air Jockey aligns the crosshairs of his scope on the man's face, vertical down the middle of the man's nose, and horizontal across the middle of his eyebrows. From his vantage point across the road, JC can see the other man still in the shack. The back of his head fills JC's scope.

All of a sudden, JC starts getting a sensation in the left side of his chest. He reaches into his breast pocket, removes a beeper, presses the button and starts reading a message that rolls across the screen.

The man using the phone is still holding the soccer ball, and starts dialing with one hand. Air Jockey starts his trigger squeeze when he hears JC whisper in his ear,

"Mac wants to go to Georgetown. Now!" Air Jockey relaxes his trigger finger, but keeps the man in his scope. That message means things have been moved up, and they don't have to secure this site any more. *I wonder why this turd didn't have a 'feeling' about this,* Air Jockey thinks.

The turd finishes dialing the number and listens for an answer. After a few rings he calls to the other officer, "No answer. What the hell is going on?"

"Who the hell cares," replies the other man as he comes out of the shack waving an envelope in the air. "I have found our pay."

"How do you know it's ours?" the other inquires.

"I counted it, and it's close enough," the officer with the envelope answers. "I think they gave a little something extra this week for a job well done."

"Lets go have a beer," the man with the ball suggests as he throws it back onto the beach.

Both men get into the police unit and divide the money. They start the car, turn the unit around and begin their beer patrol. When the police unit is out of sight, JC and Air Jockey leave their camouflaged positions and start moving toward the location where they left the two Jeeps. Along the way they discard the extra camouflage they used around the shack.

When they reach the vehicles, everything looks the same as when they'd left them yesterday. Both men quickly remove their weapons and kill suits and put them into the soft luggage. Next they remove the cammies and put on the civilian clothes. With all of the camouflage used to hide the Jeeps removed, JC asks, "Ready?"

Air Jockey nods. Both men get into and start the rented Jeeps. JC slowly guides his through the woods and to the dirt road, with Air Jockey right behind him. Once they get to the main road, they drive just over the speed limit to get back to the airport. After turning in the Jeeps and depositng a round of complaining about how those rich bastards are driving them crazy, JC and Air Jockey return to the plane.

Mac is standing at the top of the steps when they arrive.

"I feel like going to Georgetown now," Mac states for appearances.

"Yes, sir," JC replies. "We got your message."

JC is the last to board and pulls up the stairway. Air Jockey is already in the cockpit at the controls; and JC joins him as he is in the process of throwing switches and checking gauges. Seconds later, the jet engines come to life. After talking with the tower, the plane taxis to its takeoff position.

"Our schedule remains the same," Mac explains. "We are just a few hours ahead of it." A few minutes later the Learjet rolls down the runway and leaps into the air.

To the casual observer, the boats give the impression of heading straight out to sea and back to Jamaica, but when they're out of range of even the most powerful binoculars, they turn east. After a few minutes they take a north-northeast angle to reach the rendezvous point with Blue Jay and Bean. It doesn't take long for the high-speed boat to approach the area where the pickup is to occur. Tic and Check reduce the speed of both boats and slowly cruise up the shoreline, waiting for a signal. After about a mile or so, the Com units crackle to life.

"Pinga cabaso." Dickhead, in Spanish.

"Puta." *Whore*, replies Tic.

Seconds later, two figures appear on the beach, removing the camouflage that helped make them invisible. Tic brings his boat to a stop and allows Check to come alongside. After securing a line to boat 1, Met transfers to boat 2 and moves to the bow of the boat. With that done, Tic slowly moves the boat toward the shore. He will beach the boat there, and with any luck will not get hung up in the sand. If he does, boat 2 will try to pull him free. Pru is on the bow of boat 1, looking down through the crystal-clear water and informing Tic of what he sees. Boat 1 moves very slowly as its bow comes to rest on the beach.

The water only reaches their knees as Bean and Blue Jay wade out to the boat. Pru is waiting to give them a hand as they approach.

"I say, chaps, what is today's password?" Pru inquires.

"Limey bastard," replies Bean. "Now give me a hand."

Without hesitation Pru starts clapping his hands together. "Good show."

"Oh, that's funny," responds Bean as they both break into laughter. Once Bean and Blue Jay are hoisted aboard, Tic puts the boat into reverse and tries to pull away from the beach. The boat is loaded with 350 more pounds than when it beached and is a little snug, but shouldn't be a problem. Tic accelerates a little, but boat 1 doesn't move. To avoid a lot of engine noise with a second try, Tic alerts Check that he needs a little tug. Check slowly pulls boat 2 back until the line attached to boat 1 is taut.

"Ready," Check informs Tic and both boats slowly increase their speed. Still, the boat doesn't budge.

"Let's try something," Tic offers. "Give some slack in the tow line. I'll get my boat up to speed, then you go into reverse and take up the slack in the line. The sudden jerk may help pull us free." Check agrees and plays out the line, and Tic once again starts to accelerate boat 1. Check can tell by the sound of boat 1's engine it's time to join the effort, and throws his boat into reverse. The towline snaps as the line again becomes taut, and boat 1 is dislodged from the beach. As soon as it's free, Tic and Check cycle down their engines and once again boat 2 comes alongside boat 1.

Blue Jay is looking at a map with Tic and confirming their destination. Tic is very familiar with the coastline of Cuba, and has suggested a small cove similar to the one they just left. Tic takes a quick survey of his boat and Check is doing the same. Check looks over at Tic and gives a thumbs-up. Tic does the same and returns to the wheel. The boats accelerate, slowly at first, and within seconds are almost at full speed.

The destination is on the coast just inside Guantanamo Province, four miles from the fence line at Guantanamo Bay Naval Base. It is nearly sunset when the boats arrive at their destinations. At this point the original plan calls for sinking the boats, walking to the fence line at the base and, after slipping through the minefields, quietly entering the base. Blue Jay has opted for plan "B." It's probably not safer or as quiet as the original plan, but:

"Fuck a mine field."

Since it will be dark soon, there is no need to camouflage the boats. Even if a patrol boat is using night vision gear, they won't be able to see the boats in the cove. The crews have drawn straws to see who will swim to the beach with a rope to secure the boats. After lodging complaints and requesting a recall of the votes, Bean is about to jump into the water when Blue Jay says, "I'll take it. I just had an idea."

When preparing for his swim, Blue Jay includes a pair of night vision binoculars and his Com unit. In the water, he swims for the shore, gets to the beach, finds a sturdy palm and wraps the rope around it twice before knotting it. The cove is small, and in order to keep the boats out of sight they have been lashed together and secured to the beach by the line tied to the palm tree. Blue Jay proceeds along the beach inside the cove to the entrance. Once there, he picks a secluded vantage point where he can watch the sea. It's around 1 a.m. when Blue Jay finally returns to the boats.

"See anything interesting?" asks Met as he reaches down toward Blue Jay.

"I think I saw plan C," answers Blue Jay.

"Is that a good thing?"

"I'm going to put you insurance people in charge of team humor," Blue Jay informs Met as he is hauled aboard.

Once the team is assembled on boat number 1, plan C is born.

"There's a Cuban patrol that comes past here every two hours, goes up just short of the naval base, turns around, and comes back past here," Blue Jay explains. "They're going to help give us a reason for the boats being so close to the base."

"Why don't I like this plan?" inquires Bean.

"I just started," Blue Jay complains.

"I don't like it already!" confirms Bean.

A little before 3:00 a.m., the two boats are in position at the mouth of the cove. Except for the night vision goggles, everyone looks like they are ready for a swimming party. Their clothes, Com gear, Berettas and other necessities have been put into the small knapsack supplied by Blue Jay before they left the barn. It also has a device to inflate one side of the pack so it can be used as flotation gear. Something you probably wouldn't need in a land mine field. One of the .50-cals has been set up on the rear of each boat. Having already finished with boat 1, Tic and Check are just completing the modifications on boat 2's steering. Bean's explosives group has also been busy, and has just completed their part.

"It's a good thing there wasn't six trucks at that warehouse," Bean comments as he emerges from boat 1's innards. "How are things going over there?" Bean asks Bris.

"We're ready," Bris replies. "It looks like they had a personal stash stored on this boat."

"If it's bagged," Blue Jay says, "bring it topside and stack it on the back of both boats." Bris disappears and returns with an armful of plastic bags filled with cocaine, and deposits them at the rear of boat 2.

"Here," hollers Bris as he throws a bag to Bean on boat 1. As Bean catches the bag, Bris orders, "Arrest that man for passion."

Met approaches Bean and says, "You have the right to remain silent. Especially after we all get killed executing plan C."

"I understand perfectly," answers Bean.

"Fuck you both, and a mine field," yells Blue Jay.

It is now 03:00, and still no patrol boat.

"Maybe the piece of shit sank?" offers Panda.

"You wish," remarks Blue Jay.

At 03:25, the patrol boat appears.

"Remember, you insurance people, just piss them off. No need to make any more widows," Blue Jay orders.

As the Cuban vessel nears, the two boats start maneuvering out of the cove. They take a straight line that will put them just in range of the .50s when they turn north. Tic and Check pick up speed as they move toward the point they will cross the bow of the patrol boat. When they reach it, they are a little shy of their mark as boat 1 turns to port. Boat 2 travels a little farther, then also turns to port. This maneuver puts a little space between the two boats, and they both increase speed to bring them just inside the range of the .50s.

As the boats reach the desired distance, both .50s open fire. It's not easy shooting, but it's a good-sized patrol boat. After the rounds start hitting their boat, the Cubans get pissed and start to return fire. They can't see the two boats, but the man on the radar set is trying to give them directions. That isn't easy with Tic and Check moving all over the ocean to avoid any incoming rounds. This cat-and-mouse game goes on until the boats are approximately two miles from the entrance to Guantanamo Bay, when Blue Jay tells Tic to go full throttle and head for a position that will put them just inside the fence line at Leeward Point. Bean has been watching for this maneuver and alerts Check, and he does the same.

The distance between the two boats and the Cuban patrol starts to open up by leaps and bounds. The team has instructions on what to do when the two boats turn toward shore. Everyone starts field- stripping their weapons and throwing the pieces overboard, scopes, ammo and all. Within a few minutes the two boats stop just offshore inside the fence line. They both make a turn that points their bows toward the sea. Tic and Blue Jay quickly work on the wheel of boat 1 while Check and Bean do the same on boat 2.

That finished, Blue Jay gives the signal for everyone to go overboard. The team slips into the ocean and treads water a short distance away. Bean is watching Blue Jay from boat 2 for the signal. The patrol boat is about half a mile away and there is some activity at the base. Blue Jay gives the signal, and both men push the throttles full ahead on the boats and take off running for the rear starboard. They don't stop when they come to the end of the boats; instead they take a big leap and curl up like they are going to do a cannon ball into a pool. The two men hit the water sort of hard, but are not hurt and the team members quickly come to make sure they are both okay.

The boats take a straight course out to sea. The patrol doesn't stand a chance of getting close to the boats, but a helicopter from the base is entering the area.

"Get ready," Blue Jay orders. Tic and Check remove two of JC's gizmos from watertight packs they have. This time, instead of flipping the switch to DIG, it is flipped to ARM and the green light comes on. Blue Jay can see the muzzle flashes from the machine guns on the Cuban patrol boat as they fire at the two boats.

"Do it." Both boats erupt into fireballs. Since the charges were placed in the bow of each boat, they sink almost immediately. By the time the Cuban patrol boat and the helicopter from the base arrive on the scene, only scant pieces of the two boats and a few bags of dope remain afloat. As the Cubans and the helicopter with its big searchlight scan the area, the team makes for the shore. The boats were in an excellent position when the team disembarked-not too far out to sea and just inside the fence line.

As they wade in toward the shore, they can see the lights and facilities on the airstrip at Leeward Point. To get where they want to be by daybreak, they have to get ashore and bypass Marine guard posts and roving patrols without being discovered. As the team rides ashore on the small waves hitting the beach, they act as though they're trying to hide in daylight. They aren't sure if the Marines on guard duty also have night vision gear. The entire team keeps their bodies submerged as they check the beach area and beyond for movement. At the top of the hill overlooking the beach, they see a Marine guard post. The guard on duty is focused on the area at sea, where all of the activity is on going. Fireballs and helicopters; it's usually quiet on this watch. The team can't seem to see if he is observing with the naked eye or if he has some type of equipment.

As they watch the guard post, two F-18s are taxiing for takeoff. When the first one rolls down the runway and hits the afterburner, it draws the guard's attention, and the team can make out his profile as he looks toward the airstrip to watch the planes take off. They see their chance, and stand up and run across the beach to the cabana area set up for the dependents on base. This gives them cover from the post above, but they still have to watch for foot patrols.

The men quickly unpack their small sacks and put on their camouflage utilities. Now, if they are detected, they'll try to bluff their way out of it by saying   they are Marine Force Recon on a special exercise, or that they're sneaking back to barracks after a wild beer bust, or returning from being with broads (which is illegal on the base), or any of a number of things Marines do on a regular basis.

After everyone puts on their Com gear, the team forms up in single file and heads for the cabana on the far left. Blue Jay quickly figures who on the team looks most like a Marine Corps officer, then tells Met to lead off. Met goes to the head of the line and looks back at the team. Once satisfied everyone is ready, he cautiously moves around the corner of the cabana. The men are spread out, so when Met steps around the corner he is out of sight for a few seconds. Suddenly, everyone on the team jumps as a strangled scream comes over their Com units. They rush around the cabana to see what is wrong, and are confronted by two land crabs hauling ass across the sand on their hind legs, their front claws snapping together.

"They almost gave me a heart attack," Met exclaims.

"I should have mentioned that," Tic apologizes. "You aren't the first one to have had that experience."

The team members look at each other and smile. To go through everything they have for the last two days, then to be shaken up by two land crabs, is hilarious.

The team reforms into single file and continues off the beach and into a lightly wooded area. They spot a sentry on foot patrol and let him pass, then continue. They circle around the bottom of the hill until they come to a dirt road that leads up to the guard post. Across the road is underbrush, and a safe haven for the team. But before they can cross the road a six-by-six truck full of Marines barrels around the curve in the road, 50 yards from their position. *Have we been discovered?* Blue Jay wonders. The team does not move as the truck approaches them. The six-by-six comes to within five feet of their position, then speeds past and up the hill.

"Move out. It's probably the changing of the guard," Blue Jay orders. Met leads the team across the road and into the underbrush. With the noise of the guard changing to cover their movements, the team proceeds north along the dirt road next to the fence line. As the sky to the east begins to lighten, the team has found a spot they are happy with a few miles up the fence line, and settle in for the day's activities.

While Mac visited with Admiral Fox the night before, he'd mentioned that JC had been a Marine Security Officer at Gitmo some years ago, and requested special permission for he and JC to drive the fence line at Westward and Leeward Point. Mac stated that JC was eager to see how things had changed over the years, which was true. And as for himself, he would like to see it for the first time, which was also true. The Admiral suggested a Marine escort, but Mac told him the use of the Jeep would be the only requirement. Besides, they might stop by the Officers Club at Marine site and cry in their beers, remembering old times. The Admiral laughed and gave Mac permission.

The next day, Mac and JC tour the fence line. They are both wearing their Marine Corps utilities, complete with the rank they'd held when they retired. After a stop at the first guard post, the message that a full bird Colonel is driving a three star General will flash up and down the fence line, notifying all posts to expect company.

JC and Mac follow the main road through Navy site and as it winds around the bay. A series of roads shoot off to the left and right: Marine site, hospital, dependents housing. The road then moves into open area.

"We called this the cut," JC informs Mac as they approach a very large hill that the main road passes through. Further on, they approach post number 6, the main gate. Each working day Cuban people would pass through here and board buses for the ride to their jobs on the base.

After stopping for a few minutes to identify themselves, JC turns left and proceeds to the water gate post. The post is situated over looking the waterway that connects Guantanamo Bay Naval Base with the larger part of the bay.

"Back in thoes days, you could see Soviet block ships unloading over there," JC points across the narrow waterway, "and at night Cuban people would show up here in little boats seeking asylum on the base. If the Cubans had caught them, it would be bad. The Marine Guards would turn off the lights so the people couldn't be identified from across the way."

"They used to come over the fence," JC continues, "until the

Cubans put in mine fields. We put in mine fields on our side to keep anyone from attacking the base out. They put them there to keep the people in."

"Then they changed their minds and let anyone go that wanted to," Mac states.

"But you had to leave all of your wealth in Cuba," JC adds.

JC and Mac's return trip consists of driving back to the main gate, up the other fence line past Mo Goti Peek, and down to a small beach overlooking the Caribbean.

"They have a lot of land crabs here, don't they?" Mac observes.

"Oh, yeah!" JC agrees. "We used to man a walking post at night out here, and more than once heard a sentry locking-and-loading on a land crab on a dark, moonless night."

Mac laughs as JC turns right and continues their tour. Around a few curves, up and down a hill, and presto, they are at the bottom of the hill at the main road.

"What a surprise!" JC says.

After Mac looks around and gets his bearings, he realizes they are across the road from Marine site, and the Officers' Club is right up front.

"You still have those birddog instinct," Mac announces.

"Time for lunch," JC announces. "All good tours schedule a lunch break." He looks both ways and crosses the road, and up the drive to Marine site. JC passes the 'O' Club's driveway and continues to the top of the hill. The road circles a large parade field. On the right side are barracks, and on the left are Marine HQ, PX, and other small buildings. JC drives slowly around the parade ground. It has been a lot of years since JC was stationed here, responsible for security and other things not so public. Being here brings back a lot of fond memories.

After lunch and a few brews, they are heading for the ferryboat landing and the ride to Leeward Point. Sixty minutes later, after a quick stop at the plane to pick up some gear, they start the Leeward Point fence line tour.

A mile into their tour, Mac and JC each put on a Com unit. Further on, Blue Jay is talking into his Com unit as JC and Mac approach his location.

"Now, Mac," he says, "I know you are not used to being on clandestine missions, so pay attention and don't screw up. We have the area marked where we want you to drop the stuff, so don't miss it."

Mac starts paying more attention to the roadside, looking for the location. The Jeep goes up a small hill, over the crest and starts down the other side. The hill is longer and steeper on this side, a blind spot to all except the roving Marine patrol. Halfway down the hill attached to a small tree is a Marine Corps poster.

"You have arrived!" the voice on the Com unit announces. Mac looks at JC, who is laughing, and says, "I guess we're back in barracks mode already?"

The Jeep stops and Mac wrestles a Sea bag out of the back, carries it into the underbrush and drops it. After Mac gets back into the vehicle he says, "I want that poster. I'll hang it in my cell at the Federal Pen if we get caught, and every day I'll look at it and laaaugh."

After retrieving the poster, JC and Mac continue their tour as the Sea bag disappears into the underbrush.

That night, JC is standing by the base shuttle bus stop at the Leeward Point airstrip. The bus comes to a halt, the door opens and nine men with Marine Corps-style haircuts pile out, talking about the upcoming liberty call. JC moves toward the men and inquires in a voice loud enough for the guard on the gate behind him to hear, "Are you the officers hitching a ride with General Mac?"

"Yes, sir," answers Met.

"This way," JC says, and leads the men toward the gate giving access to the airstrip. JC passes the guard and flashes his ID card. The others, still jabbering about their liberty call, do the same with their fake IDs. Once through the gate, they proceed to the plane.

Air Jockey is standing inside the door as the men file on board.

"If I had a dog with a hair cut like that, I'd shave its ass and make it walk on its front paws," he comments.

"Well, how have things been back here in the air-conditioned Jet?" inquires Panda.

"It was okay," answers Air Jockey. "Air conditioning is nice when you're having a few brews in a hot climate."

"Is that what air conditioning is? Ya dickhead," Panda retorts as he and the men put the garment bags in the back of the plane, then collapse into seats.

"Mac should be here soon," JC announces. "We are scheduled for takeoff at 20 hundred."

The team members are either in the middle of a nap or thinking about taking one as the Admiral's staff car pulls along side the Learjet. Two men are laughing as they get out of the front seat. Admiral Fox decided to drive Mac to the plane himself. He and Mac go back a long way, and sometimes had to bend the rules a little to accomplish their missions. It wouldn't be a good idea to share some of the subject matter with a staff car driver with big ears.

The Admiral checks out the plane as he walks Mac toward the boarding ramp.

"I see you have passengers," the Admiral observes.

"Yeah!' Mac replies, "Since there's no off-base liberty, I thought I would give a few officers that are next on the list for liberty call a ride."

The Admiral, who had served long tours in Naval Intelligence on his way to the two-star rank, remarks, "Some of them are so excited about it, they seem to have passed out." Mac looks at the windows of the plane, then looks back at the Admiral, who is now walking back toward his staff car.

"Foxie! What's the matter?" Mac inquires. The Admiral opens the door to the staff car and turns to face Mac.

"I don't want to see something I am not supposed to see, and wind up under a D.C. bus the next time I am in Washington. See ya, Mac," he says as he gets into the car. "I'll check in with you when I get back to the States."

"Looking forward to it," Mac replies, and waves as the Admiral drives away.

JC joins Mac outside the plane.

"Everything okay?"

"Yes," answers Mac. "His name isn't Fox for no reason. He doesn't know what's going on, but he knows I wouldn't use his base if it wasn't for something important."

"What about if he knew it wasn't a U.S. Intelligence operation?"

"I don't know how he would react to that," Mac says. "I'm sure he is aware of the drug-running operation in Santiago. He will put the last few days' activities together and figure that it was taken out because it was funding something else, and let it go at that." Mac then turns and walks to board the plane.

At 20 hundred hours, the Learjet is airborne and heading for San Juan. A half hour into the flight JC notices Mac has been very quiet and seems sad ever since the plane took off. Sitting next to the general, he starts a conversation by saying, "Good and bad news about the .50s ."

"What?" asks Mac, coming out of deep thought.

"The .50s," JC repeats. "Both Pru and Met give high marks on their performance and accuracy. The bad side is that they are now in the possession of an arms dealer."

"What arms dealer?" Mac inquires, now fully alert.

"Charlie Tuna," answers JC.

"Charlie Tuna?" Mac erupts. "Is he in the Cuban mob or something?"

"Not exactly," replies JC. "Do you remember that tuna fish commercial on TV, some years ago?"

Mac looks puzzled for a second, then with dawning understanding says, "Tell me you are kidding!"

"I am not kidding," JC assures Mac.

"Tell me you're kidding anyway," pleads Mac. "And the MP5's?"

"Same."

"The Model 700's?"

"Both Blue Jay and Bean give high marks," JC replies.

"But gone to Charlie too," Mac interrupts.

JC shakes his head yes.

"But we still have the Berettas."

"Oh, well," Mac says, "As long as we still have the handguns. Do you know the shit I am going to hear from JJ Moneybags about this?!"

"Do you want me to come with you when you tell him?" JC offers.

"No, no," Mac replies. "I'll just tell him the truth: the weapons were given to Cuban freedom fighters after they helped the team get through the mine field during a hell of a firefight with the militia."

"Happy to see you are sticking with the truth, sir," approves JC.

Two seats behind them, Blue Jay looks at Bean and says in a low voice, "Fuck a mine field."

"You and management," Bean answers. "Will it ever end?"

"Fuck you too," Blue Jay says as he rests his head on the back of the seat and closes his eyes for a quick nap.

Several days after the Cuba project, Dunn is at home. He takes a bunch of keys out of his pocket, selects one and unlocks the door to his study. This place is strictly off-limits to everyone, except when he is present.

He notices something in the middle of his desk. It is a 30.06 round standing upright on its base. Dunn picks it up and starts to inspect it. As he turns the 30.06 he notices what looks like a firing pin strike on the base. Dunn is puzzled by the round and how it got on his desk, then mutters:

"Blue Jay!"

Dunn immediately picks up the phone and punches in a series of numbers. After two rings, a voice answers.

"Hello."

Dunn recognizes the voice answering the phone and immediately goes to the subject matter.

"I hate to bother you at home, but I have a problem I would like you to take care of."

"What is it?" the voice inquires.

"I was just testing some of that 30.06 ammo I purchased from your company, and found some that misfired. If I sell this shit to my customers, they are going to start buying somewhere else. Don't you have any quality control when you manufacture these rounds?"

Thirty minutes later he hangs up the phone, knowing better inspection will be performed on the ammo he purchases.

Dunn is still holding the 30.06 round in his hand. He looks at it and mutters to himself, "I wonder if he returned that mop and bucket like a good lad." He smiles and stands the round up on its base alongside the pen set on his desk.

Everyone is back at the barn after some well-deserved time off. The team, Top, The Ladies, Mac and JJ are all having breakfast together for the first time in a long while.

"I say, Top!" starts Pru. "Did I tell you Met and I saved the day on the last project?"

"Here, here," agrees Met. Pru continues.

"We kept the Cuban navy at bay so these chaps could escape." Even Met is surprised with this one, but quickly recovers and says,

"Yes, Chief, it was again our great marksmanship that saved the day." The Top bends his head down and laughs as he waits for the rebuttal he knows is coming. He doesn't wait long.

"Here we go again with this shit," Panda says.

"With a round that big, anybody could hit anything," adds Bris.

This signals the start of another round of The Bullshit Derby, and a lot of laughing.

About an hour later, Mac starts tapping a knife on his water glass and asks for everyone's attention.

Everyone stops what they are doing and turns toward him.

"Thank you," Mac says. "I have an announcement. Since you children did so well on the last project and have been forgiven for giving all of your weapons to the Cuban freedom fighters, the board has decided to give you another project. But it will not be as easy as the last one."

There ensues a short period of time when you could have heard a pin drop...then all hell breaks loose. Everyone has something to say, and says it at the same time.

"I knew you'd be pleased," Mac says. "We'll talk in the team room after breakfast."

Mac keeps stirring them up, and it is hard to figure out who is enjoying it more, him or them.

JJ is enjoying the fun as much as everyone else as he looks around the room at what he and Mac refer to as "the kids." He prays that all of the same faces will be there, stirring things up and laughing after the next project is completed.

CHAPTER TEN

A ll team members are assembled in the briefing room, going through their reviewing process for their next project, when JJ and Mac appear. The team members look up, expecting one of them to start their usual battle of words, but notice they both have serious looks on their faces.

"May I interrupt?" JJ asks.

JC looks puzzled as he yields the floor.

"First of all, men," JJ starts, "all projects are on hold for the time being."

The team members look at each other, wondering what the reason could be for the halt.

"This morning, terrorists flew two commercial air liners into the World Trade Center towers, and another into the Pentagon."

The team members all know these terrorists are fanatics. They also know about the foiled plan in France where the terrorists planned on using a commercial jet in a terrorist attack. But with something of this magnitude, where thousands of innocent people are the target, their reaction is shock and surprise.

After the initial shock, the team members reflect back to the World Trade bombing. The apparent objective of that act was to make one tower collapse into the other and bring them both down onto other smaller buildings with no warning at all. The terrorist planner estimated over two hundred thousand casualties. These are not the acts of sane people, just another case of sociopaths hiding behind a cause to do what they like to do best: kill people.

The team members are just coming out of their thoughts as JJ says,

"We are not abandoning our projects. We are merely going to stop for a while until we can get some good intelligence on what is going on. I know the money doesn't matter to you, but you will still be compensated for your services. You can stay here at the barn or if you have other things to take care of, feel free to do so."

"With that said, Mac and I would like to join you and watch CNN to catch up on the events of this morning."

JC picks up the remote, turns on the TV and punches in 26. As the screen comes to life, the first thing they see is a replay of the second plane crashing into the tower.

"My God," says a voice in the team. A few moments later, the first tower starts to collapse.

"I can't believe this," JJ says in disbelief.

"I hope everyone got out," offers Mac.

A short time later the second tower starts to collapse. No one in the room is talking; their eyes are glued to the screen. After what seems to be a very long time, JC breaks the silence,

"These terrorists call themselves warriors. Is that the act of a warrior, killing innocent and defenseless people by the thousands? I don't think so."

"I can take an educated guess as to who is responsible for this," Check adds. "It is not the act of a true Muslim. It goes against everything that Islam represents."

A while later, Top arrives.

"I have lunch prepared, if anyone feels like eating," he offers.

"Yes, thank you," JJ answers the Top.

The Team stands and starts slowly moving toward the door. Tic and Pru stay seated, both in deep thought. Benz and Check go over to Tic, and at the same time Bean approaches Pru.

"You guys all right?"

"I know a lot of people that worked in those towers," answers Tic.

"I have some British friends that worked there as well," Pru adds.

The rest of the team overhears the conversation and moves back into the room around the two men.

"Can we do anything?" they inquire.

"Hopefully they all got out," replies Tic, "but thanks for asking.

"Yes, that is very nice of you all," adds Pru.

"Hey, we're a Team," confirms Panda. "We'll help you find out about your friends tomorrow." The rest of the team agrees.

JJ and Mac are standing in the doorway, and just look at each other. They will also make inquiries the next day about the friends of Tic and Pru.

Six weeks have passed, and JJ is conducting the first board meeting since the World Trade Center attack. All financial, logistics and other issues have been addressed.

"I guess that brings us to the big question: are we going to stay active with the projects?" JJ looks at each man for a yes or no answer. All say yes without hesitation.

"We are all in agreement then; we will continue. I will now open the meeting for suggestions on what the next project will be."

Everyone has an idea or suggestion on this topic, except Dunn. He is usually in the middle of these discussions, but this time he sits in deep thought.

"What's the matter, Gil?" JJ asks him during a quiet moment. "You seem to be preoccupied about something."

"Sorry about that," replies Dunn, "I've been kicking something around for a few days."

"Care to share it with us?" JJ inquires.

"Ah, you would probably think I'm over the edge on this one."

"We are all friends here," JJ says. "Give it a shot."

"OK," Dunn concedes, "but I'll tell you up front, it's a lot of maybes and what-ifs."

"Go for it," JJ encourages.

"Well, here goes," Dunn says. "There's an old crony of mine, still at the Agency, that has a theory about some of the hijackers. It all started late one night when he was scanning through incoming tips from the public about what they thought could be suspicious behavior. One of the tips sort of amused him at first, but then he started to think about it as he walked to the parking deck."

"The tip claimed to have seen one, or possibly two of the hijackers together, a few weeks after the planes crashed into the towers. He thought, one look-alike is always being reported, but two, and together, was a rare occurrence. So knowing he wouldn't sleep thinking about it, he went back to his office and dug the tip out again."

"There was a name with it, so he ran it through the computer and the name came up on his screen. He's a former employee of U.S. Intelligence, and the dates put him in his late 50's. So we have a man with a creditable background, at an age where he probably doesn't get overly excited about things. With that the wheels started spinning. When he brought it up at the Agency, they thought it very unlikely. The FBI didn't even want to hear about it, with good reason, so out of frustration he called me."

"Between the two of us we have a lot of blank spots. So here goes: a few facts and a lot of what-ifs. I like to be moving and writing when I'm trying to make a point," Dunn says as he turns to a blank page on the flip chart and picks up a black marker.

"First, the two hijackers in question are Marwan Al-Shehih and Hamza Alghamdi. According to reports, they were on the United Airlines flight #175 that crashed into the World Trade Center."

"Second, Al-Shehih was on his cell phone with Atta at a time when both should have been seated on their fatal flights. As you know, Atta was supposedly on American Airlines flight #11, that also crashed into the World Trade Center."

"Third, Atta left a will and other documentation in a rental car at the airport."

"Fourth, reports keep coming in from foreign intelligence about Atta. Belgium, The Netherlands and even Spain are sharing with the U.S. Intelligence about Atta's dates and movements. He seems to be out in the open, but we notice some holes here and there where he dropped out of sight, then reappeared in another city or country."

"Let's look at these four items," Dunn adds as he takes a sip of water.

"The first one speaks for itself.

"Second, were Atta and Al-Shehih confirming by cell phone they were ready to carry out the mission or that someone else was ready to carry out the mission?

"Third, Why were Atta and some of the other hijackers so careless about their identity and other documentation? If a terrorist organization was going to claim responsibility it would be understandable, because they know the FBI would trace them back to an organization. But Bin Laden is not claiming involvement. Were they careless mistakes, or were they leaving a trail of their identities for a reason?

"Fourth: Atta seems to get around a lot. My guess is he is a good planner and organizer. Do I think they would take a man like that and fly him into a building? No. They may be crazy, but they are not stupid."

"You asked for my two cents, but I'll give you a buck and a quarter," says Dunn as he turns toward the flip chart. "I will focus on Atta, but the reasoning applies to the other two as well. Let's say Atta is a big help in planning and organizing the World Trade Center disaster. Following his usual MO, he is out and about in plain view for all to see. He's in and out of the U.S., Canada, and Europe. Now he leaves a trail right into the airport the morning his flight is scheduled to take off. People see him, security cameras see him; *everybody* sees him."

"Now let's talk airport security, or lack thereof, for a minute. O'Hare in Chicago and Logan in Boston. That's easy," Dunn continues. "O'Hare is bad, but at 3 a.m. at Logan, a monkey could be trying to fuck a football in front of the back gate and no one would even notice."

"With help from inside the airport grounds, an Atta look-alike enters the back gate between 3 and 4 a.m. and stays out of sight until the time for the morning flight. At boarding time, the other hijackers mill around a door next to the ramp and block the view of the airline personnel and cameras. Atta, of course, is next to the door and bends down to tie his shoe. When he reappears, it's the Atta look-alike. After switching places with the look-alike, Atta puts on the overhauls the other man was wearing, then proceeds down the steps to ground level. The help I mentioned is still in place, and has briefly obstructed the view of any surveillance cameras, then helps Atta get off the airport grounds."

"The call to Al-Shehih was to make sure he was also successful in leaving the airport. After the two crashes, all of these men are assumed dead and are free to continue their next deed."

As Dunn brings the presentation to a close, he expects to get a lot of harassment from the other men, but is surprised when Wilson says, "At what location were the possible sightings?"

"A small town outside of Philadelphia," answers Dunn.

"Any sightings of Atta?" Howard inquires.

"None reported that I know about," Dunn replies.

"I know how I feel, but I'll pose the question anyway," states Dawson. "If these sightings are for real, what would our course of action be? Kidnap and interrogate them, turn them over to the FBI or dispose of them?"

"We are not in the kidnapping business," interrupts Mac.

"And I don't think the FBI would understand about our projects," continues Dawson, "if we turned them over."

Everything is quiet for a few seconds, and then Mac speaks up.

"Well, JJ, counting Dunn's buck and a quarter and two cents from each one of us, there is about a buck thirty-three in the pot. I think we're shy two cents."

JJ looks up. "I guess I'll have to be the two cents of reason."

"I'm sure you all realize what this means," he continues. "This project will probably take place inside the U.S., and if detected, could mean total ruin for everyone and possibly prison. This would not only affect you, but also your families."

"I don't know about the others," Howard speaks up, "but I set up private funds for my entire family before we started the first project. That leaves only myself I have to worry about. I say lets do it, if the team agrees."

"How about the rest of you?" JJ asks the others.

"We feel about the same as Howard."

"And you, Mac?" JJ asks.

"You know where I stand."

"Yes I guess I do."

"What about you, JJ?" Dunn inquires. "You sound a little unsure about this one."

"I was thinking about all of you," JJ explains, "and I will do the same thing at the team briefing."

"When I started this," he went on, "I had no idea that terrorists would be capable of executing a plan like the one we experienced six weeks ago. Toward the end of Gil's presentation, my vote was already cast for presenting it to the team."

"I thank Gil for bringing this to our attention. I think all of us here feel the need to check the information out, and if it turns out to be a wild goose chase, that's okay. I guess we have a new project," confirms JJ.

"Now for the basic plan. The team will probably take apart and reassemble the parts they like, and change the parts they don't like."

"This project will be different from the others. They have to verify the sightings one way or the other and, if Dunn is right, decide the best course of action to take. The initial planning consists of transportation, weapons, surveillance equipment, human surveillance and intelligence gathering. The resources for the first two are already in place. As for surveillance equipment, JC will come up with some types of gizmos. In intelligence gathering, Dunn and the team will have input. That leaves only human surveillance," JJ announces.

"I guess Blue Jay is the logical choice," offers Wilson.

"I would agree, if the project weren't inside this country," JJ says. "He is known to U.S. Intelligence, and probably the FBI. If he gets caught, it could jeopardize everything."

"If it is strictly surveillance, I can't see any problem," offers Howard. "Even breaking and entry would be a local police matter."

"But even if he is picked up on a security camera, or if the FBI has a place under surveillance, he could bring unwanted attention to himself," JJ argues.

"He won't," Dunn states.

"How do you know that?" JJ presses.

"I just know," Dunn reassures him. "And besides, if we don't select him, he'll do it anyway. Then we'll have two out front, instead of the one out and one covering situation we usually run."

"Let's look at this from another angle," Dawson says. "Dunn knows Blue Jay, from somewhere, and vouches for his ability. Blue Jay also found out who we were, and knew that Wilson was having a problem. He was present when the problem was fixed, then he surprised all of us when he walked in here and questioned us about how we handled it. I say he has the skill."

"Good points," JJ concedes,

"Do all agree?" Yes is the decision.

"That should do it," says JJ as he looks at Mac and asks, "Will you guard the plane again, Mac? You never know, it may go to a dangerous place like Detroit."

"Yes, sir!" Mac replies.

"You're enjoying jetting around the world with the team, aren't you?" JJ asks.

"Yes, I am," Mac confirms. "Since I will be guarding the plane again, what type of weapon will I be using?"

"We will cover the weapons type at the team meeting, the way we always do," JJ answers, a little annoyed.

"Yes, sir. Oh, and I sure hope those Cuban freedom fighters don't show up again," Mac adds. "I know how upset you got about the weapons situation the last time."

"Meeting adjourned," announces Howard, and all of the board members stand and start moving toward the door. They all recognize that Mac just rang the round-one bell between JJ and himself.

Things seem to be getting back to normal. Ever since the World Trade Center attack, no one has been quite themselves. That is one of the objectives of terror, to pull down the morale of the people. But in the words of the man:

"After a period of mourning and sorrow, it's time to get back to normal, or as close to it as possible. That doesn't mean forgetting. That means get back to normal and finally wipe out terror everywhere."

The next morning, JJ and Mac meet with the team. JJ has presented the overview and Mac is now into the detail portion. It has been established that JC and his gizmos will handle technical surveillance. Air Jockey will provide transportation, of course, with JC as backup. The Learjet and an additional helicopter will be at their disposal. The team will decide on weapons later.

Blue Jay will be the front man, with Check for backup, on human surveillance. Check will translate for Blue Jay if needed, since he is Arab and can speak or figure out several languages from that part of the world. With the *what* and *why* portion complete, Mac continues with the *where* and *when*.

"The possible sighting of Marwan Al-Shehih and Hamza Alghamdi took place 40 miles outside of Philadelphia, Pennsylvania, in the small town of Oxon Hill. Al-Shehih and Alghamdi drove up in front of a SwiftFood to pick up a third man who is employed there as a cook."

"Alghamdi was driving a white Toyota when they arrived, but got into the back seat and allowed the man employed at the SwiftFood to drive. Al-Shehih was seated in the passenger's side reviewing papers all the while."

"As you all can see, verification will be the first objective. I realize at this point in the past we've bowed out," Mac continues, "but since this is our first project on U.S. soil, JJ and myself will be joining you in your team meetings if you all decide to go ahead with this project. I think a smoking break is in order, then JC can continue the meeting."

Thirty minutes later, JC calls the meeting back to order.

"First, are there any questions?" he asks. No hands are raised.

"None? Then I guess it's time to vote on the project. Those in favor?" Every hand is raised. "The team votes yes," JC announces, and planning begins.

"The objective of the first phase for this project should be fairly straightforward. Gather intelligence in the area of the alleged sighting of Al-Shehih and Alghamdi.

The results should be one of the following: a mistake or look-alike, the people in question have moved on-in which case we will try to locate them for verification-or the sightings appear to be legitimate. If we feel it is Al-Shehih and Alghamdi, we will keep them under surveillance while we verify our findings and try for additional intelligence.

"Mac has informed me that we are not in the abduction or the notify-the-authorities business. For one thing, there is too much visibility involved for the team with either option, especially in the U.S. Once we are sure it's them, we'll make a decision on what to do."

"We don't want too many new faces around Oxon Hill or the SwiftFood, but we don't want the same faces around all the time without good reason either, so that will be our first item of discussion. We also need to get photos of the SwiftFood and the area 360 degrees around it. Maybe a video taken from a car driving around the area wouldn't hurt. Could Pru and Met take care of that?" JC inquires.

"No problem," Pru answers, and Met agrees.

"I have everything you will need in my security hutch," JC offers, "and The Top will handle any film and developing you require. I think we can schedule our next meeting for tomorrow afternoon." Seeing no one has a problem with that, JC asks Pru and Met to join him in the security hutch.

It is 1 p.m. the following day, and the team is filing into the meeting room. Pru and Met had wasted no time on their assignment. They had all of the pictures and videos they needed and gave the Top back the rolls of film to be developed six hours after he gave it to them. Then they reviewed the video. If there were any problems, they could go back in the morning before the meeting. When the pictures were developed Pru, Met, Top and JC selected the ones to be enlarged. The enlarged photos are posted around the room. When the team is seated, JC calls the meeting to order.

"I'll make this first statement for our two new visitors," JC acknowledges JJ and Mac. "The way we are starting this project," JC gestures toward the pictures posted around the room, "may seem like overkill for a possible sighting situation, but like the man said, better safe than sorry.

"In this case, if we go in half-assed to see if the sighting is legitimate, we may alert the terrorists and they'll haul ass. Remember we are at home and feel safe. They are in a foreign country on a mission. They're watching everything that moves, and making an evaluation on whether it's a threat to them. We do the same thing in the same situation. The difference between us and them are that if we're found out, we will eventually be killed. If they're discovered in this country, they will be arrested." After a pause, JC adds, "Unless we find them first."

"With that said, lets get to it," he suggests, as he walks over to the first of two enlarged photos. This one is the SwiftFood in question. The second photo is a quaint little flower shop next to it.

"This situation presents an opportunity for surveillance. Take note," JC returns to the first photo, "with the exception of the flower business, the SwiftFood sits by itself. We should also be able to set up something in one of the distant buildings around SwiftFood that will give us a clear view."

JC moves to each enlarged picture, expressing his ideas. The team just listens, not taking notes or asking questions. JJ and Mac get the impression that JC was the main man when it came to planning, and that the team seemed to go along with anything he said. Once JC has reviewed the last enlarged picture, he returns to the front of the room,

"Now, I will cover what little information we have about the sighting of the possible terrorists. They were seen around 4:00 p.m. on a Wednesday, apparently picking up the cook from work. Assuming they are Al-Shehih and Alghamdi, the cook is one of them: a sleeper agent, or a dupe?"

"If these people show again, and if they resemble the people in question, we will photograph and videotape the shit out of them. Then we will keep them under surveillance. We will require rental cars from a three-state area, Pennsylvania, New Jersey, and New York, from all different rental agencies. Weapons will be .22 Black hawks with silencers, and shotguns for backup. If we require anything additional, it will be American-made only. Since the barn is approximately 15 miles from Oxon Hill, we'll continue to use it as home base."

"Before we get into the who's and where's, are there any questions?" JC inquires.

After a second of silence, the team fires questions like rounds from a Gatlin gun.

"Holy shit," JJ comments to Mac. "No notes and no questions during the presentation, but hold on to your hat at the end."

With a big smile on his face, Mac shakes his head in agreement.

JC is answering or making notes for further discussion on questions as fast as they come. At the end of the barrage, JC continues with the meeting.

The following day the items for further discussion will be addressed, as will any other issues that spring up. The day after that-Friday-everything should be in place.

Mid-afternoon at SwiftFood is the slowdown time, between the lunch and dinner hours. There also seems to be less traffic during this time. Less traffic is a plus for the painter that has set up across the street from the quaint little flower shop and is in the process of creating his next masterpiece. I guess they don't have quaint little flower shops in France?

One block away, a stockbroker is considering office space in the upper floors of a building on the hill behind SwiftFood. At the same time all this activity is going on, a blue Mazda pulls into the SwiftFood parking lot. After parking the car, two men get out and walk through the entrance of the restaurant. They order a pizza, and then sit at a booth where they can watch both the entrance and a bit of the parking lot.

The two men have eaten half the pizza they ordered when Panda spots the front end of a white Toyota in the driveway of the entrance. After alerting Benz, Panda watches the entrance. A few seconds later, the door swings open and a man who looks very much like Alghamdi enters and walks to the counter. The man tending the counter seems to know him, and calls to the cook preparing the food in the kitchen area. Panda gives another casual glance at the man at the counter. As Benz goes to take a bite of pizza he inquires, "Yes?"

"Close enough," replies Panda.

After taking a bite out of the piece of pizza, Benz proclaims he is full and places it back onto the plate.

"Me too," Panda chimes in.

"Your turn to pay," announces Benz.

"I paid last time," Panda argues. After a brief discussion Panda agrees to pay; it will give Benz a chance to get some close-up shots with the camera he has concealed in the big, floppy leather hat he is warring. It draws a lot of attention, but between the hat and the dark sunglasses, Benz gives off a 'don't fuck with me' appearance, and people with good sense usually don't.

Panda walks to the cashier to pay the bill while Benz positions himself close to the man who looks like Alghamdi. The man is yelling for the cook to hurry up when he turns and notices the hat. He smiles and says, "Nice hat."

"Pardon?" Benz inquires as he moves closer to the man for a good shot.

"The hat," the man says. "It's nice."

"Oh!" Benz says, "my lucky hat," and both men smile.

"Ready?" Panda inquires.

"Yes," Benz answers, and bids the man good-bye.

As Benz and Panda approach the double glass doors, they can see a man sitting in the passenger's side of the Toyota, reading something. They exit the SwiftFood, and Benz starts talking about the best route to Atlantic City from Oxon Hill. This is a news flash for Panda, but he goes along and offers different directions. Benz, quite convincingly, acts pissed off and raises his voice. Panda stays with the program until finally Benz says, "Let's ask someone."

They make a show of looking around and discovering the man in the Toyota, who is already aware of why they are approaching him and is quick to say he doesn't know. Panda and Benz aren't put out by his attitude. All they really wanted was a decent close-up picture.

Benz and Panda thank the man and walk toward their car as Benz starts yelling again and lapses into Japanese. It looks like Benz has won the argument as they get into their car. The man that looks like Alghamdi, now joined by the cook, come out and get into the Toyota as Panda and Benz pull out of the driveway and continue up the street.

As Benz drives, Panda gets on the Com unit and says two words: "Close enough." Four cars parked in different spots in the area start their engines. No American-made cars; they're all upper-class foreign models, with no bright colors-a Mercedes, an Audi, a Lexus and a Porsche. Between switching off positions when following, not driving any mid-range U.S. models and being in touch via Com link, the four hope to have a good chance of remaining undetected.

The white Toyota rolls to a stop at the end of the restaurant's driveway. After looking both ways, the driver turns left onto South Main Street.

"Heading North on Main Street," the Com unit crackles. The Mercedes, that had been parked in the lot of a professional building one block south, pulls onto the street and drives two blocks behind the white Toyota. Main, Green and Ashland streets all intersect about a block away. The Audi parked on Green Street and the Lexus on Ashland Street have their engines running, but hold their positions until they see what the Toyota has in mind. The Mercedes, and the Porsche that just showed up behind the Mercedes, will start the initial tail and switch off if needed.

The white Toyota passes through the first intersection and stops for a red light at the second. When the light turns green, the Toyota turns right onto Oakland Avenue.

"East on Oakland," the Com link echoes. The Lexus pulls away from the curb and crosses Main Street at the intersection, continuing north on Ashland Street. The Audi stops at the corner of Green and Ashland, turns right and is about a block behind the Lexus as they parallel the Toyota on Oakland avenue.

The Toyota continues on Oakland as if heading for the city limits and then, where Oakland Avenue meets East State Street, comes to a halt at the stop sign and sits longer than the usual amount of time. The Mercedes slows a bit, but has probably been seen and taken out of surveillance. The Porsche, two blocks further back, pulls to the curb.

When the Toyota finally moves, instead of turning right to leave town, it turns left. The Porsche communicates the turn, then pulls away from the curb and speeds down Oakland Avenue. After the Mercedes stops at East State Street, it bears right. The Lexus, followed by the Audi, turns left onto Church Street and will pick up the Toyota where Church and East State intersect.

Seconds later, "No Toyota" comes over the Com unit. The Porsche, holding at the stop sign, quickly turns left and drives past a big church looking for it.

"Come on," the driver mutters, "where did you go?" Just before East State Street turns back to the west, he notices a street that turns off to the right. He wouldn't have noticed it if he wasn't traveling slowly and looking around.

I wonder, he thinks to himself. He turns onto the street, shifts down to a lower gear and lets the Porsche do its thing. As it passes Spruce Street he can see the Toyota about a block away, and immediately brings the car down to a normal speed as he announces, "Maple Street" into the Com unit.

After checking their locator devices, the Lexus and Audi take a parallel course on Belmont Avenue. At Spruce Street they turn right, and at the next block take a left onto Maple. They are two blocks behind the Porsche and closing the gap, when the target reaches East Road and turns right. The driver of the Porsche sees the other two coming into position and continues across East Road. The Toyota speeds up after the turn and has a good lead on the Lexus and the Audi before they reach East Road.

"Lost visual," the Com unit announces as the two turn onto East Road.

The Toyota turns left on East State and gets the green at the next traffic light before the two surveillance cars can catch up.

Satisfied no one is following, the target resumes its original route.

The Oxon Hill area is expanding by leaps and bounds, and the new office complex on the hill overlooking East State is a good example. Nice new buildings, with nothing out of place...not even the man sitting in the Mercedes.

"What do have on your mind, peckerhead?" he mutters before picking up a Com unit and saying, "North on East State, approaching Swamp Road intersection." As the Lexus and the Audi reach East State, the man in the Mercedes watches the Toyota through field glasses.

"Proceeding straight through the intersection," the Com unit informs everyone. The driver of the Porsche is going for the Oxon Hill land speed record as it tries to get back into position and manages to catch the red light at the intersection of Swamp and East State. A Lexus and an Audi pass by in front of him, followed at a distance by a Mercedes. When the light turns green, he turns left and takes up position a short distance behind the Mercedes. At this point, the chase turns into a normal ride down the highway.

The Toyota passes through Wellington and continues east on 202. As it goes up a steep hill outside of Warren, the left turn signal starts blinking. The Lexus behind it passes on the right and proceeds down 202. The Audi puts on his left turn signal and stops behind the Toyota, and the other two cars stay in line behind him. When the Toyota makes a turn onto Route 131, the Audi also turns. The Mercedes follows, and the Porsche continues straight ahead. At the next intersection the Lexus and the Porsche turn left onto Street Road, travel one block and turn right onto 131, about a half-mile behind the Mercedes.

Four miles along, they have passed through Hartsburg and are starting down a long hill. Everyone in the surveillance cars is familiar with this hill. It is only three miles from the barn, and they have all traveled it for business or other reasons since joining the team.

Almost at the bottom of the hill, the Toyota turns right onto what looks like a one-lane road. The Audi speeds past the turnoff and takes a right at the bottom of the hill, onto Route 64. The Mercedes goes all the way down and crosses the bridge into Jersey. The Lexus also continues to the bottom of the hill and turns left, then right into a custard stand at the intersection. The Porsche holds position at the top of the hill.

Ten minutes later, it has been determined they are either visiting friends, or this is where they're staying. The driver of the Mercedes gets out of his car and walks to a pay phone, drops in some coins and dials a number.

"Hello," a female voice answers.

"It's me," he says. "Have you forgotten our dinner date at The Riverview Inn?"

"Oh, I'm sorry," the female voice apologizes. "I was visiting with my sister, and forgot the time."

"Well, bring her along," he offers.

"Will it be all right?" the woman questions.

"I insist."

"We'll be there soon; goodbye," the woman says and hangs up the phone.

Thirty minutes later, Lady1 and Ladya are walking across the Riverview Bridge, admiring the Springburg Inn just off the end of the bridge.

They look like tourists from the big city checking everything out, and are not afraid to ask anybody about anything. After checking out the Inn, they look across the street at a group of buildings bunched together, and immediately cross to investigate.

They first look at the buildings along Route 64, then walk around and up the road between the houses. They see the white Toyota parked in front of one of the small houses, but keep walking and looking at everything. When they run out of houses they come back down the hill, taking note of the house where the target is parked. They reach the bottom and proceed to the custard stand for some refreshments.

As they approach, the Lexus pulls out of the custard stand parking lot, turns left and proceeds across the bridge to Jersey. The ladies order food and drinks, then take a seat at one of the outside tables with a clear view of the houses and very slowly consume the food they ordered.

This will be the surveillance point if the Toyota leaves. From now on, someone will be in the area at all times.

It is sunset, and the Ladies have just about finished their meals when a van pulls into the lot and parks next to the pay phone at the southwest corner. The van is parallel to the buildings the Ladies are watching, and blocks their view. A man gets out and walks to the pay phone, puts in a number of coins, dials a series of numbers and talks for a brief time. He then hangs up and walks to the ordering window at the custard stand.

The Ladies have finished their food and decided to leave. They cross the street and walk toward the bridge. Halfway across, Ladya, still looking forward, says, "Did you notice that rough-looking turd in the van?"

Lady1 smiles as she replies, "Yeah, and I'll bet he'll complain about the food."

As Top takes a seat and waits for his order, Blue Jay and Check are in the back of the van behind darkened windows, photographing and making videos of the houses and the surrounding area. By the time the Top is through choking down his food, it is nightfall. He returns his tray to the stand and heads for the van. Once inside, he starts the engine and pulls out of the parking area to a stop sign, turns right, and continues up the hill. At the top of the hill the Porsche is parked with its hood up in a driveway that was supposed to have been the entrance to a new housing development until it went bankrupt. The van pulls into the driveway next to the Porsche. The side doors of the van slide open and two men get out. As Check closes the door, Top hands a container to the driver of the Porsche, then pulls away and continues his journey back to the Barn using another route.

When Blue Jay and Check are in position, the Audi will return to home base. Wildman in the Porsche will take up a position across the bridge in Riverview, and if the Toyota leaves, he will follow.

Forty-five minutes later, the Porsche is parked in Riverview and the wildman is enjoying the meal Top prepared for him. Blue Jay and Check have checked out the area and are snooping and pooping around the house to select a place for one of JC's listening gizmos. No bugging of the actual house or the Toyota will be used. If these guys are the real deal, they will be constantly checking for devices and will run if they find any.

After placing the device, Check listens to everything that is being said. By morning, with the listening gizmo in hand, the two have departed and will be picked up on a side road south of the buildings. Blue Jay and Check have not heard anything out of the ordinary.

The car surveillance the next morning follows the Toyota into Philadelphia, then breaks off surveillance when it appears the occupants of the Toyota are checking for a tail.

The group spreads out in the Philadelphia center city area early the next morning and waits. At around 10:30 a.m. the Toyota is spotted driving around Independence Hall, but is not followed when it leaves the area.

Watching the SwiftFood only during the day and the house only at night leaves some large holes, but with such a small group, the risk of detection is too great to employ additional surveillance.

This routine continues for two more days. Then, early one evening, JC calls a meeting of the entire team.

"Here is what we have to date," he announces. "Blue Jay and Check have found nothing out of the ordinary, but the way these people move around is very suspicious. The commute from the SwiftFood to Springburg and the visit to Philadelphia prove that."

"The two men look very much like the two in question, but we have nothing concrete. The board has connections, but they are also drawing a blank. Any input?" he asks as he gestures to the team.

"If they are Al-Shehih and Alghamdi, I have a feeling we better do something soon," offers Tic. "It has been almost two months since the World Trade Center, and Bin Laden has probably already scheduled his next big event."

"I am afraid we all agree with you on that," JC answers, but how can we speed up our findings, one way or another?"

Benz raises his hand.

"Yes?" JC says.

"Why don't we try to make them a little nervous?" Benz suggests.

"How?"

Fifteen minutes later, Benz has explained his idea, and the team agrees.

"It's good that you and Panda are teaming up again," JJ says to Benz. "If you want to converse in Japanese, no one will know what you are saying."

"Including me," says Panda.

"After hearing about your SwiftFood visit, I was under the impression you did," apologizes JJ.

"No," Panda clarifies. "When he is yelling, I drop and shake my head. When he is smiling and yelling, I just laugh."

Everyone in the room cracks up, including Benz.

"It will be all right," Benz reassures Panda, "unless we run into Rions," he adds, purposefully mispronoucing Lions.

The team again laughs as Blue Jay and Check follow JC to the Com hutch.

An hour later, Blue Jay and Check are on their way to their nightly surveillance duties. Tonight they will come in from the south and leave up the hill to the west. They take different routes at different times, in case the locals are observing them.

The van comes to a stop on the same side of the road the Audi occupied the first night. They will stay there until they get a voice check from JC's new gizmos, then leave until the following afternoon. As usual, the two men are very cautious as they travel the quarter-mile to the house. Once there, they place several listening devices around the house and then move off a short distance to communicate with the van.

"Can you hear what they're saying?" inquires Blue Jay.

"Yes," is the answer, and the van departs from the area.

Blue Jay and Check begin the usual nightly routine: Check listens for info, while Blue Jay keeps watch and looks around for anything different in the area.

When the sky is starting to get a bit lighter in the east, the two men climb into the Lexus.

"Anything new?" asks Bean,

"Same old, same old," answers Check.

"We'll see what today brings," Bean replies as he slowly pulls onto the road and heads south on route 64. A mile down the road he turns on the headlights and heads for the barn.

CHAPTER ELEVEN

At 4 o'clock the next day, Benz and Panda are again eating at the SwiftFood when the white Toyota pulls up in front. This time the driver comes to the door, opens it and yells for the cook. When the cook acknowledges, he closes the door and returns to the car.

That's their cue. Benz and Panda go to the cash register, pay the bill and walk out through the glass doors. Once again, Benz starts a directions argument. This time, it is Philadelphia. As they are talking, Benz pretends to just notice the white Toyota and waves to the man on the passenger side.

"Let's go ask our pal," he says.

The two men approach the passenger side and ask about the best route to Philadelphia.

"Don't you know your way around here at all?" inquires the man in a very disturbed voice.

"Yeah, buy a map," adds the man sitting behind the wheel in a wiseass manner.

"Well, that is one of our problems," Benz explains. "We're actually terrorists sent here to blow up the Liberty Bell, but our maps got all wet when the submarine dropped us off."

The driver immediately looks at the other man, but the man sitting in the passenger seat stays cool.

"That's not funny," he says.

At that moment a voice breaks the tension as the painter, walking up the drive to the SwiftFood for a cold drink, says "Good night" to the cook, who has just come out of the door. Bris has made friends with the SwiftFood crew when he wasn't busy creating his masterpiece.

As the cook approaches the car, the man sitting behind the wheel gets into the back seat and the cook takes his place. Before he can start the car, Benz is at it again.

"You know," Benz observes, "the more I look at you, the more you look like that hijacker Al She-he, Al Shrib, or whatever his name is."

Panda gets a tighter grip on the revolver in his coat pocket. If the guy in the back seat even farts, he's a goner. The painter has stopped to wipe the sweat off of his forehead with a handkerchief, halfway between the car and the door to the restaurant. If his new friend the cook does anything stupid, he's a goner too.

After what seems to be a long time, but is actually a few seconds.

Panda looks at the man in the back seat and affects a look of surprise. He then starts to persuade his friend to leave the men alone as he pulls on his sleeve. Benz starts insisting the man looks like one of the hijackers, and Panda continues to pull. Staying very calm, the man in the passenger seat instructs the cook to start the car and leave. By this time, Benz has lapsed into Japanese and Panda is pretending to understand every word. The Toyota pulls away as Bris waves goodbye, then heads for that cold drink.

The same people in different model cars-all except for the Porsche, which has only changed its color-take up surveillance. Somehow, Air Jockey has convinced the powers that be they need a Porsche in the mix.

The surveillance to the house proceeds without incident. When the three men enter the house, the people in the van are listening, but nothing out of the ordinary is discussed. A meal is prepared, and they make small talk and watch TV. Since the listening devices are in place, Check and Blue Jay are manning the headphones instead of doing night surveillance. At 11:30 p.m., Bris joins Blue Jay and Check just after the three occupants of the house retire for the night. Blue Jay takes off his earphones and looks at Check and Bris.

"I don't get it," says Blue Jay.

"Maybe they are just look-alikes?" suggests Check.

"Maybe," agrees Blue Jay, "but if they are, why didn't they mention anything about the incident at the SwiftFood?"

"Maybe they talked about it in the car on the way home," offers Bris.

"Even so," Blue Jay replies. "Benz was just going to make them a little nervous, but he jumped so far into their shit that I thought a gun fight was going to break out right there. And by the same token, wouldn't innocent people be shocked enough by the incident to at least bring it up once during the night's conversation?" Blue Jay picks up the Com unit and asks, "Anybody on?"

Answers, varying from yes to sort of, come back over the unit.

"Everyone home except Jockey," Blue Jay announces. "Same routine as last time."

When 3:00 a.m. rolls around, Jockey is sipping coffee in the Porsche, and Blue Jay is getting antsy.

"I'm having one of those feelings," Blue Jay announces into the Com unit.

"Ah shit," the man in the Porsche comments.

"Bris," Blue Jay says, "since Check and I have been doing recon at night and are used to the area around the house, you take over for him on listening. If you hear anything, relay it to Check."

"He and I are going to go snoopin' and poopin'." Bris acknowledges and takes over the earphones.

By 3:15, Blue Jay and Check are on their way to the house when

Bris comes onto the Com unit.

"I hear movement."

"Maybe it's just a head call," Blue Jay suggests.

"It was that at first, but the movement isn't stopping," Bris observes.

"Any talking?"

"Not yet."

Blue Jay and Check pick up the pace. Blue Jay instructs Bris to wake up the barn. Everyone there is standing by, knowing that tonight this thing was going to go, one way or the other.

JC hangs up his cell phone and suggests, "Maybe we should take a ride to Riverview. It's nothing yet, but if it develops into something, we'd better be closer."

Bris' voice floats over the Com link again.

"Check, I caught a few words, but they were talking very low. I think it was Philadelphia, Washington and I am not sure about the third. It was gee-hod or something like that."

"I think that might have been Jihad," Check says as he and Blue Jay stand from their kneeling positions and head in a straight line for the house, an eighth of a mile away.

"Holy shit, you're right," Bris erupts.

"Notify the barn," instructs Blue Jay. He then inquires, "Jockey, you on the Com?"

"My engine is running," is the reply. JC and the other team members are halfway to Riverview when his cell phone rings again.

"It's in motion," JC alerts the others, and the two cars pick up speed on the narrow dirt road to Riverview and the bridge to Pennsylvania.

As Blue Jay and Check approach the house, it appears to be completely dark inside. The two men stop and drop into a kneeling position as they survey the area.

"Bris, can you hear anything in the house?" inquires Blue Jay.

"Just movement, no talking."

"Why don't I like this?" Blue Jay whispers over the Com unit as he looks at Check.

Check shakes his head in agreement.

"We better be prepared," instructs Blue Jay as he takes out the .22 Blackhawk and attaches a silencer. When Check has done the same, Blue Jay whispers, "Let's do it."

The two approach the house from different angles, always keeping track of the other's movements through the night vision gear. When both men reach the house, they are around six feet apart and checking out all the windows.

At the far end of the house, they notice a crack of light at the bottom right-hand corner of the window. It looks as though they've put something over the inside of the window so the light wouldn't show.

"Looks like they're spooked," Blue Jay whispers, and the two men start moving toward the light.

As they pass the middle window, they notice the bottom half is all the way open. Check motions to Blue Jay to make sure he sees it, then continues moving in a sidestep so he can be aware of Blue Jay's position while keeping an eye on the open window. The two men are halfway to the last window when Check turns to look at the open one and sees the cook leaning out, bringing a sawed-off shotgun up into firing position.

"Shotgun! Open window!" Check yells into the Com as he brings the Blackhawk up to shoulder level for his first shot. As Blue Jay turns toward the window, he is moving into position to fire his first round when he hears the muffled snap of Check's weapon firing. Before the cook can shoot, the first round hits him in the chest.

Blue Jay has already raised his left arm horizontally across his chest. He quickly raises his gun hand and fires when his right arm comes in contact with his left hand. The cook is hit again in the chest. Each man fires one more round. If the man is on drugs, the .22s may not bother him a whole lot, and he has a shotgun. The next two are killing shots even if the man is on drugs. The two then run to the open window, and Blue Jay quickly looks in and ducks back. Both men look in and scan the room.

A second later, the door to the room flies open and Alghamdi appears to see what the commotion is all about. He takes one glance and darts back the way he came. Blue Jay and Check swing their weapons toward him for a shot, but he is gone. Check gives Blue Jay a hand up and he goes through the window and into the room. Check then takes off running to enter through the front door.

Blue Jay knows Alghamdi went, back to his right, but where is Al- Shehih? He moves slowly across the room and looks both ways in the hall outside the door. Alghami is in the room to the right, but is Al-Shehih somewhere in the dark to the left, with another shotgun? *Better safe than sorry,* Blue Jay thinks. He stays low and moves quickly toward the room to the left. The door is halfway open, and Blue Jay sees no one in the doorway. He moves to the doorway and looks in. No one. If he is in the closet or under the bed, he'll have to wait. Blue Jay pulls the door closed tight. If he hears that doorknob turn or any noise from inside the room, he'll send a shitload of rounds flying.

Blue Jay then turns his attention to Alghamdi in the front room and moves cautiously down the hall. There was a lot of movement in that room when he first entered, but now it's quiet.

This is an old house, and between the way it was built and the fact the wood is drying out, things don't work the way they should. Blue Jay is just about to swing around the corner into the lighted room when the door he'd just closed decides the strain of staying shut is too much, and opens just a hair to relieve the stress.

Blue Jay hears the squeak of the wood and immediately turns and fires two rounds at chest level through the door. A second after he fires, what feels like a ton of weight hits him from behind, and he goes flying down the hall and to the floor. The blow almost knocks him out, and as he is trying to recover he looks back toward the lighted room and sees Alghamdi. He holds a large brief case in one hand, and points a 9mm automatic at him with the other.

As Blue Jay tries to raise his weapon, Alghamdi squeezes the trigger, and a round goes through the floor just above Blue Jay's left shoulder. Alghamdi tries to fire again, but the 9mm has a jam and will require two hands to clear it. Not wanting to put down the briefcase, he unlocks the front door, opens it, and disappears from view.

A second later, Blue Jay hears a crack and Alghamdi comes flying through the door backwards and falls to the floor. He recovers quickly and tries to pull back the receiver on the 9mm to clear the jam, but is stopped when two rounds enter the front of his head.

Blue Jay isn't surprised when he sees Check's face appear around the edge of the door.

"You all right?" Check inquires.

"Yeah."

"Al-Shehih?"

"Don't know," replies Blue Jay. "Let's look."

The two men check out the house, but don't find anyone else.

"Where in the hell did he disappear to?" Blue Jay mutters as both men return to Alghamdi.

"What's in that briefcase?" Blue Jay inquires as he rubs the back of his neck.

"Think it's booby-trapped?"

"Hard to say."

"Shall we take a look?" inquires Check.

"Go ahead," grants Blue Jay as he looks through Alghamdi's pockets for info.

"Is this what I think it is?" Check asks, not believing what he is seeing. Blue Jay quickly moves to the briefcase for a look.

"Holy shit," he exclaims. "Let's check the Toyota." Both men head outside with the briefcase in hand.

"Nothing," Blue Jay exclaims, and starts talking into the Com unit.

"We have Alghamdi, but we need to locate Al-Shehih really, really badly." The team knows what that means.

"Jockey, stay in place and watch the bridge." Blue Jay continues over the Com. "Tic, call the barn and tell Mac that JC is bringing a present for him. Then go outside the van and set up security for Route 64 and the field around you. JC, are you on?"

"Yes," a voice responds.

"Meet us at the custard stand."

"Got it," JC replies. With all of the instructions given, Blue Jay looks at Check and puts his hand over the mike on the Com unit. Check does the same.

"We'll take this, meet JC at the custard stand and tell him we think it's a briefcase nuke. He'll take it from there."

"OK," answers Check.

"I'll walk ahead to the custard stand in case Al-Shehih is still in the area," Blue Jay adds, then he walks down to Route 64 and crosses to the sidewalk on the other side. After checking behind the bushes, Blue Jay motions for Check to cross.

The two men act as if they are out for an early morning walk, nothing out of the ordinary...except for the briefcase and the .22 Blackhawks they carry at their sides.

Blue Jay is 20 yards ahead of Check when they arrive across from the custard stand.

"We'll wait here for JC," Blue Jay says. "Too much light over there, and we haven't cleared that building yet."

As the two are waiting, Blue Jay hears what sounds like a garage door opening. He looks in the direction of a house just off the end of the bridge and, after alerting Check, decides to investigate.

He starts crossing the road and is in the middle when he sees a man on a motorbike coasting down the driveway next to the house. When the man sees Blue Jay, he immediately starts the motor and turns left toward the bridge.

"Jockey, get the car on the bridge!" Blue Jay orders. "Motorbike's coming; may be Al-Shehih."

The Porsche is on the bridge in seconds, and JC is just turning onto Bridge Street two blocks from the bridge.

Al-Shehih notices all the activity. He turns the bike on a dime and starts back the other way.

This guy has ridden a bike before, Jockey thinks.

As Al-Shehih flies off the end of the bridge Blue Jay is waiting. He wants a sure shot, because the item attached to the front handle bars of the bike looks a hell of a lot like a big, heavy briefcase. The rider is staying low and behind it.

Blue Jay figures he will nail him when he goes by, but the biker has other plans. He again turns on a dime and heads for the sidewalk that goes across the bridge. As the bike approaches the bridge, it heads for the stairs leading to the towpath below. At that same instant, the Porsche comes to a halt and Jockey jumps out to see where the bike went.

When Blue Jay gets to the Porsche, Jockey is just returning.

"He's heading south; let's give a go," Jockey says. The two men don't hesitate. They climb into the car, put on their seat belts, and the Porsche screams off.

"Bris, can you hear the bike on the towpath?" Blue Jay inquires.

"Yes, he's coming this way. Shall I throw something his way?" asks Bris.

"Not a good idea," answers Blue Jay.

By this time, Check has told JC what is in the briefcase and JC comes onto the Com.

"Bris, not a good idea at all."

JC, Check, Pru and Met take the briefcase back to the barn, and the second car joins the chase.

The Porsche and the Audi are heading south on Route 64. This road runs parallel to the towpath, but the path runs out of sight in several places.

"Bris, get on the path in case he doubles back. If he does, whatever you do, don't hit the briefcase on the front of the bike," suggests Blue Jay.

"What's with the briefcase?" inquires Air Jockey.

"Remember hearing in the news about the Russian briefcase nukes?"

"Say no more," answers Jockey as he shifts into a higher gear for the straightaway ahead.

The Audi comes to a halt beside Bris, who is on his way to the towpath. Benz jumps out to join him, and the Audi returns to the chase.

"If he was on a Harley sportster I wouldn't even try this," Jockey says, "but I'll give this rin-din-din a run."

As the Porsche goes into a sharp curve at the end of the straightaway, Blue Jay thinks they're going a little to fast, but keeps it to himself. Air Jockey shifts down and the car takes the curve like a road magnet, and in no time is at the 90-degree turn following the curve. Jockey shifts down again, hits the brakes, turns the wheel to the right and the Porsche goes into a slide. Off the brakes, floor the gas and they miss a building by a coat of paint, then take another slight curve to the left.

"I'll bet if someone in that house was up taking their morning piss, they're taking a shit now," Blue Jay remarks.

"It's cake," Jockey replies.

The Porsche is on a straightaway and hauling ass again. As they approach the lighted area of the toll bridge entrances, Blue Jay says, "Remember down here: the road winds up a slight grade and at the top there's a small bridge overlooking the towpath?"

Jockey shakes his head yes.

"We'll stop on the bridge and see if we're still in touch." Jockey again goes through his slowdown routine and stops on a pin in the middle of the small bridge. He quickly rolls down the window and listens. He didn't have to listen long. A few seconds later, the bike comes rolling down the path, ducks under the bridge and continues south.

"There he is, the little rin-din-din fucker," Jockey announces. He lets out the clutch and the chase continues.

"We need to get onto that towpath," Jockey suggests as they come off the bridge, around a curve and onto another straight stretch of road. As they come out of the next turn, they are entering the borough of Kingston.

"I think I know a place we can get on," Jockey says.

In another three blocks the Porsche goes into a power slide onto a side street that leads to the path. A short block, a left turn and they are on it. The Porsche picks up speed and they spot the bike, a block away.

Three blocks later a real case of wonderment occurs for Blue Jay as the car approaches a street bridge that arches over the path and the canal. *Is the path wide enough?* he wonders. *Jockey seems to think so, he is shifting down for more speed.*

The Porsche just makes it through, but half of the tires on the passenger side must have been hanging over the edge.

From this point on, the buildings on both sides are closer to the towpath and the canal. Another bridge appears, and the margin for error is even smaller. As the car passes underneath, Blue Jay swears the only things touching the ground on his side are the insides of the tires.

Between the buildings passing by in a blur and his ass hanging over the canal half of the time, Blue Jay doesn't know whether to pull out his gun and shoot Jockey or shoot himself.

"Holy shit, exclaims Blue Jay.

"It's cake," Jockey echoes.

The motorbike reaches the other end of the borough where the path ends, then continues on the other side of Route 64. The bike slows and moves down a set of steps to the street, proceeds about an eighth of a mile down 64, then gets back on the towpath just as the Porsche is sliding to a stop at the end of the borough.

Jockey looks at Blue Jay and says, "Do you get the feeling this guy has a plan?" Blue Jay shakes his head yes.

"Well, fuck a plan," Jockey announces as he puts the car in reverse.

"I can't get through that guardrail, but I'll raise hell with somebody's household fence." Jockey stops the Porsche, turns the wheel toward the street and rolls through a side yard. A little fence crunches under the car's wheels and they're on the street heading south. An eighth of a mile later they pull into the driveway of a restaurant, then back onto the towpath.

Al-Shehih has a big lead, but they can still see headlight glow from the bike. Half a mile later, the light snaps off.

"Can you see him?" Jockey asks.

"No, it went out," replies Blue Jay.

They slow down when they approach the area where they think the bike disappeared. Blue Jay says, "There," as he points to a light in the water.

Both men get out and take a closer look.

"I don't buy it," Blue Jay says.

"You can say that again," agrees Jockey.

As the men look around the area, they can hear police cars in the distance.

"We have to get," says Blue Jay. Both men climb into the car and drive off.

After a little maneuvering, to get around a 'Do Not Drive On The Towpath' barricade, they head west over the hill.

Blue Jay takes out his cell phone and dials a number.

"Yeah," a voice answers.

"Bean, we need you to birddog for us," says Blue Jay.

"No shit," Bean replies. "You have so many people in Kingston out and about, it looks like New Years Eve."

"Meet us on Aquatong Road just before it crosses Route 202. From there, we'll go cross-country to the Spanish Town Bridge and cross into Jersey," Blue Jay instructs. After meeting, the two cars proceed to the Spanish Town crossing, the Audi in front checking for the law and the Porsche a quarter mile behind. It's the long way around, but the team doesn't need any attention drawn to the Porsche.

When the two cars come to a stop at the barn, it's full daylight. JJ and Mac emerge to greet them and suggest breakfast after a quick shower. They want them refreshed for a team meeting; they all have to brainstorm about Al-Shehih's plans for the nuclear device. They have bits and pieces, but need to put it all together with some added insight.

Air Jockey was right when he suggested "this guy has a plan."

Al-Shehih does have a plan. After he dumps the bike in the canal, he walks south another quarter of a mile and retrieves a bicycle he had stashed in the woods for just such an emergency. The plan is to peddle down the path to Morrisville, then over the bridge to Trenton, NJ.

JJ has asked Top to set up breakfast in the team room this morning so they can get a head start on the day.

"You men go ahead and get breakfast," JJ says. "I am going to cover some items from yesterday. First, we proved the sighting was legitimate. It was definitely Al-Shehih and Alghamdi. Second, we know they had at least one briefcase nuclear weapon that is now in good hands. I don't mind saying I'm glad it's off the property," confesses JJ.

"Third," he continues, "we are assuming Al-Shehih escaped with a second briefcase weapon. Fourth, Al-Shehih and Alghamdi were taking day trips to Philadelphia to look around. And fifth, last night the listening devices picked up the words Philadelphia, Washington and Jihad."

"The conclusion is," JJ says, "Al-Shehih and Alghamdi were

going to place nuclear weapons in or around Philadelphia and Washington, D.C.

"As for the two cities in question, the board has contacts who have other contacts that have alerted the FBI to the briefcase. The state and local police have also been notified. The FBI was a bunch of non-believers, until the briefcase was put on the table and opened. Then they were digging out pictures of Al-Shehih as fast as they could."

"Our contribution will be to try and figure what Al-Shehih will do next, and try to stop him. What was his original target? Will he now switch to another, since his long-range plans have been interrupted?"

"I now open the floor for ideas. Yes, Bris?"

"I think maybe Philadelphia."

JJ writes it on the board. "Why?"

"They already hit Washington once, and our government was born in Philadelphia."

"Good point. Anyone else? Met."

"New York City is in range, but I don't think he will hit there again. They want a new target." Met suggests.

This goes on for 30 minutes before JC says, "You're awfully quiet, Blue Jay."

"Just thinking," he replies. "These are all good reasons on why or why not a city will be hit, and that's what makes it so hard."

"I look at it this way," he continues. "We can almost be certain that Philadelphia and Washington, D.C. were the original targets. The impression I get is that Al-Shehih was the senior man of the three at the house. And if you are the senior man on a mission, and the two targets are the birth place of a country and the place where all of the current leaders are, which one would you pick for yourself?"

"What makes you think he will stick with

Washington?" asks Mac. "Since the mission is blown, he may just settle for Philadelphia. It's closer, and easier."

"Not him. We known he's a cool customer. Benz proved that for us. That cool exterior will get him to Washington, and if you focus on his eyes in that picture you can see somebody that wants to blow the shit out of something big. That leaves the White House or the Capitol building. I vote for the Capitol building," Blue Jay concludes his opinion.

"Good reasoning," JJ agrees. "With this size group, we have a one-city, one-building limit. Shall we vote?"

"You know," Pru says out loud. "He does have the look of someone that wants to blow the shit out of something big."

"I agree," adds Met and the remainder of the team also agrees.

"Washington it is," confirms JJ.

"I would like to add something else," Blue Jay requests. "When we were chasing Al-Shehih down the towpath last night, he was determined to stay on the same course. Several times, he had enough of a lead on us to drive down an alley where we could not follow. Instead he stayed on the towpath, then discarded the bike in the canal. I'll bet he had something stashed in that area that would transport him to Morrisville, over the bridge to Trenton and to the train station. And what is the first thing you see when you come out of the front door at Union Station in Washington, D.C.?"

"The Capitol Building," exclaims Check.

"Let's do it," JC orders. "Civilian suits, .22 Blackhawks with silencers. We'll take the Jet. JJ, can you ask the board members to pull some strings to get us into Reagan National?"

"No problem," answers JJ, "But don't leave without me."

"Are you going?" Mac inquires.

"It's my plane, isn't it?" JJ snaps, "It was my idea that brought these kids together, wasn't it?"

"Well..." Mac starts to say, but JJ cuts him off.

"Well, hell's bells. If you people go up in smoke, I don't know if I could handle losing all of you...with the exception of you of course," JJ says, looking at Mac. "Anyone can go that wants to go."

Top and the Ladies look at each other, nod and start taking off their aprons as they walk toward the door and their quarters in the house. Mac is dumfounded as JJ walks briskly to the house to make some calls. As Top walks past Mac he inquires, "Is that the first time you only got ONE word in?"

"Yes, I believe it is," Mac muses. "You don't suppose it's a bad sign, do you?"

Thirty minutes later, everyone has reassembled in the barn. Mac and JJ are the last to return. As they walk into the training area, Mac announces, "Well, don't you all look spiffy. Like a bunch of Presbyterians going to a wedding."

"You're dressed a little on the reverse side, aren't you, Mac?" Panda inquires.

"Yes, laddy," Mac replies, "and with good reason."

JJ looks around at the assembled team and says, "It looks like everyone is here. Let me cover a few points, then I'll turn it over to JC."

"First of all, where is the Porsche?" Air Jockey speaks up.

"We stashed it in the same building as the panel truck, with a cover on it. Since no one will be here," JJ continues, "what about security?"

"For basic security, the gate at the end of the lane will be locked, and of course we have the stickers on the windows and doors saying the buildings are protected by a security service."

Top informs JJ.

"What happens if an alarm goes off, and the security service shows up?" asks Met.

"They won't show up," answers Top. "We just have the stickers, not the service. But it's good enough for the average person just nosing around."

"For the more serious felons, JC has modified our silent alarm system that alerts us to unwanted visitors. The system will now broadcast a message outside that the person or persons are trespassing, and that the police have been called. We can also monitor the area from a PC on the plane, and if all else fails, encourage them to leave with some other things."

That has lawsuit written all over it, JJ thinks, *but no time worry about that now.*

"The only time we won't be monitoring is when we are all off the plane in Washington."

"Thank you, Top," says JJ. Now, I have one last thing to add. Due to the potential of what could happen in Washington, this one is on a strictly volunteer basis. Top and the Ladies didn't sign on for this type of activity, and no one will think badly of them if they change their minds. As for the team, you have already done your part. You proved the sighting of Al-Shehih and Alghamdi were legit, retrieved a nuclear weapon, and due to your efforts, have alerted proper authorities about possible targets. That goes for all of you, and again, no one will think badly of you if you decline."

JJ then pauses a few seconds, and asks, "Would anyone like to change their mind?"

After another pause, Pru raises his hand.

"No problem, Pru," JJ assures him. "Like I said the team has already done its share."

Pru fixes JJ with a puzzled look and says, "I was just wondering if we will require the long guns in D.C."

"You and those fucking long guns," Panda responds.

"We do save the day," Met insists.

"Well, put their asses up someplace high so they can watch over us all," says Air Jockey, "like on the top of Washington Monument…on the outside."

"OK," says JJ, "I guess it's time to turn things over to JC."

JC comes to the front of the room and starts calling out a checklist. As he reads off each item, everyone responds yes or no. "Com units. Weapons with silencers. Everyone except JJ and Mac, you will be doing surveillance inside the Capitol building, and you'll have to go through metal detectors." JC then puts two bags on the stools next to him.

"Everyone takes two pairs of latex gloves and one of those fake DEA IDs that Bean got off the dope boat in Jamaica. If you're challenged by Capitol police, tell them you have been pressed into service due to the high alert situation, then bitch about being called in. It should get you through.

"We have made arrangements for transportation in Washington, and will go into more detail about that and other things during the flight to D.C.."

"Now, everyone except JJ and Mac put on a pair of latex gloves. This will be for the plane and the vans in D.C. When we get off the vans, take off the gloves. If things go really bad, JJ's and Mac's prints will be the only ones on the plane, and they can say Mac was the pilot."

JJ looks at Mac and says, "Well during all those hours you were guarding the plane on foreign shores, you should have picked up something about flying a plane. What do they call the steering thing in the movies, a joy stick?"

"He was probably studying his own joy stick," says a voice in the group.

"I knew this crowd wouldn't let me down," laughs JJ.

"At ease, at ease," Mac commands in a military voice.

"Don't you have any control over these hooligans, Captain?"

JC finishes putting on his gloves and asks, "Any questions?" When no one speaks, he adds, "Lets do it."

Everyone leaves the barn and gets into the four vehicles parked outside. Top, in the last car to leave, locks the gate and activates the modified security system. The drive to Mercer Airport will probably take longer than the flight to Washington.

No speeding; police stops will cause unwanted delays. The four cars pass through Pettyville, heading south on Route 29. Seven miles further they are driving through Washington Crossing.

As Mac looks out the side window at the Delaware River he thinks: *Ah, those brave souls that crossed this river in December, then walked to Trenton and fought a battle. Things have changed a little. Instead of walking, we are riding to catch a jet. Instead of an enemy armed with flintlocks and cannons, we are facing one with a briefcase nuclear weapon. This new enemy of America claims to be honorable and holy, but they are neither. There is no honor in killing innocent people, nothing holy about performing these deeds in the name of a religion that denounces such things. No, it's just another case of crazy scum tying to take over, for whatever reason. But like the man said, we have to keep working for it, because freedom is not a gift.*

JC's voice suddenly interrupts Mac's thoughts.

"What's the matter, Mac? You have a serious look in your eye."

"Nothing," Mac tells him. "Just thinking."

Five miles down the road, the four cars are parked by the hanger and everyone piles out.

"JC," Bris announces, "the next time you see that look in Mac's eye, you know, sort of ignore it."

"He can get on a roll," JC admits.

Mac just looks at both men. Bris starts to laugh and, putting his hand on Mac's shoulder as they walk toward the plane, says, "Mackeee!"

"Damn kids," Mac mutters.

As soon as the plane is airborne, JC continues the briefing.

"If we are right in our thinking about Al-Shehih, he went to Trenton to catch a train to Washington, D.C. His arrival time in D.C. will depend on how he traveled from outside of Kingston to the Trenton train station. Walking would take approximately five hours. Motorbike on the towpath: one hour. For the hell of it, let's say three hours."

"If he started at 4:30 a.m., that puts him in Trenton by 7:30, on a train between 8 and 9 and at Union station by noon. It is now 9:35, and if the board connections are still working, we should be on the ground by 10:30. Three vans will be waiting at the hanger, and we will proceed to the Capitol Hill area."

"We will not take up surveillance next to the Capitol building itself. We'll be a block away in each direction. JJ and Mac will take up surveillance inside the building, and the remaining fourteen of us will handle the outside."

JC unrolls a large sheet of paper containing his drawing of the Capitol grounds and the surrounding area.

"The Capitol is here in the middle," he starts, "and we will set up on these four streets: Constitution, Independence, First Street Northeast and Third Street Northeast. We will keep one person on each corner at all times. This will give us surveillance on parts of two streets using the person on the corner. The remaining 10 will be spread out along the streets."

"Constitution and Independence are longer than the other two, so there will be three on each of them, and two on First and Third streets at all times. We will also rotate clockwise every 30 minutes. That will give us seven hours before the same faces start showing up. Any questions?"

Met raises his hand and asks, "Are two people inside the Capitol building enough?"

"With the small number we have to cover the outside," JC answers, "two will have to do."

There will actually be six in the building. The board feels the same as JJ, and Dunn has set them all up with Com gear of their own. JJ and Mac will serve as relay points, and be hooked into both Com links.

Another question is raised. "What action should we attempt first?"

"Be absolutely sure it is him," JC starts his answer, "and if he has the briefcase, plug him, take the case and leave the area."

"If he doesn't have it, get it out on the Com link and we'll wing it. Either way, since we are all on the link, the rest of us can show up quickly to give assistance. We also don't know if he is going to hook up with a cell for assistance, so if you see him, let everyone else know immediately."

"Anything else? No? Then, good luck," JC offers. "I'm going to relieve Mario Andretti at the controls for a few minutes. After last night, I think he needs a nap."

Everyone thinks that's a good idea. Taking a 10- or 15-minute snooze break helps a lot when you've been up for a long time.

At 10:40 a.m. the Learjet comes to a stop at the hanger in D.C. As the turbos of the engines cycle down, the door to the plane opens and JJ steps off, followed by the others.

"The keys should be in the vans; take your choice," offers JJ.

They load up and take off for the Capitol building. At the airport exit, they head north on the George Washington Parkway, then Route 395 takes them to the area. The vans get off 395, and after a series of turns pull to the curb on C street Northwest.

They are one block off Constitution Avenue and the Capitol, but the big office buildings block the view. The group splits up into three smaller groups and proceeds to Constitution via Second Street, First Street or New Jersey Avenue. Once there, the individuals in the three groups proceed to their first positions while JJ and Mac head for the Capitol building.

After the two men pass through security, they head to meet with the board members, who are already in the building. They find the rest of the group standing in the Rotunda, and they exchange cordial greetings as though they are on business. As Dunn hands JJ and Mac the Com gear the board will be using, Wilson is looking up at the massive dome.

"You know, when I was a kid this dome reminded me of the inside of a great space ship," he remarks.

Dunn looks at the dome and says, "Well, if things don't go right today, we may be riding this fucker to the moon!"

"Oh, that's funny," replies Wilson.

"Dunn, have you figured out the best positions for us?" asks JJ.

"Let's take a tour," answers Dunn.

Minutes later, everyone inside and outside the building are in place.

Eight hours pass with no sighting. Did they guess wrong? Is he going to lay low for a while, or even worse, hit another target?

"Guess who's on the front page?" drifts over the Com unit.

Blue Jay is covering 3rd street. He walks to the corner of 3rd and Pennsylvania to buy a paper. As he unfolds it he is greeted with a full-sized picture of Al-Shehih, but with a slight twist.

Apparently this is Al-Shehih's twin, who is also a terrorist, and has been put on the top of every FBI most-wanted list. *This guy doesn't have a twin brother,* Blue Jay thinks. *That's FBI PR in action.*

That's why he didn't try during the day. His face was probably all over CNN and all the other TV stations.

When Blue Jay looks up from reading the paper, his pupils are still adjusting from the white newspaper to the darkness of the night as he glances down Pennsylvania Avenue.

There's a man walking up toward Third Street, carrying a briefcase.

Why do I have this feeling? he thinks as he lowers the paper to his side.

The walking man takes one look up toward the corner of Third and Pennsylvania and has an immediate flashback to Springburg, and the man in the middle of the road.

Al-Shehih stops, puts down the briefcase, puts his foot on it and pretends he is tying his shoe, all the time looking at the man at the corner.

Blue Jay is still trying to focus when traffic congestion blocks his view. When it moves, the man is gone. Now Blue Jay really has a feeling and speaks into the Com unit.

"Blue Jay; may have something, not sure, proceeding down Pennsylvania Ave."

JC instructs Air Jockey, on the corner of Constitution and Third, to back up Blue Jay, and adjusts the others to cover the vacant areas. Air Jockey relays, "Crossing Third, will continue on Constitution until it intersects with Pennsylvania."

Blue Jay has a hard time getting across Third Street, but finally makes it. He has now completely lost sight of the man with the briefcase. When he reaches the corner of Pennsylvania and Constitution, he looks up Constitution and sees Air Jockey walking toward him. He then looks across to the other side of Pennsylvania Ave and slowly scans back to the right, reasoning that if this works in the countryside, it should work in the city. His scan pays off, almost at the very end.

"Holy shit," Blue Jay announces, "this guy is halfway to Sixth and Pennsylvania already. No conformation, but he's moving fast for some reason."

Air Jockey approaches him, and they both move across Constitution and break into a run in pursuit of the man with the briefcase. When the man looks back and sees them, he also takes off.

"He's running," Blue Jay relays into the Com unit. "His secondary may be the big W."

"Bris, Check," JC orders, "get to the vans, take two of them and try to intercept that guy." Bris and Check take off, but it will take awhile to get them and make their way downtown.

Blue Jay and Jockey are slowly gaining on him, but at each intersection he has the green light, and his pursuers have to fight to get across on the red. The chase continues for another three-quarters of a mile down Pennsylvania Avenue.

"He's crossing 14th, and we're half a block behind," Blue Jay relays into the Com unit.

When Al-Shehih is in the middle of the block, a van comes flying down 15th street and blocks the intersection at 15th and Pennsylvania. Al-Shehih immediately cuts across Pershing Park toward the next intersection on 15th street when another van heads down 15th and blocks that intersection. Al-Shehih looks around quickly for alternatives, and notices the Willard Hotel, across the street from the park. Running to the street, he crosses and almost gets run down by oncoming traffic.

Blue Jay and Air Jockey are racing through the park as Al-Shehih reached the other side of the street.

There is some sort of exclusive affair going on at the Willard tonight. New, expensive cars are lined up down the block, waiting for valet parking.

Al-Shehih walks up the line past a Mercedes, a Cadillac, and a Continental. He stops at a Ferrari, pulls the door open and orders the driver out. When the driver objects, Al-Shehih puts a .38 to his head.

"No problem," the man says as he gets out. His wife tumbles out of the passenger's side. Under other circumstances, Al-Shehih would have killed him, but this time it's faster for the man to vacate under his own power. Once he is out, Al-Shehih is in and the red Ferrari pulls out of the line and heads for 15th Street.

Bris, who had gotten out of the van to join the pursuit, gets back in and is attempts to completely block the intersection, but the Ferrari squeaks by and flies up the street.

"Put on your rubbers Jockey," Blue Jay instructs, "it looks like we're going Day-Day in the car."

Both men are putting on their second pair of latex gloves as they run up the line of cars and stop by a dark blue Porsche.

"We need your car, sir," Blue Jay says to the driver. "Police emergency." He flashes his phony DEA ID.

"I don't give a damn what it is, you ain't getting this car!" the man replies.

"Ah, get the fuck out!" says Air Jockey as he points the .22 at the man's head.

"You won't shoot. You're police officers," The driver of the Porsche informs Air Jockey.

"Did you ever see a police officer with a silencer on his gun?" Air Jockey asks. He shows the man the weapon, then puts it back to his head.

"I'm out," the man gives in as he opens the door.

"Help the lady out," Blue Jay tells Air Jockey, "I'm wheeling this time."

"Ah, shit!" exclaims Jockey as he runs to the other side of the car. No need to help the lady, she is already out and on the sidewalk talking to the lady from the Ferrari.

They aren't stupid. It's simple math: Man with gun, minus one new car, equals insurance money plus another new car. The two men in the Porsche pull up to the corner.

"He turned up New York Avenue," Bris yells.

"You guys get scarce," Blue Jay orders, then the Porsche screams away and up 15th street.

A few blocks later they turn onto New York Avenue. "I wonder why he didn't blow it back there? He was only a block from the White House," Jockey inquires.

"It probably wasn't set up to blow on demand," Blue Jay guesses.

"What do you mean?"

"I have a feeling this guy is not your basic crazy," Blue Jay explains. "He's more of a set-it-and-forget-it guy. He probably isn't part of the brainwashed, blow-yourself-up crowd. But I don't think we'll be that lucky next time. He's probably trying to set it up to blow on demand right now."

The Ferrari races up New York Avenue, but with the volume of traffic, Al-Shehih has been unable to work on the briefcase. He slows down as he goes around Mt. Vernon Square and turns onto K Street.

Blue Jay and Jockey have a slight advantage, for now. They know what Al-Shehih is driving, and he is not aware they are pursuing…yet.

The Porsche has been pushing hard coming up New York Avenue, and has closed the gap. As they slowly navigate Mt. Vernon Square, they check each street for signs of the Ferrari.

"Pay dirt," says Jockey, and they turn onto K Street.

"Get JC on the cell phone and tell him it looks like Al-Shehih may be heading back to the Capitol building," Blue Jay instructs.

As K Street turns into Mass Avenue, Jockey relays the message to JC and stays on the line for any updates.

"He is turning onto Third Street, and probably Route 395. He's either coming back at you or trying to make an escape into Virginia or Maryland," Blue Jay announces, and Jockey relays it to JC on the cell phone.

Seconds later, both cars are headed south on 395.

"If he tries to exit in D.C., I'll try to block him," Blue Jay informs everyone. "If he is trying to escape, I'll let him get to a less populated area in Maryland or Virginia before we act." Blue Jay gets into position to strike if necessary, but not to close.

It looks like Al-Shehih is indeed trying for the escape, until the C Street exit gets closer. When the Ferrari's speed begins to taper off, Blue Jay knows Al-Shehih is going for the Capitol. He shifts down and floors the Porsche, and the car responds as if it has been launched from a mini-catapult.

Since Al-Shehih had not been challenged, he believed he wasn't being pursued, and therefore isn't driving too aggressively. As he approaches the exit, a dark blue Porsche appears out of nowhere on the passenger side of the Ferrari and blocks him from turning onto the exit. This startles him for a moment, then he thinks it was just a traffic incident...until he sees the Porsche remain in position.

"What are ya gonna do now, *asshole*?!" Blue Jay thinks.

It's too late to turn onto the exit, and Al-Shehih realizes what is going on. He shifts the Ferrari into a lower gear and punches the gas, and the two sports cars fly down 395 like twin bullets. The Ferrari decides to take 295 toward Anacostia, and the Porsche is right with it.

When they reach South Capitol Street, Blue Jay anticipates Al-Shehih's try for the exit and blocks him again.

"Boy, this guy is determined," announces Blue Jay. "Away, away, you fucking rug merchant."

The two cars continue side by side down the middle of the Southeast Freeway when they both realize they are rapidly approaching a car in the lane they are sharing.

The Ferrari veers to the left and the Porsche to the right, passing the other car on both sides simultaneously. This causes a vacuum powerful enough to shake the shit out of the old couple driving it, but no harm is done.

As both cars pass the old couple, Al-Shehih sees the Third Street exit, drops back behind the Porsche and slingshots off the highway.

"This rug weaver is pissing me off," announces Blue Jay as he stands on the brakes and the Porsche comes to a stop in a straight line.

Luckily, Ma and Pa Kettle are the only ones on the road at the time, and after being passed, seeing the Ferrari fly off the exit and witnessing the Porsche screeching to a halt, the old gentleman pulls over to the side of the freeway and stops the car. He'll just wait until the crazy people move on.

Blue Jay throws the Porsche in reverse and drives faster than anyone has a right to until he gets back to the exit. He then shifts into first and flies off the exit.

When Al-Shehih left the highway he'd nearly lost control, but after completing a 360-degree spin, he starts the Ferrari again and heads for M Street.

The terrorist has a two-block lead on Blue Jay and Air Jockey as they fly down M Street southeast. If the cold war were still on, the people at the Navy Yard might think they were incoming cruise missiles.

As the Ferrari approaches Second Street Southeast, Al-Shehih spots two people crossing the street. He swerves and almost jumps the median strip that would put him in the path of oncoming traffic. Blue Jay notices all the activity, passes Second Street and turns onto New Jersey Avenue a few yards beyond.

"What are you doing?" Jockey asks.

"New Jersey Avenue runs at an angle to Capitol Hill," Blue Jay answers, "and I think I know what this asshole has in mind.

The Ferrari continues up M Street and makes a right turn at South Capitol Street.

Meanwhile, the Porsche is burning up New Jersey Avenue. L, then K Street flashes by. After passing Garfield Park, Blue Jay lets off the gas, shifts to a lower gear, hits the brakes. He turns the wheel to the left, then the right, and slides onto E Street. Off the brakes, on the gas and the Porsche heads for the intersection of E and South Capitol, a short distance away.

"When I stop, you get out," Blue Jay orders Air Jockey. "You have been keeping JC up to date on the cell phone, so he knows what's going on. The main thing I want you to do is get that briefcase at any cost, no matter what happens. He may have armed the device and might try to set it off; who knows."

Blue Jay and Air Jockey, just off Capitol Hill, and are again in range of the team's Com units.

"JC, you there'" asks Blue Jay.

"Standing by," confirms JC.

When Blue Jay gets to the intersection he stops, even though he has the green light.

"Out," he orders. Air Jockey gets out quickly, steps to the sidewalk and moves closer to the intersection. Holding his gun down at his side, he waits to see what Blue Jay has in mind.

Traffic coming in toward the Capitol is light; outgoing, on the other hand, is crowded-the exact opposite of morning traffic patterns.

Blue Jay creeps up slowly into the edge of the intersection and looks down South Capitol Street for any signs of the red Ferrari. *Either he got slowed down in traffic, or I missed him,* he thinks.

Just then he sees the car out from behind a big truck as Al-Shehih changes from the left to the right lane. He also notices that his traffic light just changed from green to amber. Blue Jay lets off the brakes and hits the gas, and the Porsche jumps into the intersection. He turns the wheel hard to the left, putting him directly in front of the Ferrari, then stops.

The truck driver can't believe his eyes. Al-Shehih can, but he has no place to go. The big truck has taken away any room to maneuver. As the truck and the Ferrari bear down on Blue Jay, tires screaming, the backup lights on the Porsche blink on and he starts hauling ass in reverse. The truck can't stop, but stays in the left lane as it passes the Porsche.

The Ferrari grinds to a halt and Al-Shehih immediately grabs for the briefcase. The cars have passed the intersection, and Air Jockey is already running toward the Ferrari, firing his weapon at Al-Shehih. Blue Jay jumps out of the Porsche and also starts firing at the Ferrari's windshield. The .22 rounds are having a hard time penetrating the glass, but if hit enough times in the same place, the windshield will give. Blue Jay pumps as many rounds as he can at the driver.

Al-Shehih can't take the bomb or set it off, so he bails out and dives under the big tractor-trailer stopped next to him, and rolls to the other side. Blue Jay and Air Jockey take a shot at him, but only hit the under carriage of the truck.

Al-Shehih jumps over the divider and passes through the traffic that has slowed down thanks to the rubber-neckers, gawking at a possible accident. Jockey starts to pursue, but Blue Jay yells, "The case."

He acknowledges, retrieves the case and joins Blue Jay in the Porsche as D.C. police cars approach the scene.

Blue Jay puts the Porsche in reverse, and when it's going fast enough performs a back turn, shifts into first and continues up South Capitol Street toward Capitol Hill. At the next intersection, he turns right onto D Street, then a left onto First and another right on C Street, where he pulls to the curb.

Air Jockey quickly gets out and starts walking to the corner of First and Independence, one block away, where he will be joined by JC and Top. Then there will be three men walking down Independence, not two like in the incident with the Porsche.

Blue Jay pulls away from the curb in a respectable manner, planning to meet with one of the vans at another location.

Meanwhile, Al-Shehih is making his escape down South Capitol Street. So as not to attract attention, he walks the long block between E and I. He acts casually as he walks past an empty playground, not unusual after dark in this part of town.

As he approaches the intersection of South Capitol and I street, he regards the Best Western Hotel on the corner. This has been his objective all along and he itches to break into a run all the way down the street, but that would defeat his efforts to not draw unwanted attention. He will enter the hotel, pretend to be a hotel guest or meeting someone for drinks, then duck out through the parking garage or the side doors.

Al-Shehih walks across the street and approaches the front door of what used to be The Sky Line Inn in years past. *I'll be back,* he promises himself. *And next time, this area will glow in the dark when I am done.* He opens the door and steps onto the highly polished lobby floor...and goes flying forward, falls on his face and slides halfway across the lobby.

Two Teflon-coated rounds have hit him in the left side of his back, penetrating any body armor he may have been wearing. The rounds then exploded inside his chest, and he is dead before he stops sliding.

A drive by shooting, no doubt.

After Blue Jay and Air Jockey have the briefcase in their possession, a sigh of combined relief can be heard over the Com units, and all start making their way to the meeting point.

Ladya catches up with Lady1 and they walk together on First Street. Suddenly, three men who had been walking toward them block their way.

"Hey, where are you mommas rushing off to?" the spokesman of the group inquires.

"We don't want any trouble," Lady1 says, throwing mugger money on the sidewalk in front of them.

The smallest of the three scurries to pick up the cash.

"That ain't nothin'," the leader says. With that, Ladya throws her mugger money down, and once again the little one scurries like a rat to get it.

"Now, maybe we can give you somethin'," the leader says.

"Like what?" Ladya inquires.

"You know," he says as he pulls on his crotch.

"You mean you want to give us what you have in your pants?" Ladya asks.

"Yeah, that's it."

Ladya replies, "Well, whip them out, we'll take 'em." She presses a button on an Italian stiletto she is holding in her hand, and a four-inch blade jumps out of the handle.

The group leader jumps back.

"Hey, I don't play that shit." He produces a blade of his own.

The man standing in front of Lady1 starts to react, but a roundhouse kick nails him in the solar plexus, and he goes down rolling and gasping for air.

"You hurt my friend," the spokesman says.

"Actually, I tried to kill him," Lady1 informs him, pushing the button on her stiletto.

"Now, what was that about carry-out?"

He sees they have messed with the wrong women, so he and the rat decide to leave.

Everyone on the Com link has heard what's going on and are rushing to the scene. Mac and JJ arrive first, but before they can all leave the area, a Capitol Hill police car approaches them.

The man on the ground is still not happy, but his breathing ability is returning. Mac turns his back to the street and instructs, "One of you ladies act like your shaken up by all of this." Ladya volunteers, but wonders why until Mac turns around wearing a priest's white collar.

"It's Father MacDougal, my friends," Mac says as the police car pulls up.

"I feel like I'm going to faint," says Ladya as she forces her hands to tremble.

"What's the problem here?" the officer asks, looking at the man on the ground.

"I'm Father MacDougal," Mac offers. "This poor child is one of my flock and she was the victim of an attempted mugging, but everything is all right now and perhaps this poor soul will mend his ways in the future."

Mac looks down the street and sees one of their vans responding to the situation.

"We're on our way home after visiting the Capitol building," Father MacDougal tells the police officer, "and here is our ride now."

"I have to make a report on this," the officer says.

"There will be no charges," Father MacDougal states.

"I have to make one anyway," the officer insists.

"Very well, then. We'll give this poor lamb a ride to the front and take her inside so she can use the conveniences."

The officer nods as another police car pulls up and stops.

As the ladies and JJ are getting into the van, Father MacDougal is on a roll.

"Bless you, my friend," he says to the driver of the van. "Bless this van. Bless all here."

"The cops aren't looking," says Bris. "Get that ham bone in here."

Three pairs of hands snake out of the van and grab Mac, and Father MacDougal disappears into the van as it drives down First Street.

"Father MacDougal?" Ladya laughs.

"I can hardly wait for my next confession with Father John," Mac says. "Impersonating a priest on top of everything else...I'll be doing penance forever."

"Mackeee!" calls Bris from the driver's seat as the van heads for the meeting place.

Blue Jay arranged for Check to pick him up outside of The Governor's House Hotel on Rhode Island, and is heading in that direction. He'll park the Porsche up in the Embassy row area and walk to the hotel. It seems like a good plan-until an alert D.C. police officer on 7th Street did a double take at the Porsche. Blue Jay was hoping it was just a second look at a neat car, but when the officer makes a U-turn and the flashers come on, he knows it's time to scoot.

Blue Jay shifts down the Porsche and turns left onto L Street, then onto Massachusetts Avenue.

"Well, the pickup plan is shot in the ass," he mutters as he approaches Dupont Circle, "and with that officer on the radio, his friends are going to be coming along soon."

Blue Jay goes almost all of the way around the circle and exits at New Hampshire Avenue. By the sound of things, a lot of help is coming. With its acceleration and road handling, the Porsche escapes the first officer easily, losing him in the circle, but the entire police force has a description of this car, for several reasons.

Blue Jay turns left onto 20th Street, then a quick right onto a cross street between 20th and New Hampshire. He pulls to the curb and turns off the lights. After taking a quick look around to make sure the police haven't followed him, he turns off the engine, grabs the briefcase, gets out of the Porsche and closes the door. He stands there for a second, getting an idea of where the sirens are coming from, and then pats the Porsche affectionately.

"Thanks, Bubba," he says, and walks to the corner and down 20th street.

By the time he gets to 20th and N streets, a shitload of police cars have swarmed the area. Blue Jay walks across the street to the Embassy Square Hotel and stands in front of it, briefcase in hand.

The doorman asks if he can be of assistance, but Blue Jay tells him he is just waiting for someone.

The added commotion indicates that the Porsche has been discovered. Police are everywhere, looking and asking questions. They pull the doorman aside and started asking him questions about the man with the briefcase.

What a dilemma, Blue Jay thinks. *Here I stand holding a nuclear bomb in my hand, surrounded by policemen, and I'm trying to look nonchalant.'* One of the officers walks over to Blue Jay and says, "The doorman tells us you just got here?"

"Yes, that's right," Blue Jay confirms, "I am waiting for someone."

"Did you see anyone running down the street, or anything on your way here?"

The officer is testing him, trying to find out if he's nervous or guilty-sounding. Blue Jay has been down this road before; the KGB was exceptionally good at it. This trick is not to be too anxious or too cool.

"No," Blue Jay answers.

"Well we have an exceptional situation in the city tonight," the officer explains. "Would you mind coming to the precinct house with us to answer a few questions?"

Fuck a precinct house, Blue Jay thinks, *not with this briefcase. I won't shoot these guys, but I may hurt them a little.* Just as Blue Jay asks for the reason and changes his position to attack, a voice yells out, "There you are! I hope I didn't keep you waiting too long?" As Blue Jay turns, he sees a man in Navy dress whites coming out the front door of the hotel.

After a quick flashback, Blue Jay shouts back, "Foxie, you old rascal. How are you?"

Admiral Fox is in town for meetings, and was on his way to a formal evening affair when he saw Blue Jay with the police officers. After studying him for a while Foxie remembered seeing him through the window of the jet in Gitmo Bay when he took Mac to the plane.

"They're bringing my car around here in a second, and then we can go hoist a couple."

The police officer is almost completely out of the conversation. "Admiral, do you know this man?" he interrupts.

"Of course I do! He's my nephew!"

The officer seems satisfied and excuses himself to continue looking for the driver of the Porsche.

A few seconds later, Foxie's car is out front. The two men get in and start driving down N Street.

"I don't know what's going on and I don't want to know, but you tell Mac he owes me big-time." Foxie informs Blue Jay.

"Admiral, I hate to bring this up, but do you read any Russian?"

"Why?" asks Foxie.

"I have a bomb in this briefcase and I'm sure it's in an okay state, but I'd like to make doubly sure."

"What kind of bomb?" Foxie inquires.

"One of those Russian nuclear briefcase deals," Blue Jay answers.

"Nuclear! What the hell is Mac into now?"

"It's a long story, sir, but Mac is involved in a good way," Blue Jay assures him.

Foxie pulls to the curb and stops the car.

"I was in Navy Intel for quite a while and picked up a few things. Lets have a look," he instructs.

Blue Jay pulls the briefcase onto his lap, opens it and turns it so the other man can see it. After a good look the Admiral says, "Yeah, it's okay. How did this thing get out of Russia?"

"I don't know," Blue Jay admits, "but this is the second one this week we retrieved."

"What!" the Admiral explodes.

"From terrorists," Blue Jay adds.

"Terrorists." Now Foxie is really pissed.

After looking straight ahead in deep thought for a while he says, "You say another briefcase was retrieved?"

"Yes."

"The disposition of that briefcase?" the Admiral inquires.

"It was turned over to our government."

"Well, there was nothing in the paper, so I guess they're going to keep it," Foxie infers. "What are you going to do with this one?"

"Give it to Mac to be channeled back to our government, I guess." answers Blue Jay.

The Admiral sits silent for a long while, then starts to speak.

"Halloween was one of my favorite times of the year when I was a kid, with the trick-or-treating, ringing door bells and running away, and stuff like that. Did you do that sort of stuff when you were a kid?"

"Yes," Blue Jay answers, not knowing where this conversation came from.

"Have you ever gone trick-or-treating on Embassy Row?"

"No," answers Blue Jay with a smile, "but it sounds like fun."

"We'll save the Russians some embarrassment, in case the politicians want to keep one of the briefcases and give the other one back while allowing one of those famous, informed sources to leak it to the media. Besides," Foxie continues, "returning it this way will really piss off the Russian intelligence and police agencies. They'll think U.S. intelligence is rubbing their noses in bad borscht."

"It may get them off their asses and accounting for all of the other briefcases. The Americans will deny any involvement, but the Russians will think it's just part of the old spy game."

"Foxie, you da Man," announces Blue Jay with a smile.

After Foxie does a few things to make the bomb completely harmless, it is deposited at the Russian Embassy with a note, written in Russian:

"Can't you homeboys keep tracked of your briefcases?"

The next day, JJ, Mac and Foxie have spent most of the day together before the jet heads back to New Jersey. Foxie is retiring next year. Maybe he'll join the board? But as Foxie would say, "I don't know and I don't want to know. If I know something I'm not supposed to, I may wind up under a D.C. bus."

Everyone has done an excellent job, and are unwinding with a Bullshit Derby during the flight back to barn.

Father MacDougal is asking for clarification from the Ladies about the carry-out situation, as Panda claims he will never eat bratwurst again.

Air Jockey makes inquires about Blue Jay's standings in the annual "JC 'Crazy Fuck' Award," after his stunt with the Porsche on South Capitol Street.

In defense, JC yells from the cockpit of the jet, "They're all pussies, Blue Jay".

Halfway home things quiet down and everyone is relaxing. Then a voice breaks the silence.

"I say, Top! Once again, the long guns got the job done," Pru announces.

Everyone on the plane looks at Pru and Met.

"True, true," Met adds as he flashes the front page of the Washington Post reporting the demise of Al-Shehih's twin brother.

"I'll be damned," says Bris.

"But can you prove it was you?" asks Benz.

"Well, we would have cut off his ears and brought them back for proof," Pru answers, "but the Ladies borrowed our stilettos."

"I'll never eat bratwurst again," Panda reiterates, and they're all off and running for another round.

When the plane lands at Mercer Airport, everyone is talked and laughed out as they pile into the cars for the ride back to the barn.

This time, Mac shares his thoughts with the others in the car as they travels up Route 29 and approach Washington Crossing.

"You know," he starts, "every time I pass through this area I can't help thinking about Washington and his men. They were hungry and half-frozen, and some of them didn't even have shoes, but they wouldn't give up-and they won a victory in Trenton that probably saved the revolution."

He looks around the car at JJ, JC and Blue Jay.

"I don't think either the team or the board will stop, as long as anyone is killing innocent people or trying to hurt our country."

He then looks out the side window of the car and says, "We're not giving up either," He gives a casual salute toward the spot where Washington's troops crossed the Delaware.

The following Monday, Gil Dunn is at his New York office, on the phone with his old crony at the Agency.

"I guess they'll listen to you next time," Dunn says. "Everything I have been seeing in the media is about Al-Shehih and Alghamdi, and how they were supposed to have been on flight #175."

"Yeah," the voice confirms. "These political dicks around here looked down their noses at me before last week. Now, they have their heads up my ass so far they can't see daylight. I miss the days when we were coming up through the ranks," he continues, "There were a lot of good people in DDP."

"Well we can thank Peanut Man and Uncle Stan, Stan for getting rid of most of them." Dunn offers. I'm surprised I survived making statements like 'Who are the assholes that think technical intelligence can replace most of the human intelligence effort?'"

"You survived because the people we reported to were good people," the crony answers, "If you had an opinion and you expressed it, that's where it ended."

"I guess you're right," Dunn admits. "Well, I just wanted to call and congratulate you on your success, and tell you that if you ever get frustrated about anything else, feel free to call."

The crony thanks Dunn for his good wishes and hangs up the phone.

After Dunn hangs up, he smiles as he thinks about the old days. Back then, his old crony DeFlipi had a knack for seeing through things others wouldn't even notice. *Ah, for the good old days,* Dunn thinks, then gets back to the business of running a company.

In Langley, Virginia, DeFlipi sits back in his chair in deep thought. *I wonder what that pecker head is up to?* He sits silently for a while longer, then gets up from his desk to check into the reported Atta sightings that just came in from Spanish Intelligence.

www.ingramcontent.com/pod-product-compliance
Lightning Source LLC
Chambersburg PA
CBHW020441180626
46812CB00003B/1342